The Rise of Draegan

The Dark Artifacts – Book 1

By

T. R. Edwards

Table of Contents

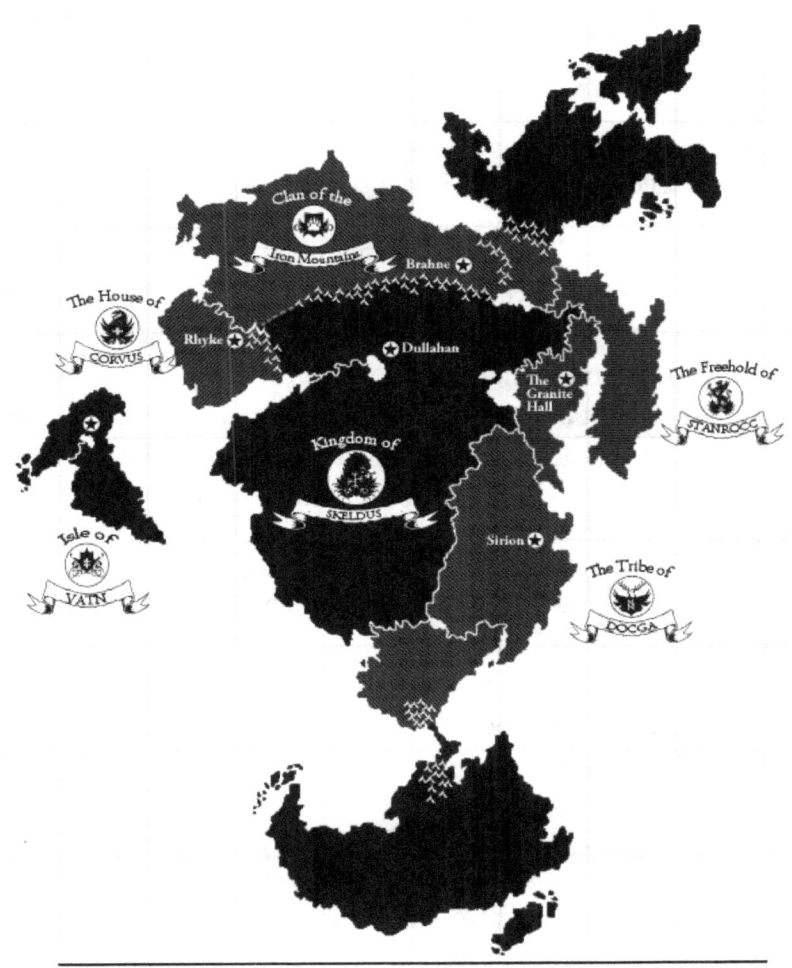

A Map of Fyrian and Beyond

Chapter 1: Wolves at the Door

The wolves pressed closer to Draegan, flanking him and matching his speed as he broke into a run up the wooded path.

"You've picked the wrong man to hunt," Draegan thought as he looked over his shoulder and quickly took stock of the situation. Several wolves hemmed him in on both sides of the narrow forest path leading to his small village in the valley. He wondered why wolves had come so far south of the Iron Mountains before the first snowfall. Only in the depths of the harshest winters had they ever hunted this deep into the kingdom of Stanrocc. And they'd never hunted men.

The wolves glided easily through the twisted oaks along the path, eyeing Draegan as he picked up his pace yet again. The wolves had been tracking him for miles and now the sun had set, making it difficult to count their numbers. Draegan wondered how much longer this could go on.

"It ends now," thought Draegan coming to a full stop in the dry dirt of the path. He crouched as the wolves came to a stop and leered at him from the undergrowth. Kneeling, he hastily drew a simple rune in the dusty path with his right hand. He held his left hand high above his head as he drew the ancient symbol. Bits of light began to appear in the air and move to a focal point a few feet above his upraised palm where they coalesced in an expanding ball. Within seconds a red globe of ethereal light had formed above Draegan's hand, illuminating a few feet into the dense brush along the forest path.

"Only five of you?" he whispered. Still holding his left hand aloft Draegan unsheathed his sword in a ruddy arc as he rose to meet his pursuers. "You won't make much sport."

With ferocious speed he cut down the wolf closest to him. Without waiting for the others to respond, Draegan dove into the underbrush and dragged a smaller wolf onto the path by its throat. As he flipped it on its back, he slammed the thrashing animal to the ground. Draegan drove his knee into its chest as a larger gray wolf leapt at him, teeth bared. In the fading light of his spell he deftly wheeled out of its path while his sword flashed through the gray beast, cleaving it in two. The halves of his attacker continued their arc and clumsily thumped into the tangle of brambles along the path. The smaller wolf had used the distraction to sink its teeth into Draegan's forearm, clawing frantically at his face. Draegan silenced his squirming attacker by skewering the animal to the earth. Looking up he eyed the remaining two wolves that paced uneasily at the edge of the trail. They turned tail and ran. Quickly pulling a knife from his belt, Draegan hurled it at the slower wolf. The serrated blade sank deep into its neck.

"Keep it as a gift, friend," Draegan muttered to himself as he gingerly extricated his arm from the locked jaw of the wolf that now lay dead at his feet. "Of all the rabbits in the forest, you chose to hunt the Captain of the Night Watch." Draegan looked at the puncture marks in his glove and grimaced. "At least one of you will live to tell the tale," he said as he turned his gaze to the wolf lying at his feet.

Draegan removed his sword from the dead wolf and wiped it off before sliding it back into its scabbard. Wolves hunting men at this time of year, this far south was odd, yet he felt something else was wrong. Draegan scanned the path, trying to peer into the darkness at the edge of the wood. His illumination spell had died out during the fight, yet he could still see. In truth, he could see farther into the dense forest than when the spell had burned brightest. Looking up the path toward the clearing he saw the sky had turned a dull red near the horizon. The sun had set only an hour ago. Taking a few more cautious steps forward he heard a low rumbling and saw flecks of red light lazily rising from the valley floor. Then he understood.

Draegan sprinted up the path toward the clearing. The forest thinned as it approached the cliff and the path turned sharply down the steep hillside, beginning its winding descent toward the village. Looking down into the valley, Draegan's fears were confirmed. His village of Draken's Hold was engulfed in flames.

Chapter 2: A Warm Welcome

Draegan stumbled and slid down the hillside grasping at roots and scree to slow his descent. "Was this the reason the wolves were pursuing him? Had they been flushed by the fire?" he wondered. Draegan kept his mind from focusing on the obvious. His childhood home was burning and he saw no signs of life. The forest behind him was deathly quiet and below in the valley the fire blazed unchecked.

Draegan slowed himself as the hillside began to level out. He was now approaching the edge of the village commons. Draken's Hold was a small village in the southern foothills of the Iron Mountains. It had been founded by his father a generation ago with a handful of other families who chose to live under harsh conditions, but with greater freedoms than those afforded to the men and women who dwelled closer to the cities and capitals. With every house and outbuilding now ablaze, it seemed to him that the entire world was burning. The roaring of the flames was deafening as timbers and roof beams burst in the heat. A dry wind blew down into the valley and lifted the thick, black smoke into the reddened sky. As embers and ash swirled around him the air cleared briefly enough for him to glimpse two familiar figures collapsed at the broken millstone that marked the village entrance. Although the fire had consumed most of their bodies, he knew them instantly. They were his parents.

Draegan sprinted across the smoldering commons toward them when a thunderous crack stopped him in his tracks. At the far edge of the village a thatched roof collapsed into its blackened stone foundation. The rush of air fanned the flames and as they briefly blazed brighter Draegan saw shadows retreating into the forest. "More wolves? What great hunger drove them that they couldn't wait for the fire to die before scavenging?" he wondered.

Rushing again toward his parents, Draegan suddenly stopped mid-stride to pick up a smoldering garment that had been partially spared by the fire. He knew his father's cloak instantly since it was the same cut and color as his own. The cloak of a Captain of the Night Watch, the King's personal guard. His father had been wearing it fastened around his hardened shoulders by a distinctive clasp ten years ago when he presented Draegan to the King to begin his formal education. It was the only time he'd seen his father in his military uniform, though he'd never seen him without the clasp.

Crouching by the stone where the charred bodies of his parents lay, he turned his face from the grizzly scene and saw the true extent of the devastation. Looking down the only road in the village he saw the bodies of the villagers not only burned, but that they had been gutted along with all the livestock. They lay strewn unceremoniously along the unpaved street. There were few signs of struggle. Blood half-filled the drainage ditch and reflected the tongues of flame as they stretched skyward. He pocketed the clasp from his father's cloak and spread the tattered cloth over the remains of his parents.

"This was no accident. It doesn't look like a raid from the Clan of the Iron Mountains. Provisions burn alongside the bodies. The rumors must be true. The land of Iss has risen from the shadows, and its dark warriors are loose in Fyrian," Draegan thought.

Chapter 3: Flight to Dullahan

There was nothing to do but return to Dullahan and the King. The village would continue to burn and he knew no magic powerful enough to stop it. The stream would serve as a fire break as would the cliff wall on the opposite side of the valley. Burying the dead would take days and if this butchering was the work of the dogs of Iss then the King and the Council must know immediately.

Taking a last look at his parents' crumpled bodies under his father's cloak, Draegan began climbing the path back to the cliff top.

With no horses left alive he'd have to take the forest path to the High Road and hope to meet a traveler heading toward the King's Road and Dullahan to take him the rest of the way to the capital. It'd be a three day journey by horse. But a horse would need to be watered and fed, and it couldn't run for three days without rest. He could.

Pausing at the top of the cliff he turned to look back down into the valley one last time. Black smoke obscured the burning remains of his childhood village. He sat down and stared at his father's clasp in his soot-stained hand, emblazoned with the crest of the kingdom of Skeldus and choked back tears of rage. How many times had he walked this path with his father? How times had he been sent to gather firewood or berries for his family? He had wanted to return triumphantly to his parents and show them what he'd accomplished in the past ten years. He had been made Captain of the Night Watch two years sooner than his father. He wanted to tell his mother that the King had chosen a bride for him. An acolyte of Vatn, like she had been. Everything he'd imagined in his future was now abruptly relegated to the past, along with his former life in Draken's Hold. But with a sudden spark of hungry flames from the valley below, he grasped the clasp so tightly it drew blood, snapping him from his tortured reverie. Draegan lifted his eyes upward, exposing his neck to the cool night air.

Draegan took the blood in his palm and pressed it into the hollow of his throat, where it pooled briefly before running in a small rivulet under his tunic, and down his chest. Standing and quickly turning his back to the scene, he took a deep breath and felt the cold air fill his lungs. As he exhaled the heat of his breath surprised him. It was hot. Burning hot. It had never burnt this much before. The blood spell would allow him to run like a horse for a few days, but he'd need to keep moving and drink the cool mountain air or his body would overheat. He had used the spell before, but only under the close supervision of his hunt masters when he trained in Docga. Now he'd need to be in tune with the ebb and flow of his body's energy or the spell would consume him from the inside. "Three days should be perfect. Just enough time to make it to the King's Road where I will be sure to meet another traveler," he thought, steeling himself for the journey.

Wasting no time, he burst down the path feeling his stride lengthen as he went. His legs felt sure on the rocky path as he ate up the ground at blinding speed. With no oversight from the hunt masters this time, it was imperative that he balance perfectly his awareness of his body and the challenges of his external environment.

A few miles down the path he passed the sprawled carcass of a dead wolf. The familiar black handle of his knife bearing the seal of Skeldus protruded from its neck.

"You wear it well."

Through the gnarled branches of the thick mountain oaks he could make out the faint, flickering starlight of the Tear of Helian high in the western sky. He set his teeth and resumed his blistering pace.

Chapter 4: The King's Road

Draegan was jostled awake by the creaking of the ox cart in which he lay sprawled. He rolled over and spat bits of straw out of his mouth as he looked around. An old man sat on the rough wood plank at the front of the cart ignoring both his ox and newly roused cargo. Draegan slumped back into the straw. "A simple cart on the King's Road. Most likely headed to Dullahan to sell straw for the horse stalls," he thought.

"I see you're up," the old man said over his shoulder.

Draegan slid out of the cart onto the road and was shocked by the pain that shot through his body. Wincing and taking a sharp breath, he matched the lumbering pace of the old ox as he approached the front of the cart.

"I am Draegan Ferus, Captain of the King's Night Watch" he said, staying a few paces distant from the ox and old man.

The old man turned slightly to cast a lazy glance in his direction, but made no reply. He resumed staring blankly at the back of his ox.

"How did I end up in your cart, sir?"

Looking straight ahead the old man replied, "Found you an hour before sunrise, smack in the middle of the High Road, a mile or so from where it meets the King's Road." He gave the ox a half-hearted crack of the whip. The ox maintained its ponderous pace.

"Poor choice to sleep it off, son" the old man said before Draegan could open his mouth. "Wolves about."

"Indeed," Draegan responded, reaching instinctively for his forearm where the bite of the wolf had left its mark. "How far to Dullahan?"

As they came around a bend, the old man pointed straight ahead where the gilded spires of Dullahan could be seen stretching upward through the morning fog to catch the sunrise.

"Ah, well, thank you," Draegan offered, but the old man appeared to be asleep. The squeaking cart continued to lurch forward and the ox huffed and voided its bowels, marking the end of the conversation.

Draegan broke into a jog to put the awkward encounter behind him, but immediately his throat seized shut. His aching muscles, flaming tendons, and creaking bones worked in concert to send a symphony of pain through his body with every footfall. He had pushed himself past the spell's limit and now his body was paying the price. Forcing air slowly through his nose and trying to move more gently, he pushed on. He'd have to keep fighting the pain until he made it to the council chamber.

He passed only a few peasants heading toward the city. He had expected more since it was day break and farmers and craftsmen from the surrounding country side usually arrived at the market early in order to claim the best stalls.

As the sky turned from the rose of dawn to the clear blue of early morning he saw Dullahan, the capital city and crown jewel of Fyrian Empire emerging from the morning mists in the distance. The sight of it made him feel some small relief.

Draegan arrived at the outer gatehouse to find the portcullis lowered. He paused for breath and then shouted up at the tower until two guards appeared.

"Open for Draegan Ferus, Captain of the Night Watch," he choked out through his burning throat. His eyes teared with the effort.

"No market today sir. Home with you," came the reply.

"Open!" he said through clenched teeth and held up his sword so the guards could see the hilt.

The guard's reply was drowned out by the groaning of the heavy chain as it lifted the iron gate. Once through, Draegan didn't bother to reprimand the guards. He expected to use his remaining energy to push his way through the crowded market and move as quickly to the Eastern Gate as possible. However the market, usually bustling with the local commerce of the countryside, was empty.

"Strange, but I suppose good luck for me," Draegan thought as he half sprinted, half hobbled between the empty stalls.

He arrived shortly at the Eastern Gate. He stared straight up at the great Lion of the East which towered five stories above the wooden market stalls. It was always awe-inspiring to pass through the grand mouth of the lion into the inner court of Dullahan, but today the mouth was closed. The city of Dullahan was thousands of years old, however, and held many secret entrances and exits and as Captain of the Night Watch Draegan knew almost every one.

Draegan followed along the wall for a few paces and stopped at a sewage grate. Reaching his hand through the grate and deep into the fetid water he felt around for a small ring. Finding it, he gave it a tug. The sewage began draining through the false floor of the drain while the grate made a quiet click. Lifting the grate and sliding it onto the cobblestones, Draegan hopped into the low tunnel and replaced the grate behind him, making sure it locked backed in place.

He moved a few feet deeper into the tunnel to make sure he was well enough under the inner wall to light the markings. Removing his glove he felt the cold from the wet stones as he pressed his palm onto the slimy rock. The wolf bite had gone deeper than he thought, he realized as he winced from the pain of contact. He felt along the wall as he walked until his hand felt a familiar indentation. Draegan traced it fluidly with his finger and the pitch black tunnel began to glow an ethereal green. The light expanded slowly from the marking and ran outward in rivulets, clinging to the mortar in the tunnel's rough hewn wall. Another hundred feet and he'd be in the inner courtyard.

He covered the distance quickly. Locking the last grate behind him as he exited into a shaded corner of the inner commons, he heard the sound of sewage being pumped back into the tunnel. Here in the inner courtyard things were livelier as the servants and craftspeople went about their morning work of preparing the castle for the new day. The sun had not yet crested the eastern wall, giving him plenty of shadow to trace its perimeter to the main gate house. The gate wouldn't be open for hours, but there was an access door for the guards he could use. He wished to move undetected, not daring to betray his presence to the craftspeople for they all knew him and would surely detain him with questions, idle gossip and small talk, but he had news of grave import for the King.

"Keys." He fumbled around his belt as he approached the door and realized they were gone. "How could I have been so careless? They must have torn off during the fight with the wolves," he thought, trying to figure out another way in that didn't involve crossing the brightly lit inner courtyard. His self-deprecation was interrupted by the creaking of the oaken door. The heavy mass of iron and oak opened slowly inward and in the darkness of the entrance he heard a familiar voice.

"Dullahan is renowned for the Four Cardinal Gates, arguably the greatest examples of ancient craftsmanship in all the cities of Fyrian, yet you choose to arrive by the sewer."

Draegan broke into a smile at the sight of a familiar face. "And I could ask why you are trying to leave by them."

Vangen motioned for him to enter quickly. Draegan stepped through the doorway and entered darkness once again. As Vangen slid the bar and turned the lock with a confident thud, he touched the wall and a series of lights illuminated their path past the exit and into another hidden tunnel. The two friends clasped hands briefly.

"The gates were closed and I didn't want to be announced," Draegan said sniffing at his clothes. "What are you doing out here this early? And why is the market closed?"

"You smell as bad as you look," Vangen said smiling. He ushered Draegan past the guard's entry door and into the dimly lit tunnel. "Your return was supposed to be weeks from now. Are you wounded?"

"Yes. Apparently there are wolves about."

"So they say. Well you limp, smell and look worse than an old stable hand. I shall take you to the infirmary. You always did make the acolytes earn their keep."

"No Vangen, I must go to the King and have him call together the Council," Draegan said, opening the latch on the exit door and swinging it wide into an unused store room on the interior of the castle. Vangen touched a stone near the exit and the lights extinguished. Locking the door behind him Vangen pushed past sacks of moldy grain and barrels of molasses to the store room's door. He peered out into the hallway to make sure it was empty.

"The King? The Council? No, I will not let you do that," Vangen said as he pulled his head back into the store room and shut the door. "I am specifically trying to stay out of the council meeting that our Highness called last night. You know how I try to limit the amount of time I spend with our wizened leaders.

"I have urgent news," Draegan whispered as they listened to a cook shuffle down the corridor on his way to the root cellar.

"Urgent news from Draken's Hold?" Vangen said as the cook's footsteps receded into the distance. "Well perhaps I should present you to the Council. It might do those old dogs some good to hear your 'urgent news' from Fyrian's other cultural capital."

Shrugging off the remark Draegan motioned for them to exit the store room. He hurried down the hall and made directly for the council chamber. Vangen followed, eyeing him curiously.

After a few minutes of stealing down twisting corridors they climbed the stairs to the landing where they saw the towering double doors of the council chamber. The doors were sealed and two guards were posted outside keeping watch. Draegan paused beneath the massive slabs of ancient marble and marveled at the intricately wrought carvings depicting the War for Athar and the Six Sages of Light battling the dark armies of Iss. Vangen moved past Draegan and stepped into the light in full view of the guards.

"Open the doors," Vangen commanded, staring straight ahead. "We have urgent news for the King," he said, casting a glance over his shoulder at Draegan who was still gazing at the door.

Both guards placed their hands on stone circles flanking each door. Blue light traced a path from each circle up and down shallow troughs in the wall and disappeared into the doors. The massive monoliths began to silently swing inward as the carved figures on each door came to life and moved into positions on each of the door's panels. It appeared to Draegan like a giant chess board resetting itself.

Vangen took Draegan by the wrist and pulled him forward. "Present yourself."

Draegan winced and pulled his arm back. "You go first. You've got rank," he said, gingerly rubbing the puncture wounds on his forearm.

The council chamber was a great circular room carved of blindingly white marble. The vaulted dome was supported on massive white columns larger in girth than any living tree. At the apex of the vault was an oculus that was beginning to catch the first rays of the day. The marble room seemed to absorb the light as it spilled down the grand sweep of the dome, causing the room to glow from within. A monolithic and simply hewn obsidian table sat in the center of the room directly above the seal of Skeldus that was etched into the floor. In the center of the table was a great crack that nearly split the black mass in half. Around the table sat five figures each in the formal dress of their kingdom. Together they made up the King's Council, and in their midst sat King Leon Atrox.

Vangen sighed and then strode directly into the chamber, his dark cloak whipping in the wake of his passage. "Prince Vangen Atrox, multiple titles and honorifics, son of his majesty Leon Atrox, High Emperor of Athar, King of Skeldus, the Lion of the Rising Sun…et cetera and so forth," he said, rising from a weak attempt at a bow and skirting the patch of light that fell on the floor. He moved to his left and leaned against a column near the edge of the room, close to the door.

"I see you've dragged a gutter rat in with you." The booming voice came from King Atrox. He was a lion of a man, broad shouldered and with a thick mane of gray hair. The king rose from his chair, shaking off the fog of a sleepless night. His heavy cloak of crimson and ermine knocked various ancient maps and dusty documents to the floor as he circled the table and headed straight for the door. Walking past Vangen he extended a hand to Draegan, an easy smile lighting the care-worn lines of his face.

"Draegan my boy! What cheer to have you here before the harvest moon. I should keep silent and thank the Sages to have you back sooner than scheduled. Why, you may even be in time to join a tournament I'm hosting at the end of the week. You'll have a chance to show these stuffy noblemen how I've raised the finest blade in all of Athar." He looked in Draegan's eyes and paused to collect himself. "Dare I ask of your father, old Havek, and Draken's Hold?"

Draegan drew a breath and held his gaze steady. "Havek and everyone else in Draken's Hold are dead, my lord. The village is burned to the ground."

King Atrox stepped back as his face tightened in disbelief. The four other council members bolted to their feet in consternation at the news, chairs scraping the floor. Draegan saw surprise on the Prince's face as he stood in the shade of a column at the entrance to the room.

"Havek dead?" said the King as he took another step back to take in Draegan's disheveled state. Draegan's face was stained with dried blood, his hair was matted and his posture was strained. His clothes were tattered and he reeked of sewage.

"I wear his clasp." Draegan fingered it where it lay at his neck. The King's mouth dropped. The council member's looked at one another in amazement.

Draegan released the emblem pinned at his neck and let his hand fall to his hilt. "The villagers of Draken's Hold were massacred by the dogs of Iss. I have seen it. The whispers are true. Iss has risen."

A gnarled hand shot forward, its finger pointing straight at Draegan. "Lies," sneered Arius Han from his seat at the council table. He pulled his gray feathered robe tightly about his bent frame and peered at Draegan over his beak-like nose with tiny, black eyes. "This is the King's Council, boy, not some nursery where your tales of Iss will find sympathetic ears."

"He doesn't lie," the King said over his shoulder as Draegan set his teeth and glared past the king's massive frame at Arius. "The clasp at his neck is proof enough. I gave it to Havek many years ago for his service and friendship during the War for Unity. If Draegan wears it, Havek is gone. It could not be otherwise."

Arius furrowed his brow and leaned forward to peer at Draegan with spiteful eyes. "How do we know he didn't simply steal it?"

"I know of only one son who would steal from his father, and it's not this one," the King said as he attempted a weak smile and laid a hand on Draegan's shoulder.

Draegan glanced uneasily at Vangen who narrowed his eyes. "You are loved by both of us, sire." Draegan said and turned to face the council members. "I saw the devastation with my own eyes. I took this clasp from the gutted remains of my father." He paused to touch it before continuing. "The village was burning when I arrived and there were no survivors, men or livestock, just like the other three villages. This was the bloody work of the raiders of Iss, I'm certain."

Baledin Stormhelm smashed his monstrous fist on the table, his bear-skin cloak lending extra mass to his already impossibly large frame. The twin braids of his red beard quivered as he spoke. "Impossible! Three thousand years ago the six Sages defeated the six Blades of Iss. The Elder Gods banished what remained of their broken armies into the shadows. They're gone. Even the land is gone, sunk into the sea. It's a tale we're all familiar with. How could they possibly rise from the sea and return from the dead?"

"And why now, when the five kingdoms are once again unified? It would seem ill timed." Tysta Hund offered while easing gracefully into her seat. Her dark hair was tied back by a thick leather band, and upon her shoulders sat a simply adorned hunting tunic fastened with delicately etched boar tusks. The first traces of fine lines around her eyes did not dim her keen glance as she eyed Baledin with caution.

"It was raiders from the Iron Mountains and nothing more," Arius said as he returned to his seat. "In a day's time my Ravens will confirm it."

"Your spies will confirm whatever they're paid to," Baledin growled. "The crows of Corvus are the lap dogs of whoever pays the most gold. And my people of the Iron Mountains would rather roast you vultures then pick lean scraps from the granite cliffs of Stanrocc, if we were interested in raiding kingdoms," he growled, eyeing Arius.

Maluk Brun pushed back his scarlet cloak and straightened his rail-thin frame. He pointed a red gloved hand at the King while brushing aside his jet black hair with the other. "Whether or not Draegan's fantasy monsters are razing villages or it's the work of malcontents, the fact remains that all the attacks have been in my kingdom. I suggest we focus our efforts where they will be of the most use. Resources should be sent where…"

"Resources?" Tysta's clear voice echoed through the chamber. "The Tribe of Docga was the hardest hit in the War for Unity. If any of the five kingdoms deserves resources, it is us, for our aid we gave Skeldus in subduing the barbarians of the north, the crows of the west and you rats of Stanrocc. Our kingdom suffered great losses and even now struggles to rebuild…"

King Atrox cut her off. "Hold, all of you! After twenty years of peace and unity you four still cannot push aside your petty differences. Perhaps I shouldn't expect you to forget so easily with three thousand years of strife and hatred gnawing at your hearts, but recall how it was only through our brief unity those many years ago that our ancestors and the six Sages were able to vanquish the six Blades of Darkness." He sighed and gathered his thoughts for a moment. "I will go with an envoy to the Kingdom of Stanrocc, and see for myself how dire is your situation." He faced the other members of the council. "A new crisis assaults us every day, though this is one for the Chronicle of Fire. My adopted son tells me the land of Iss has risen from the shadows. I trust his words. The rumors of its dark warriors pillaging our land are at last confirmed in my eyes."

He threw his heavy cloak over his shoulder and cracked his back. He twisted the royal signet ring of Skeldus he wore on his finger and it flashed like fire in the warm glow of the room. "Twenty one years ago I spilt my blood to unify the five warring kingdoms. After such a short lived peace we now face the threat of an ancient evil that nearly destroyed the whole of Athar. The Sages test us. We will prove worthy. When I return we will make ready for war."

Draegan began to protest over the riot of voices from the council. "I should go with you. As Captain of the Night Watch it's my duty to protect..."

"You'll remain here with the Council and make necessary preparations. I will not attend your wedding dear boy; please forgive me." King Atrox looked across the glowing white room into the shadow behind the column. "Vangen will lead in my absence."

"I have no use for these diplomats," Vangen said as he glanced around the chamber. "I would send them all home and seal this blasted room as my gift for your return."

The King glowered at Vangen as he strode out of the room. "This is why you're staying Draegan. My child still needs wise council."

Chapter 6: The Encounter

"Faster," yelled the king as the convoy left the Eastern Gate. "I grow impatient." The sun had just set and King Atrox had wanted to start his journey to the kingdom of Stanrocc while there was still light.

Upon leaving the council chamber the King had spent the larger part of the afternoon assembling a team of five Night Watchmen and an gathering an emissary from Stanrocc who could serve as a guide through its stark terrain and barren cliffs. Unfortunately the diplomat had taken far too long to pack for the journey and prepare his horse.

Thus it was an impatient king that hastily exited the mouth of the Lion of the East and sped through the empty market expanse accompanied by six riders on their dark mounts. The hooves of the horses echoed off the high walls and the torches cast long wavering shadows as the rider's cloaks cracked and whipped behind them. They streamed out of the castle and through the outer gate, dark shadows speeding into the growing blackness.

The King's Road was lit by twin columns of ten foot iron braziers that marched along side it for a few miles outside Dullahan, but soon the riders had put the sleeping city and its flickering sentinels far behind them, and the country side moved from open pastures to rolling hills.

After several hours of hard riding, the group came to the stone marker that stood where the High Road split from the King's Road.

"We turn here," announced the King, breaking the silence.

"My liege, The Granite Hall is a few days journey directly down the King's Road. I urge you to begin your tour of the Freehold of Stanrocc at our capital city…" the emissary pleaded before the King cut him off.

"We make for Draken's Hold. I wish to bury a dear friend."

The horsemen spurred their steeds up the High Road in a burst of steel scraping upon cobblestones, and then all was silent as the forest swallowed them. Moments later an old ox cart creaked by and turned laboriously up the High Road after them.

It was well past midnight when the silence was broken again.

"In all our haste we've forgotten to eat," the emissary said, looking at the other riders for support. No one made eye contact. After a lengthy pause, he spoke again. "While I understand your Majesty's need for urgency in this matter, perhaps it would be best to attend to our stomachs?"

"We're all tired and sore," the King said, "but warriors of Iss are attacking my Empire. A missed meal is the least of my concerns. If we keep this pace we'll make Draken's Hold in two days. Tighten your belt. You can enjoy your warm meal while I dig a grave." The king urged his horse forward and the rest of the party moved quickly to match his pace.

As he passed, a member of the Night Watch tossed an apple to the emissary. The emissary called his thanks but missed the catch. The apple rolled to the edge of the path. The night watchman shook his head and spurred his horse onward yet again. Once the group had moved deeper down the road and into the black forest a curious wolf emerged from the hedge, sniffed at the apple and began loping after them.

It was an hour before daybreak when the group at last stopped to water the horses. Riders and mounts alike drank greedily from the mountain stream that ran alongside the High Road. The horses were covered in lather and after wiping them down they walked up the bank and back onto the road. All had remounted and were about to continue on, except for the emissary who seemed to be struggling with his saddle.

"Shall I water your horse and have you drink from my skin just to keep you from slowing us down?" the King said turning his horse around to address the struggling emissary.

The King's rising frustration was quickly diverted by the sight of a pack of wolves loping up the road behind them. The emissary was fumbling in his saddlebag for his sword and stammering nervously to himself. The King wheeled around and yelled to the Night Watchmen to form up around the emissary when he noticed an enormous wolf blocking the path ahead. Something was wrong. Leon had never seen wolves hunt like this.

"Steady men. Torches high, let's get a good look at what we're up against," Leon said trying to calm his nervous horse.

The pack of wolves down slope had grown in number as more joined their ranks from the thicket along the path. Ahead, the giant wolf paced across the path as if it was waiting for the men to be flushed into its jaws. Viscous saliva fell from its bared fangs on the dry dust of the road.

"We charge the lone wolf in front of us on my command."

As if it understood the King's order, the monstrous beast moved slowly to stand erect on its hind legs. Silhouetted by the faint moonlight the men watched in disbelief as the wolf began to change shape.

"What foul sorcery is this?" the King yelled, holding his torch higher over his head. A biting cold wind suddenly blew down the path, rattling the dried leaves that still clung to the branches of the mountain oaks. The torches guttered and went out.

Swallowed in darkness, the forest erupted with panicked screaming, steel beating against steel, and fangs rending flesh. Horses reared in terror and threw their riders. Men slashed blindly in the dark, crying out. Their screams were cut short by the snapping of massive jaws.

As quickly as it began the chaos was over. Within a few moments the forest was once again host to the sound of crickets chirruping. A slight breeze carried dead leaves across the scene of the slaughter. Not a trace of the party remained, save a signet ring bearing the sigil of Skeldus still attached to the king's dismembered hand.

Chapter 7: Vangen Rising

"Draegan, I have need of you," came the whisper from the shadows. As Draegan walked down the dimly lit hall he realized the voice originated from the alcove near the door rather than from his bed chamber. "Couldn't wait for me inside, Issa?" Draegan said, peering expectantly into the shadows around the alcove. He smiled to himself. Marriage had been kind to him so far.

"Has one week of marriage softened your brain so thoroughly?" Vangen said stepping from the shadows. He seemed more agitated than usual. "Perhaps I should not be relying on you after all. Now make haste and keep quiet."

"Oh, it's you. It's only been a week, Vangen. What is so pressing that I need to leave my bedchamber?" said Draegan tightening his robe against the sudden cold in the hallway and motioning toward the door.

"I am calling an emergency meeting of the Council. I need you there and I need you presentable." Vangen snapped.

"Why do you require my assistance? Surely running the empire for a few days hasn't proven so difficult that you need help from the Captain of the Night Watch." As Draegan looked at Vangen more closely he realized something was truly amiss.

"My father is dead. Rather 'our' father is dead. Now come quickly," Vangen urged in a rasping voice barely above a whisper.

Draegan stumbled back toward the door and fumbled for the latch. His head was swimming. Not finding the lock he turned and opened the door. "How do you know Leon…" Draegan began to ask as he turned around to face the empty alcove. Vangen had already gone.

Issa stirred slightly in the bed as Draegan staggered into the room. She was beautiful in the soft glow of the dying firelight. Not wanting to wake her he slowed his pace, gathered himself, and changed into his uniform as quietly as possible. He took his father's clasp from the mantle and fastened his cloak. It was his clasp now. He gave the coals a few gentle pokes and took one last look at his new wife before he crept out of the room and shut the door softly behind him.

He fastened his belt and sword as he broke into a jog and headed toward the council chamber. Leon Atrox was dead. He wondered what wrong he had done the Sages that they would take his adoptive father so quickly after they had taken his parents. Burying his self-pity he told himself that there must be a miscommunication somewhere. It would be resolved before sunrise. Then he would be back in bed with Issa.

Draegan arrived at the massive carved doors of the council chamber just as they were parting for Vangen. The stone figures reset themselves as the colossal slabs swept silently open.

"Perfect timing," Vangen said straightening his inky black cloak. "We are the last to arrive. Stay silent and follow my lead, brother."

Entering with an authority Draegan had never seen him wield before, Vangen strode into the silent chamber and circled the massive council table, finally settling into his father's chair. Draegan took his position to Vangen's right and a few steps behind him. The other council members who had risen to their feet as Vangen entered now moved to sit.

"Remain standing. You will want to hear this on your feet, I assure you," Vangen said leaning forward on the table and clasping his hands.

"His majesty Leon Atrox, High Emperor of Athar, King of Skeldus, Grand Warden of the Four Gates, the Lion of the Rising Sun, and my father, is dead."

Draegan bit his tongue and winced. Hearing it this time, in this room, it felt official and cold. He gripped his gloved hands behind his back and straightened his posture. He thought of the implications for the kingdom. He set his jaw and stared ahead, trying to focus as the council erupted into fervent shouts of disbelief.

Arius's raspy voice carried over the outpouring of questions from the other council members. "It is true. The House of Corvus has seen it. Our Ravens have reported it."

"And I have confirmed it," Vangen said standing up from his chair while motioning for the others to sit. He placed the royal signet ring of Skeldus on the polished black surface of the obsidian table. "The spies of Corvus who have seen this have been properly disposed of. I assure you that only those within this room know of our King's departing."

"The crows of Corvus can be bought. We all know it Vangen," Baledin said pointing a finger at Arius. "Your spies will spew whatever bile they're paid to."

"What are you suggesting? That the Prince emptied the King's coffers and paid the Ravens of Corvus to spread rumors of his father's death so when Leon returns from Stanrocc in another week he can witness his own funeral?" asked Tysta, eyeing Baledin as if he were a child.

"I think…" Baledin stammered.

"No, you rarely do," Vangen said. Turning to face Tysta he said, "thank you for your clear thinking, Tysta. I urge all council members to follow your lead," Vangen said casting a glance in

Baledin's direction. "I will continue acting in my father's place until next week when we will announce his passing to the Empire. There will be an official mourning."

"There must be a funeral as well, your Highness," Maluk said. Vangen turned to him and smiled slightly.

"We recovered only his hand and this ring on the road to Draken's Hold in Stanrocc. With no body, there will be no ceremony. Once the mourning period is over I will be crowned in his place. Then you may have your pomp. What the five kingdoms need now is strong leadership."

"This is highly irregular, Vangen," Baledin said in his most diplomatic tones. "Telling us such outrageous news without proof and expecting us to swallow it. I just can't fathom…"

"There is little you can," Vangen said icily. "And it will please me to be referred to by my title. King or His Majesty. Either is fine, do you not all agree?" Vangen said looking at each member in turn.

Vangen continued as he began slowly circling the table.

"We cannot afford to become mired in details and cling to procedure as justification for accomplishing nothing. The hand of Iss has reached from the shadows and taken two great men from Fyrian. Leon is dead. Havek is dead, and three Stanrocc villages are left utterly ruined," Vangen said looking at Draegan.

Draegan bowed his head and smoothed the black and silver shirt of the Night Watch before clasping his hands behind him once again.

"We speak of funerals. My father spoke of war. We will honor him with great deeds. We must strike back and end this swiftly."

"Only one who has not suffered through war would speak of it so lightly," Baledin said, folding his arms across his barrel chest. "And this nonsense of Iss. We have no proof. I don't believe that two of Fyrian's greatest warriors were felled by shadows from the history books."

Vangen turned to face him. "And what would the Bear of the North council? Our villages burn. My father is dead. This is the work of Iss as plain as the beard on your face. While we sit here and debate, they act. Would you have me build roads for their armies straight to the five capitals? Shall I throw wide the gates and hand the four keys and my father's crown to their general? Shall I invite them to the coronation ceremony?" Vangen stopped opposite Baledin, hands on his hips and waited for his response.

"I honor your father and would gladly follow him to battle. He truly was the Lion of the Rising Sun. Since the founding of the five kingdoms three thousand years ago, he achieved what no one else had, peace and unity, and I respect him for it. I won't throw it away on baseless claims of an ancient evil risen from children's story books," Baledin said, never taking his eyes off Vangen.

"Your kingdom has not suffered these raids, nor was it host to the loss of two of Athar's greatest heroes since the Six Sages walked Fyrian," Maluk said.

"Twenty one years is too short a time for Fyrian to enjoy such a hard won peace, my liege," Tysta said trying to diffuse the tension, "though if Iss has returned…" she continued.

"If?" snapped Vangen. Calming himself he continued. "The council hungers for proof and thinks I hunger for war. Then so be it. You will have your proof. We will sit here and debate for another week until my father fails to return. We will remain idle and solemnly weigh the grave implications of going to war while the beasts of Iss continue to burn our land and our subjects scream for deliverance."

Vangen mockingly bowed to Baledin. "I will prove a patient King. We will wait one week and reconvene to discuss our options." Vangen walked toward the door. "Open for the King," he called and motioned for Draegan to follow him.

Turning back toward the council members he said, "Until then I leave you in your marble tomb to furrow your brows at one another and make your flowery speeches. I have an empire to protect, and much planning for the inevitable," and walked through white doors into the darkened hallway.

Once he heard the ancient mechanisms of the great doors stop moving and he was sure they were once again sealed, Draegan spoke.

"I've never seen you handle the Council like that. Typically you hate anything to do with them and are barely capable of more than a few words."

Vangen blinked as if awaking from a dream. He looked at Draegan, half smiled and said, "Follow me to my study. I will be busy tonight and throughout this next week. I will need you at my side." He waved his hand as he strode down the dark corridor, his cloak snapping behind him. "Flowers will be sent to your wife."

* * *

Minutes later, Draegan shut the solid door of Vangen's study behind him and let his eyes adjust to the dim light coming from a few sputtering candles. Charts and maps hung like tapestries on the walls. Tables edging the room overflowed with moldering books that poured onto the floor making it difficult to navigate a path to the desk where Vangen now sat. The air was vaguely musty, but it was the chill that Draegan noticed the most.

"I'll light a fire," Draegan said looking around for kindling. Not finding any he put his hands directly on the logs and began murmuring.

"You never could do that one properly, brother. Your skill with a sword is known by all, but magic is one of the few things where I proved more capable than you," Vangen said from behind a pile of tomes on his desk. Holding up his hand and tracing a quick pattern in the air, the logs began to glow from within. By the time Vangen had dropped his hand and returned his attention to his book, a fire had taken hold and the logs cracked and threw sparks onto the hearth.

"Move those books, quickly," Vangen said. "You would have me lose thousands of years of wisdom so you could warm your bones."

"So this is what you've been up to these last few years?" Draegan said looking around. "Do you hate the sun so much?"

"I hate what has become of the empire. I have seen it crumbling from within. Bureaucracy and diplomats. You see how petty those in the Council are and how quickly the old hatreds flare. The foundations my father laid twenty one years ago have become weak. You have seen that tonight. And now we are assailed from without."

"I can still hardly believe he's gone," Draegan began.

"Let us not speak of it. We must focus instead on what must be done and make ready for the inevitable. They cannot see it, but I have. You have. They think this is a ploy for power, and I fear some will make certain to take advantage of the situation. This is why I need you, Draegan."

"I hardly think the Night Watch can stand against the warriors of Iss," Draegan said trying to peer out of a lone window so covered in soot it was darker than the wall.

"I will be direct with you and trust that our shared upbringing will lead you to the same conclusion I have reached." Vangen pushed aside a stack of books and looked at Draegan.

"You have been in the Council Chamber these past few months and heard the rumors. But only you have seen firsthand the rumors are true. The butchers of Iss, banished to the void from Athar three thousand years ago by the Elder Gods of Light, have returned. I too have seen this."

"Iss fell three thousand years ago under the might of a unified Fyrian and it shall once more," Draegan said pulling a chair close to Vangen's desk and spilling a few hundred books in the process. Vangen winced.

"The Six Sages led Fyrian then. Our magic was more powerful then, yet even so we barely forced a victory. Iss is testing us now and we have failed. They have killed the one man that could have led us to another certain victory. I know that I am not my father. The council has no great love of me, nor I for them. The great Council my father assembled to hold the peace will crumble. If the five Kingdoms abandon the Empire once again we will be fragmented. Then it will not matter if the Sages themselves came to lead us in battle. We will be conquered."

Draegan looked down. Although he wanted to rebut Vangen's words, he knew what he said was true.

"We cannot win without unity," Vangen continued. "Our fathers fought for it and we must prevent it from slipping away. But this unity has never been more fragile. A week from now my father will fail to return from his trip to Stanrocc. A week later I will be crowned King. With me at the head of the Empire the Council will begin to fall apart and other alliances will be made. Some will remain loyal to the Empire, others will dissent. The House of Corvus and Arius will stay loyal as long as we have gold to line their pockets. The Tribe of Docga and Tysta will stay loyal but they are weakened from the War for Unity. I can't speak to the Clan of the Iron Mountains or the Freehold of Stanrocc. Baledin dislikes me and Maluk is impossible to read."

Vangen pulled a parchment from underneath pile of books and spread it on the desk.

"But all is not hopeless. I have seen more than I let on, Draegan. My father always thought me buried in these books and chided me for not being more like you. While you were out gaining fame as the greatest swordsman in the five kingdoms at father's tournaments, I was here, waiting, learning, listening. And these walls do talk, if only you would stop to listen. Though I have learned much, I do not think twenty years of peace can stand against thousands of years of hatred. The seeds of destruction were sown when our fathers built this Empire. Without my father at its head, the Empire will be seen as weak. When we announce my father's death the wheels will begin to turn against me."

"You think your life in danger?" Draegan asked. "From whom?"

"From everyone but you," Vangen said rising and walking toward the fire. Draegan felt a chill in the wake of Vangen's passing. The fire did little to take the bite out of the air.

"You are the only one I can trust. I cannot handle everything on my own, so I need your help. I want you to put together a small team of Night Watchmen. The best, the bravest, and those loyal only to you. You will serve as my right hand, my sword and my shield. As Sage Skeldus bore the Great Aegis in the War for Athar, you and your men will bear the shield that protects me, protects the kingdoms, and protects our tenuous peace."

"But that is already the mission of all Night Watchmen."

"The Night Watch has a storied history. They are bound by oaths to the Kingdom of Skeldus. You will instead be bound by oaths to me. You will be tasked with things that would be beyond the training of a typical Night Watchman. You will walk the gray line between black and white because we alone understand that in order to preserve peace extreme measures need to be taken."

Vangen motioned for Draegan to join him by the fire.

"You would test the limits of my discretion, Vangen," Draegan said rising from his chair. Moving toward the fire he continued, "I don't pretend to understand how a few Night Watchmen can shore the cracks you see in the Empire. How will being your lapdog prevent the destruction of the Empire?"

"You will be my Graywalkers, a corps of elite soldiers who will solve issues before they become catastrophes. You will move swiftly and with the authority of the King. You will take measures that would lead to scandal if you were to be found out. But history will prove you heroes when Fyrian defeats Iss again," Vangen said looking into the flames. Blinking quickly and looking up his face softened.

"Here, I gift you my cloak as a token of the bond we share in our mission to preserve the Empire," Vangen said taking off his cloak and handing it to Draegan.

Pausing, Draegan took the clasp out of his cloak and reached for Vangen's gift.

"My father was a very generous man to give such a gift to Havek," Vangen said eyeing the seal of Skeldus carved into the silver pin. Draegan put the black cloak over his shoulder and fastened it with the clasp. He shivered slightly. "I would have expected it to be warmer."

"It has some special properties that in time you will come to thank me for," Vangen said, turning to the dying fire. "It is an ancient relic of a bygone era, infused with arcane magic. It will be a willing servant as your powers in the magical arts grow," Vangen said looking back at Draegan. "And they must grow, for force of arms will be of no use against Iss or against the fall of Fyrian."

"I never was as good as you at magic. You seemed always to have a gift."

"Gift? No I just practiced more. While you and father were out hunting for sport, and besting foes in mock combat, I was here, training in my own way." Vangen walked over to a table and began sifting through books.

"Here is something they never taught us in any of the capitals," Vangen said, handing a thick leather bound book to Draegan.

"The Chronicle of Fire tells only part of the story of the War for Athar, the six Sages and the Founding of the five Kingdoms. This is our shared history and we all are taught it since childhood. But history, my brother, is penned by those who lived to write it and only offers a single view of events. There are other tales to be told of the War and the Founding. The White Temple in Vatn houses many books that have never seen the light of day, and for good reason, for they would incite the minds of those who read them."

"This is from the archives of Vatn? But how did you ever come to possess..." Draegan said before Vangen raised his hand.

"You never knew my mother. Perhaps you recall her funeral, when your father brought you here from Draken's Hold to pay his respects. I believe it was the first time you had ever come here, in fact the first time you had ever left home."

"And it was the last day I saw my father alive," Draegan said touching the clasp at his neck that now fastened his brother's dark cloak around him.

"Lawai Atrox of Vatn," Vangen said staring past Draegan, lost in memory. "She was an acolyte of Vatn, the same as your wife, Issa and your mother. When I was a child I was very sickly. We both know how disappointed my father was by my weakness. But my mother saw to it that I strengthened my mind. It was through her love and training that I gained access to things usually hidden from men. These are all I have left of her," Vangen said looking at a stack of tomes on his desk.

"When she returned to the White Temple in Vatn once a year to offer prayer to Helian, she would procure certain volumes from the archives for me. I would stay up until dawn copying them, learning their every nuance. When she visited the temple again I made sure that it was my copies that she took back, while I kept the originals here. I am certain my early copies were crude, but no one was the wiser because these were old, forgotten tomes that would never be missed. But I learned much that was hidden. Still, I thirsted for more."

Vangen walked back toward his desk. "Once my mother passed away, I traveled to Vatn once a year to pay my respects, and to comb through the archives. I have kept my copying tradition alive," he said running his hand over an ornately wrought book on a lectern behind his desk.

"Stealing from the acolytes of Vatn?" Draegan said in shock. "You should've simply asked and they would have given them to you with blessings. The priests of Vatn know no hate or greed."

Vangen smiled thinly. "Perhaps, though perhaps not when it concerns these particular books. They were hidden away deep in the archives, buried far beneath the White Temple. Some were bound by powerful seals. Others remain inaccessible still, in parts of the archive that are protected by such formidable magic that they are cut off, even to me."

"You should not be surprised that the priests of Vatn can weave more powerful signs than you. They're the greatest mages in Fyrian, Vangen."

"Are they? I have their books. I have their knowledge. I have the means to put such power to proper use, unlike the acolytes and priests who cannot see beyond their alabaster walls."

"Teaching and healing are noble pursuits," Draegan offered.

"And where was Vatn during the three thousand years when the five kingdoms were at war with each other? Sequestered from the world. They kept all this to themselves," Vangen said, motioning at the collection of books strewn about his study, "occasionally sending an emissary to try and negotiate peace. But it was only for show. They had the power to end the bloodshed centuries ago. Now I have that power. And you and your Graywalkers will be the hand that wields my blade."

Draegan stared at Vangen, shifting beneath the cloak. His new garment seemed less comforting than it should have been, considering its weight. "I wish to be excused, my wife awaits and dawn approaches. If I am to be your hand I must prepare. Finding a few of the best men from an elite corps requires time and thought."

Draegan looked toward the fireplace as if it could offer some small warmth.

"Your cloak can cast shadows," Vangen said breaking the silence. "It will prove invaluable in your new work."

Draegan shifted uneasily under the cloth. Vangen explained as Draegan stared at the cloak questioningly. "You know the spell for drawing light from darkness to illuminate dark places. This mantle simply does the opposite. It constantly draws darkness to itself."

Seeing that Draegan didn't fully understand, Vangen offered a demonstration. "I'll cast the illumination spell and as the room grows brighter you will remain in shadow." With a few words and a snap of his fingers the sputtering candles in the room erupted with enough light to rival the noon day sun. Vangen raised a hand to cover his eyes, but as soon as the light flared up it was gone.

"The cloak has absorbed it."

"How did you cast that spell without drawing the rune?" Draegan said once his eyes adjusted back to the dimly lit study.

"There are few things I excel at, but magic is one of them. The cloak holds other secrets as well. You will learn of them once you are ready. But for now, read this book. It was the very first my mother brought back from Vatn. And choose three of your best men to join you. I'll send for you in two days for your first task. A humble one I assure you."

Draegan reached for the musty tome. "So it begins. What would you have us do?"

"I need you to assassinate a member of the Council."

"I'm here." Draegan whispered from outside the barred door to Vangen's study.

Locks clicked and bolts slid with a resounding thud. "Enter," came Vangen's voice. The door swung in and Draegan saw Vangen hunched over his desk, examining a pile of scrolls by the light of a single candle. Though it was well past dawn, not a trace of the rising sun entered the stale cavern Vangen used as his study. The candle's flame danced in the moving air as Draegan stepped into the study, casting exaggerated shadows on the maps hung behind Vangen's desk. The door swung shut by itself and latched securely.

"A nice touch, is it not? I built it to operate from my desk," Vangen said, looking up from his work. "I have a very valuable collection here," he said motioning to the piles of books, "and things can have a habit of walking away in this castle, if they are not closely guarded."

"I have brought you back your book," Draegan said straightening his cloak, "and done as you ordered."

"So what do you say of the hidden record that the priests of Vatn have kept in their crypt these thousands of years?" Vangen asked, lighting another candle near Draegan with a snap of his fingers.

Draegan moved the pile of books that had accumulated on the only other chair in the study, over the past two days and sat down. "Heresy. I can't believe it and yet here in my hand are the words written by Sage Vatn the Pure herself. Why have we been told that Iss was banished to the shadows? Why hide the fact that while Iss was swallowed by the sea, fragments of the land still exist?"

"And what of the account of the Dark Artifacts?" Vangen asked, his eyes gleaming in the faint light. "If remnants of Iss are still very much part of this world then it follows the Dark Artifacts might remain as well. Those who seek power would seek the Artifacts if they but knew where to look. This is why the books were hidden and sealed away. And I believe this to be the key to the destruction of Iss, and our salvation."

"How do you mean?"

"Three thousand years ago the triumphant six Sages met here in Dullahan at the end of the War for Athar, in our very own Council chamber," Vangen said, motioning behind him. "They began to negotiate how best to divide the spoils of their victory. The Elder Gods of Darkness, bitter at their defeat in the ten thousand year war corrupted the Artifacts of Darkness with their foul magic. The Artifacts poisoned the minds of the Sages who carried them as symbols of their victory over the six Blades of Darkness and the armies of Iss. Sage Vatn discovered this as the negotiations became more hostile, and retreated to her island, leaving the other five Sages to begin their bloody three thousand year war." Vangen leaned forward slightly. "But you'll recall the Chronicle of Fire does not mention the Artifacts after the failed Council of Dullahan. They seem to slip from the pages. But weapons of such power don't easily fade into obscurity. During the Sundering of Athar and the Fall of the Sages, the Elder Gods of Light discovered the treachery of the Gods of Darkness and in retaliation banished the followers of Iss to the shadow realms and sunk their lands into the seas. All assumed the Artifacts went with them into the deep." Vangen smiled slightly and leaned back. "But perhaps they did not. Perhaps they are still here."

Draegan furrowed his brow and eyed Vangen with interest.

"I believe Iss has come here and is searching for the Dark Artifacts. Once they have gathered these ancient weapons of great power, they will invade in full force and it will be too late for Fyrian. But if we move quickly, we may still be in time."

"In time for what, exactly?"

"To find them first. To gather them to us. It is only through finding the Dark Artifacts ourselves that we can prevent Iss from amassing enough power to overwhelm us. We at least stand a chance in battle if they cannot make use of the Dark Artifacts."

"But they are poison! If the Sages couldn't find a way to destroy those cursed weapons what hope do we have? Indeed we would be doing the servants of Darkness a favor by gathering them all in one place." Draegan tossed the book onto the desk. "I think your plan is folly."

Vangen looked at Draegan for several moments. "I appreciate your council, but in this instance I will follow my own wisdom." Vangen motioned for Draegan to sit. "I know I need not have your agreement to have your loyalty. But let us speak of other pressing matters. Tell me of the men you've gathered for your Graywalkers."

"We lost five good men in addition to our father, the King, in the hills of Stanrocc," Draegan said, not noticing the anger that flashed across Vangen's face, "but the Night Watch is an elite unit, so I had little trouble gathering men to avenge them."

"How much do they know?"

"Nothing, save that I need them. They are to gather tomorrow night for a special detail when they will be given more information."

"Excellent," said Vangen, smoothing a blank scroll on the desk. "Their names?"

"Gron Thaldin of the Clan of the Iron Mountains, Aran Hund of the Tribe of Docga, and Ceredyn Arcanis of the House of Corvus. All good men, all highly skilled, and all honor bound. I would trust them with my life."

"And so you shall, many times," Vangen said leaning back in his chair. Without his usual cloak Draegan could see how gaunt and stretched Vangen appeared in the flickering light.

"I know little of Gron Thaldin. Another bear from the north I presume?

"Yes, a beast of a man, the strongest in the Night Watch, and a good friend. He takes orders without complaint, a rare trait."

Vangen nodded and continued, "And if memory serves I believe Aran Hund fought with our fathers honorably in the War for Unity."

Draegan smiled briefly. "For someone always shut away in his study you know a great deal of the people in this castle. Yes he did serve, and well. He was very young then but proved himself capable. Since then he has only grow wiser and more proficient in his craft. He is a great woodsman and tracker and has mastered what little magic remains in the Tribe of Docga," he said, unconsciously rubbing his throat as he thought back to the aftermath of the *staminis* spell he'd used to run from Draken's Hold to Dullahan.

"It is my business to know things. Yours to do things," Vangen said, scratching words on the scroll on his desk. "And of Ceredyn I have heard strange tidings. He used to be a Raven of Corvus before he left their nest to roost with us in the Night Watch. I should like to know why. I become wary when a spy breaks his allegiance."

"I was unaware. I should like to know too. However he is the most skilled mage we have in the Night Watch. In fact he is the most skilled mage I have ever seen."

"For someone always beyond the walls of this city, you have seen little then," Vangen said as he smiled. "So these three men will be joining you, the most accomplished swordsman in the five Kingdoms. You were undefeated in every tournament father placed you in. The Little Lion of Skeldus father always called you. I hope they prove worthy of your company." Vangen finished his writing and looked up. "Now to your first mission."

"Yes, the assassination. Committing murder and treason against the Council is a grave action. Is there no other way?" Draegan asked, trying to read the scroll on the desk in the faint light.

"We both agree that Iss is a dire threat to the Empire. The Council does not, but in time they will change their way of thinking. However, I fear the Empire of Fyrian will collapse into five bickering kingdoms long before they recognize the menace of Iss." Vangen rolled the scroll up and moved it aside.

"The five kingdoms were bound together through respect for my father. I am clearly not my father. Among the kingdoms there is no great love of the sickly, dark son of the Lion of the Rising Sun. They think me weak, so the tenuous ties that bind the five kingdoms in peace will be severed when I assume the throne."

Vangen stood and walked to a table where he began sifting through books.

"Iss must become the common enemy that binds the Empire together, as my father was the force that bound them before me. But the servants of Darkness do not see this. They do not obey my commands. So we must force their hand," Vangen said depositing an armful of books on the desk.

"You would have war so soon? Even if it were possible we don't know where their forces are, what numbers they have, or even the strength of our own Empire. We are still rebuilding from our father's war," Draegan said leaning forward in his chair.

"You are too dramatic Draegan. We don't need a war. A simple death will suffice," Vangen said sitting once again.

"How will killing a Council member solidify the five kingdoms?"

"You will assassinate me."

Vangen continued before Draegan could put together the thoughts racing through his mind.

"Do not worry, you will not be successful. You will attempt to assassinate me, and you will make it look like the work of Iss. When I survive the people will rally behind me as the victim of the evil machinations of the warriors of darkness. My cries for war will be much harder to brush aside," Vangen said folding his arms across his chest.

"But this is madness brother. I wouldn't know where to begin if I even thought for a moment your plan had merit. Wouldn't your assassination attempt make you appear even weaker in the eyes of the Council?"

"Perhaps, but you get ahead of yourself so easily. We have time until my coronation, when you will attempt to assassinate me. Until then read these," Vangen said pushing a small stack of musty books and scrolls toward Draegan.

"These are ancient accounts written by a priest of Vatn during the War for Athar. They contain first hand descriptions of the methods and magic of the warriors of Iss. A rare find indeed, for his personal comments in the margins recreate the spells they used in great detail. With these, the account becomes a manual of shadow magic. Blasphemous to think it was rotting on a shelf in the White Temple," Vangen said smiling to himself.

"Once you've understood these codices, I want you to train your men in the tactics they describe. After you have mastered them we will move forward with my attempted assassination. You and your men will practice your new skills in the northern towns. So far only Stanrocc has suffered from these attacks. Baledin must become a believer in the peril Iss presents. And he is a hard man to win."

Draegan looked at the books and then at Vangen and furrowed his brow in disgust. "This cannot be done."

"If this proves beyond your men, replacements can be found."

"My men will obey me without question, but I will not obey you, brother. You have found the limits of my discretion. You'd have me murder innocent people using the foul methods of Iss solely to push Baledin to your side. Do you hunger for war so desperately?"

"You witnessed the brutality of Iss when you saw the horror in Draken's Hold. Would you wish the same on countless other villages? We both know what is coming. The sooner the council is convinced the sooner we can act. The sooner we act, the more deaths we prevent. Would you have us sit here arguing until the Four Gates are overrun? We'd be no better than the council. When we trained in Docga, one of the first lessons we learned from the hunt masters was how to treat a bite from a tree viper."

"Cut off the finger to save the hand," Draegan muttered. "Yet there must be another way."

"I wish there was. I do not revel in bloodshed. But you saw Baledin in the Council Room. There is no love lost between us. And Maluk is right in saying that his kingdom bears the brunt of the suffering. The rest do not understand the threat Iss poses. They are men of emotion, not logic, so they must be made to feel it. Do not think I have not already given myself the same council that you gave me now. A hundred times have I sought another way, but there is none. There are countless men, women, and children spread across the five kingdoms whose lives I would forfeit if we do not act now. If a few villagers are the cost for an Empire it would be folly not to pay the price."

There was a long pause as Draegan considered his words. "And I must pay it," Draegan said, finally staring at Vangen.

"The Graywalkers will be the instrument of salvation for Fyrian. It will not be pleasant work, but there is no other way to secure the safety of my empire."

Draegan crossed his arms and sat unmoving.

"Let us speak of something else for a moment, then. I neglected to tell you one of your cloak's greatest secrets." Vangen opened the top book on the stack he had given Draegan. "Here it is," he said pointing to a rune drawn on the margin of a decaying page. "Or rather here is part of it. It took me weeks to decipher the missing pieces."

"That is like no mark I've ever seen," began Draegan, forgetting his unease.

"It is the tongue of Iss. And with this mark you can use your cloak to shadow walk."

Draegan peered at the rune again in the dim light. "Show me."

"I already have. In the alcove near your bed chamber door I have drawn the full mark. In truth, I have many drawn in hidden spots all over the castle. With the cloak you can move between any other mark of your choosing in an instant. Did you not notice that one moment I was behind you telling you to prepare for the council meeting, and the next I was gone?" Vangen said, his eyes glinting with amusement.

"So that was how you moved so quickly," Draegan said eyeing Vangen with curiosity.

"Unfortunately part of the rune is missing from the text, and so the completed rune is my best educated guess. To make the two parts work together requires a small bit of effort. You must trace the sign with a bit of blood."

"Blood magic? This magic is banned for a reason Vangen," Draegan said, shutting the book with alarm.

"How does it differ from the *staminis* spell we learned from the hunt masters? Is it not made more potent when drawn with the caster's blood?"

"I don't have the words. It just feels wrong."

"You must push aside your feelings. The empire cannot afford your naïve scruples." Vangen paused and put a hand on Draegan's shoulder. "I know you to be a good and honorable man. This is why my father loved you, and why I trust you with the safety of the kingdoms, brother. What you and the Graywalkers will do is absolutely necessary for the Empire. We seek to preserve peace and protect ourselves from Iss. We cannot afford to limit ourselves when we should instead seek the use of all tools to aid our effort. Would you have us fight the coming war with one arm tied behind our collective backs?"

"If I agree and we do these terrible things for the empire, then how are we any different from Iss?"

"Our purpose, Draegan." Vangen rose and turned to a pile of books behind his desk. "We seek peace and stability. They seek power and dominion. No matter the methods we use, these two purposes will always divide the light from the darkness."

"And if I refuse?"

"You know the truth. You've seen the storm that is coming. If you don't try to stop it the blood of the five kingdoms will always be on your hands. Would you rather that or the blood of a few villagers?"

Draegan took the books and without looking at Vangen, left the study.

Chapter 9: A Storm Gathers

"Then burn it to the ground." Draegan was finishing the last hieratic symbol when Ceredyn gave him word that the other Graywalkers were done and waiting for his command.

The small village in the valley erupted into flames. From the hillside Draegan watched the shadows dance on the opposite slope. The forest was unusually quiet and from this distance the burning buildings seemed almost pleasant. Embers and smoke began to rise from the valley floor and Draegan followed them as they lazily ascended into the starry autumn sky.

As the fire spread and grew in intensity the cracks and pops of burning roof beams echoed in the still night air. No villagers or livestock made a sound, for Draegan and his Graywalkers had already dispatched them with the ease of men used to killing. Draegan caught a whiff of smoke. Something stirred in his memory.

It had been a long, hard year since Vangen had told him it was necessary to cut off a finger to save a hand. He and his Graywalkers had razed a village in the Iron Mountains. And then another. In the past year he and his Graywalkers had cut off enough fingers to make saving the hand pointless. Vangen had given him more and more ancient books and taught him the workings of the dark magic of Iss, which proved useful in his assassination attempt. Vangen had spoken of purpose and peace while ordering the deaths of his most vulnerable subjects.

Draegan understood the importance of maintaining the threat of Iss in order to unify the council. His work had convinced all the council members save Baledin of the notion that Fyrian must take the war to Iss before it was brought home. The five kingdoms had unified behind their new King. And now, with the subtle smell of burning oak in the cool autumn air, he understood the last piece of the puzzle that had been plaguing him. Vangen had lied.

"Graywalkers, to me," Draegan commanded, scratching a strange rune in the dirt. Within moments Gron, Ceredyn, and Aran were with him on the hilltop overlooking the conflagration below. Draegan pulled his cloak tighter to him, though it did not shield him from the bite of the night air.

"During this past year you have proven yourselves loyal to me without fault," Draegan said turning to address each man. "Now I ask for something that is beyond even what you have given."

"We are yours to command," Aran said looking curiously at Draegan.

"What would you have us do now?" Gron asked while tightening the fasteners on his belt.

"Go home, quickly. Prepare packs for a long journey. Make peace with what little faith you have left in humanity."

"A long journey?" Ceredyn asked. "Does the King know of this?"

"He will in moments. If I do not contact you within the hour, head west to the Spire of Heaven Mountains. Wait for me no longer than a day. Be swift, be silent, be unseen," Draegan said while crouching to the ground and retracing with his finger the strange symbol he had drawn when his team had arrived. As he finished, his cloak seemed to swallow him as a black mist rose from the rune, enveloping everyone in darkness. When the breeze blew the mist away a pocket of cold air was all that was left of Draegan.

"I always thought he should teach us that one," Gron said shaking his head and tugging reflectively on his thick red beard.

Draegan stepped out of the shadowy alcove near his bed chamber. He pushed open the door expectantly, but was met with disappointment again. It had been many months now since Issa had returned to Vatn to pay her offering to Helian. The few times Draegan returned home and opened the door he hoped to see her, but every time he was met instead with emptiness.

Shaking off his momentary sorrow he quickly moved through the room packing scrolls and books in a small bag that he attached to his pack. He stuffed his larger pack with supplies and checked to make sure he hadn't overlooked anything. During the past year his room had become almost a mirror image of Vangen's cramped study. Maps and charts hung on the walls, books and scrolls littered the floor making it almost impossible to walk anywhere. The bed was still made and buried in notes and piles of documents. Even the air had begun to take on a musty quality.

The thought of becoming Vangen's protégé left him cold. Now he had business to attend too. He locked the bedroom door, dumped his pack in the darkened alcove and strode down the hall.

As he approached the familiar iron-barred door of Vangen's study he saw it was slightly ajar. Taking another step toward it, the door began silently swinging inward. A single candle lit Vangen's face as he hunched over a giant codex on his desk.

"Back so soon?" Vangen said, not bothering to look up. Draegan stepped in and heard the door's mechanisms lock into place behind him.

"I wish to speak to you Vangen. Directly," Draegan said removing his gloves and tucking them into his belt.

"Please sit," Vangen said motioning to the chair as he rose. "I will light a fire. You always did enjoy them more than I."

"I shall stand, brother."

"Well then, what? Are we to stand here and look into each other's eyes until we fall asleep?"

Draegan took a step forward and thrust his finger at Vangen. "You murdered my father and mother and burned Draken's Hold to the ground. You murdered your own father who had adopted me as his son." Draegan narrowed his eyes and glared at his brother. "There is no threat of Iss, and you are mad. You must step down as King."

A thin smile spread across Vangen's face. "Oh I wish I had stayed sitting for this. I feel as though I may faint." Vangen sat back down and put his feet up on his desk. "You have stunned me. Where do I begin? Shall I pretend to take your accusations seriously by answering them or address the larger issue of your obvious insanity? And it must be insanity, for otherwise I would have to kill you for treason. The priests of Vatn are on call in the infirmary. They have special teas that can calm…"

"I know the truth Vangen. I am only guilty of not deciphering it sooner."

"Please help me to understand," Vangen said taking his feet off the desk and leaning forward into the faint candle light. He flashed a wicked smile.

"I am Iss. I and my Graywalkers are Iss. Iss has not attacked the Empire since we began our campaign to convince the Council. If there is no Iss then there are no Dark Artifacts and no threat, save that which I am responsible for causing. You have used me to gain the power you always lusted after."

Vangen slapped his hands on the heavy desk top. "Even when it's right in front of you, you still fail to see it." He stood up and looked at Draegan with a cruel smile. "No dear brother, it is not you, but I that am Iss. I am the threat that binds the Empire in peace. I am the common enemy but also the salvation of Fyrian. And though the servants of Iss are truly only a memory, the secrets their land contains are very real."

Vangen turned around and pulled a heavy black box off the lectern behind him. He set it on the desk and opened the lid. "You have not yet seen this," he said pulling an intricately carved sword hilt from its heavy felt wrappings. Figures writhed in agony along the grip and guard. Where the blade should have been there was only an empty gaping mouth.

"Your antique collection is the least of my concerns."

"Soon it will be your greatest. Watch." Vangen held the bladeless hilt upright in front of him and drawing his other hand down the length of the imaginary blade Draegan watched as a black fire burst forth from the hole that had been empty moments before.

"Carnis Fornax," Vangen said, admiring the black fire that leapt forth from the hilt in lieu of a blade. "One of the Artifacts of Darkness. Carried and put to great use by Fet Reth the Eater of Souls during the War for Athar." Vangen shifted his gaze to Draegan. "They say the sword holds the soul of every man it's killed, and with each death the bearer of this magnificent weapon grows more powerful."

Draegan's eyes were wide as he stepped back and reached for his own blade.

"A test? You may be a master swordsman, but I have not spent all my time in this study during the past year either, Draegan." Vangen stepped around the desk. "In fact I have become quite proficient. Though I doubt this blade would be a fair match for yours, no matter our relative skill levels."

"Impossible." Draegan took another step back. The greedy flame of Vangen's blade lit the room with a menacing black glow. Vangen pointed the formidable sword directly at him. Though he was several feet away he felt an icy chill throughout his body, as if all his warmth was being drawn out toward the weapon.

"I learn something new about this sword every day. I can feel it hungering for you," Vangen said while bringing the weapon back under his own eyes. "I have been experimenting with this Artifact, but have neglected to use it as it was originally designed. I can feel its thirst. Compelling."

"So the six Artifacts of Darkness exist?" Draegan began looking around the room nervously.

"Oh yes. You wear one even now. The Chronicle of Fire calls it the Shadow Walker. Gifted to Dalken Tor the Burning Shadow by the Elder God Vyr during the War for Athar. I do miss it. It would make gathering the remaining four Artifacts so much easier." Vangen lowered the blade and smiled at Draegan. Holding out his hand he said, "Would you be so kind?"

Draegan unsheathed his blade in the wavering black light and began chanting.

"I thought my study to be the one place in this castle where I was safe from such plots. I see now I was mistaken." Vangen began circling Draegan and moved slowly toward the door.

"Surrounding yourself with this darkness has poisoned you against reason, Vangen. You sought stability. I thought our purpose was peace," Draegan said keeping his eyes on Vangen while trying not to stumble over the books strewn about the study. "And now you would throw it all away for power."

"You know as well as I do that peace cannot be achieved through the council. My father kept them bound together through force of will, but they are petty and bickering, and their short-sighted self interest will destroy what our fathers fought so hard to achieve. Thousands of years of hatred and war between the five kingdoms cannot be undone by one man with good intent. Only a king can keep order, and only a powerful one at that. The feeble attempt my father made at placing a council at the head of the empire was destined to fail. Five kings cannot share rule of an empire. There is only room for an Emperor." Vangen flashed a wicked smile as he stood between Draegan and door.

Draegan looked toward the soot stained window. "You seek dominion over Fyrian as surely as the Dark Artifacts seek dominion over you."

"You are wrong Draegan. I shall control the Artifacts. I have plumbed their depths and discovered powers hidden within them that even those who once wielded them could not make use of. Once I have them all I will be a force none dare oppose. My word will be law and the law will be obeyed."

Draegan gripped his sword with both hands and shifted his weight to his back leg. "You would be our Emperor? You know what is best for Fyrian?"

"Yes," Vangen said feinting at Draegan, his eyes wide and white in the dim light.

Draegan leaned back feeling the air in front of his face chill as the blade passed by. "Then I must stop you," Draegan said as he sprung off his back foot and leapt at Vangen. His blade came down in a vicious arc.

"Such hate behind that blow. Do you mean to kill me? Foolish treachery," Vangen chided, catching Draegan's assault with the burning black blade. With a flick of his wrist Vangen sent Draegan and his sword stumbling backward. Draegan tripped over a stack of books and caught himself on the desk.

"This sword lends great power, indeed," Vangen said slowly closing the distance between them. "Come now. I expected more from the most celebrated swordsman in the Empire. I suggest you do better than that if you want me dead. I wonder what father would say if he could see how easily I toy with his favored one."

Vangen raised his blade and it came down so quickly that Draegan barely had time to raise his sword in defense. He caught the black blade before it split him in two but the force of the blow drove his own weapon into his shoulder. He felt the warm blood trickle down his arm even as his own blade felt icy from contact with the dark souls of Vangen's sword.

"With only half effort I strike like ten men. Skillful swordplay cannot hope to overcome such a weapon," Vangen said raising the sword again. Draegan rolled out of the way as the blade sunk into the desk. He gripped his sword in both hands and felt the hilt become slippery as the blood from his wound ran down his arm. His eyes darted around, looking for a possible escape.

"We are too high up for you make use of the window, and I must inform you that the door opens only at my command," Vangen said pulling his sword from the desk. He turned to face Draegan. "I will make it painless."

As Vangen pulled back his arm to strike, Draegan slammed his left palm onto the leather cover of an ancient tome atop a stack of books. Keeping his hand on the book he looked up and saw the black fire of Carnis Fornax howling through the air toward his face. Then he saw nothing but darkness.

In a rare moment of surprise, Vangen looked to where Draegan had stood moments before. He examined the cover of the book. Bending over he snapped his fingers and a red light illuminated the room. On the cover of the book a bloody print of the shadow walking rune glistened in the red light. "Perhaps I did choose well," Vangen said smiling.

"Let the hunt begin."

Chapter 10: The Clouds Break

Draegan hit the back of his head against the stones in the alcove. Realizing where he was he stopped ducking the blade that no longer threatened him and rubbed his head. Sheathing his sword, he picked up his pack and shouldered it in one motion. He winced from the fresh wound in his shoulder. He'd tend to it later, once he was beyond the castle walls. For now, he had to move as quickly as possible. Vangen had most likely erected magical barriers to prevent his escape, but he had no other option. Placing his bloody hand on the wall he muttered a few words and was again swallowed by darkness.

"Graywalkers, to me," Draegan whispered into the cold night air. No response. He peered around the corner of the stone wall that hid him from the torchlight. The sound of boot heels scuffing the courtyard cobblestones echoed in the stillness. "They must have left ahead of me," he said while pulling a piece of paper from his pack. He needed to find his small company and quickly, before Vangen could raise an alarm and send men and hounds after him. Draegan crumpled the paper in his hand and kept squeezing it until it ignited. He blew the burning embers out of his palm and watched them rise slowly, then whip toward the tear of Helian which had begun rising.

"West. Just as I told them. Good dogs." Draegan rose from a crouch near the rear of the Night Watch barracks and peered around the corner again. No alarm torches had been lit and the two sentries walking the upper wall were talking quietly. Still some time.

Draegan lifted his finger and traced a rune on his neck. He wished he had a horse, already feeling the exhaustion creeping into his bones. He took a deep breath. The cold air helped wake him up as he once again placed his bloody hand on the cold stone wall of the barracks. Darkness swirled around him again.

***

Vangen smiled as he looked out of his study window. Below him in the outer courtyard he saw a dark shape hunched near the Night Watch barracks. "Predictable." As he turned from the window to his desk the clear glass panes became pitch black. "Gather your friends and head to Vatn." Vangen slid his hand down the length of the blade from the tip to the hilt and the black flame receded into the grip. "I hope you prove good sport for my Reavers, Draegan. I'll give you until sunset tomorrow for the sake of our father, then no quarter."

***

"Rise and shine." Draegan's eyes snapped open. He couldn't see anything in the darkness as he reached for his blade. His other arm felt tight and stiff as it shot to his boot for the dirk hidden there.

"Sit still before you ruin Aran's bandaging." Draegan blinked as he recognized Gron's voice. He blinked again, and after a moment his eyes adjusted to the darkness. He stood up. "How long…where…" he began before Gron cut him off.

"We found you an hour ago. Passed out a few feet off the side of the King's Road. You got ahead of us somehow."

Ceredyn continued the explanation. "We left before you as instructed and moved west. Aran picked up a blood trail a few miles back, and I located you with a *topos* spell. You placed no barrier spells to protect yourself, an oversight we have corrected since finding you and bandaging your wound."

Draegan looked down at his hand in surprise. He saw the palm of his left hand was completely bandaged. He pulled his glove from his belt and slipped it on.

"Interesting scar," Ceredyn said. He pulled his knees to his chest, making his slight frame even more compact. His dark eyes moved unblinking from Draegan's bandaged hand to his face as his thin lips curled into a slight smile. "I'm beginning to understand you."

"You think that looks good, you should see some of mine," Gron offered, his giant grin flashing through his red beard in the moonlight. He hooked his thick hands in his massive leather belt, drawing a deep breath and holding it, looking expectantly at the others. Exhaling he asked, "So where are we going?"

"And why?" Aran asked looking directly at Draegan. "You've always been clear with us in the past."

"I will tell you and then you must decide as you wish. But hear the whole story before you choose." Taking stock of the situation, Draegan adjusted his cloak and checked his pack and weapons. Flexing his bandaged shoulder he looked through the trees and saw the braziers of the King's Road burning in the distance.

"I am now an enemy of the Empire. I have turned against my brother, who has gone mad and killed my father as well as King Atrox. Vangen has succumbed to the foul arts and practices blood magic. He is versed in the magic of Iss. The threat of Iss is a lie. Iss is still in the shadows, and he uses its false threat as a means to keep the council occupied while he gathers the Artifacts of Darkness to himself to rule all of Athar. Vangen is the true enemy. When I questioned him about this, he agreed and attacked me. I fled and now head west to Vatn where I will gather the remaining lost books of Iss and then proceed to beat Vangen at his own game, by obtaining the Dark Artifacts first."

Ceredyn and Aran stared dumbfounded at Draegan as Gron burst into laughter.

"I didn't get much of anything past 'enemy of the Empire,'" Gron said wiping a tear from his eye. "Why are we going to Vatn?"

"King Vangen has orchestrated the myth of Iss to keep the Council occupied while he hunts the Artifacts of Darkness. We were never under attack from Iss. The four of us were, in truth, all that exists as Iss. He used us to kill innocent people so he could force the council to lend him more power. Vangen is mad, but he is also exceedingly powerful and cunning. I believe he can and will do what he says. If I find the four remaining Artifacts first and destroy them I can limit his reach, which is all I can hope to do now."

"You claim the Dark Artifacts are real but Iss remains nothing more than a myth. How can this be?" Ceredyn asked.

"I have no authority to answer that save this." Draegan reached for his shoulder and said, "This wound was given indirectly by Carnis Fornax, the fabled sword of Fet Reth and the most sinister of the Six Blades of Darkness. The Chronicle of Fire tells how Fet Reth used Carnis Fornax to slay an entire legion of Sage Stanrocc's soldiers in the battle of Kiarn For. Vangen now wields this fiendish Artifact. I have seen its black flame and felt its unrelenting hunger as it tried to pull the life from my blood." Touching the clasp on his cloak he continued, "In truth I wear an Artifact myself. A gift from Vangen, it is the Shadow Walker, worn by Dalken Tor during the War for Athar. A dangerous garment, but it has its uses and proved itself invaluable in saving my life tonight."

"So that's how you can do it," Gron said snapping to attention. Ceredyn eyed the cloak and nodded to himself in understanding as he pulled his hood over his jet black hair, tucking a few strands behind his ear.

Aran, who had been gathering dry tinder while Draegan spoke, placed the branches and twigs in the middle of the group and squatted over the pile. Holding his hands on the wood, it began to glow and caught fire. He stood up to his full height and cracked his back. He was almost as tall as Gron, but his sinewy frame made him appear much smaller next to Northerner's bulk. Though he was twenty years older than the others, he possessed incredible stamina and could move like the wind through the forest as can many of woodsmen from the Tribe of Docga. Looking down at Draegan he said, "I served with your father as well as King Leon in the War for Unity. They were great men. You have brought no shame to their memory and so I will continue to serve with you now."

Aran pulled the hood of his cloak up over his salt and pepper hair. "I will follow where you lead. If you are an enemy of the Empire, I am as well. If you seek the Dark Artifacts, I will hunt them with you."

Gron stepped over to the smokeless fire and joined Draegan and Aran. He was as wide as them both, a massive beast from the north, though he was quicker to laugh than to anger. "I wouldn't want to let Aran and you have all the fun," he said grinning through his red beard at them both. "Hunting the legendary six Artifacts of Darkness? Well that'll make good tavern talk," he said hiking up his belt, dangling its two hatchets, "now where did you say they were?"

"We head to Vatn to raid the archives of the few remaining books concerning Iss and the Artifacts. I must have more knowledge of these weapons before I begin hunting them."

"The archives of Vatn," Ceredyn said standing slowly from the log he was sitting on, "are said to contain all the knowledge of the Sages since the War for Athar. I'd gladly become an enemy of the Empire for a few hours in there." His unblinking eyes stared off into the distance as the firelight lit his frail features from below, making him appear even more thin and spectral.

"I don't ask any of you to accompany me on this quest. That you have done so willingly speaks to your character. The oaths you have sworn to me as members of the Graywalkers are void."

"What choice do we have? If we return to Dullahan, Vangen will kill us or we will just be sent right back out to hunt you, no doubt," Ceredyn said. "I have less fatal ways to spend my remaining years."

"Then let us move now. We can make the mountains by dawn. Dullahan still sleeps. I've heard no horns announcing the opening of the gates at this late hour. I don't know why Vangen waits, but we should make use of the time," Aran said, kicking apart the fire and watching the light die out.

"I agree. We must make haste while we can. You all know the *staminis* spell. Tonight we use it and push for the Spire of Heaven Mountains," Draegan said rubbing his burning throat.

"And then through the wetlands of Corvus. The crow's flying home," Gron said slapping Ceredyn a little too hard on his shoulder.

Ceredyn pitched forward before catching his balance. "Maybe I'll return to the Rookery and leave you three on your own. I don't know if I can handle this oaf for much longer." He pulled a small curve bladed knife from his belt and pricked his finger. He traced the symbol on his throat. "This always makes my head spin."

The other three were already ahead of him, running at full speed down the King's Road.

Chapter 11: The Enemy of Fyrian

"Really Vangen. At this late hour?" Arius said as Vangen's footsteps echoed in the vast empty space of the white marbled council chamber. "What is it now?"

"Greetings Arius," Vangen said sweeping past him and settling into his chair. "You may all be seated."

Baledin looked around the chamber and missing Draegan said, "I see you've let your lapdog sleep through this meeting. Or is he out chasing rabbits for you?"

"Such a natural segue. The wonders that spill from your mouth. Thank you Baledin. My 'lapdog' is the reason for this emergency meeting," Vangen said looking at each council member.

"Draegan has betrayed me. He has rebelled against the Empire and taken some of his Night Watchmen with him. They fled west only an hour ago, heading for the Spire of Heaven Mountains and presumably the kingdom of Corvus."

"My Ravens have reported nothing," Arius said looking around the table. "I assure you this is the first I'm hearing of it."

"Of course it is. It only occurred an hour ago, and in my study at that. Not even your network of Ravens works that quickly. Draegan tried to kill me. When this failed he fled with three of his men."

"Your own brother tried to kill you?" Tysta asked, eyeing him suspiciously. Vangen set his jaw at the word 'brother', but let the anger pass. "And you say he failed? Draegan is one of the best swordsmen in the five kingdoms."

"He is also a master of the Dark Arts," Vangen said rising from his chair and removing a leather bound book from his cloak. He threw it into the middle of the table with a resounding thud. The council members stared in silence.

"That is his blood mark. He dropped the book as he fled. It contains ancient runes and other foul information pertaining to Iss and their dark magic."

"The council members recoiled at the site of the book. Baledin broke the silence.

"You bested Draegan, bloodied him, and forced him to flee?"

"I am not the child you seem to think I am Baledin," Vangen snapped. "A simple spell will confirm the truth of the matter of the blood. The rest will be revealed in a few days. Draegan is now an enemy of the Empire. I suspect that he has been tainted by his contact with the dogs of Iss. Whatever the reason, he must be brought to justice for his attempt on my life. Make it known throughout your territories. Anyone who aids him or his men is a traitor to the Empire."

Arius looked up at Baledin from the thin sheet of paper he had placed over the book. "The blood is Draegan's. No question. But where did he acquire such a rare book? I should like to have it sent to the Headmaster of the Rookery. Outside of the priests of Vatn he's the most knowledgeable on ancient matters."

"The book stays with me," Vangen said picking it up from the table and tucking it quickly away in the folds of his cloak.

"How did he get past the Western Gate? It closes at sunset and remains closed until dawn. Has the Night Watch reported anything?" Tysta asked, shifting in her seat.

"There are many ways out of this antiquated castle other than the Lion's Mouths. But Draegan left by sorcery. The mark on the book is a rune of Iss. It allows him, with the aid of his dark cloak to walk through shadows. That is how he appeared unannounced in my study. It is also how he left."

"If anyone was a master of the Dark Arts I would've thought it to be you," Baledin said. "Not the golden boy."

"One day I would like to peer into that skull of yours. I truly do not know if you meant to insult me or compliment me. I doubt you know either."

Arius rose. "Even if he is using dark magic, four men are hardly a threat to the Empire. He has fled and can do little, especially once we announce his treason to the people. What does he plan to do that has you so concerned that you drag us from our beds?"

"He wants what everyone wants," Vangen said looking around the room, "my throne." "He seeks power and an army. He hunts the Dark Artifacts and will wield them against the Empire of Fyrian. He must be stopped. He has gone mad."

"Probably from the company he keeps," Baledin muttered a little too loudly.

"Ha! Baledin, you shock me. Such wit." Vangen turned to face the other council members as Arius sat back down. The Council members shifted uncomfortably in their chairs. "I am glad you find this amusing. Forgive me if I'm unable to take Draegan's betrayal so lightly. Our Empire is under assault from Iss, and my adopted brother seeks to deliver it into their hands using the Dark Artifacts. I trust your good humor will see you and the Clan of the Iron Mountains through the coming war."

Baledin folded his arms across his massive chest. "The Dark Artifacts aren't real, Vangen."

"If you believe that, mighty bear of the North then you are a fool. He was wearing one of the Dark Artifacts even as he tried to end my life. His cloak is the Shadow Walker previously worn by Dalken Tor, one of the six Blades of Darkness and their most cunning general. Would it not follow that if one is real they all may be real? And with his book," Vangen said, gesturing at the spot on the table where a bit of blood still lay, "he may be able to discern where the other Artifacts are hidden."

They stared at each other until Tysta spoke up. "What can we do my liege?"

"As I have said. Make the announcements to your kingdoms. Ensure that every villager knows not only his face, but the pain they will suffer for aiding him." Vangen circled the table and headed for the great double doors that sealed them in the room. "I will hunt the four traitors myself."

The doors began swing open. "You may retire," Vangen said as he strode out of the chamber and was consumed in the darkness of the hallway.

***

Vangen waited for his eyes to adjust to the darkness of his study as the door locked behind him. He walked over to the lectern behind his desk and moved the wooden box to his desk. He opened the lid and removed the heavy felt that covered the hilt of his bladeless sword. Snapping his fingers over his head and slowly lowering his hand to the box, Vangen picked up the finely wrought hilt as all the books and clutter of his study arranged themselves against the edge of his circular study, clearing a large space in front of his desk. A green light began to emanate from the mortar joints in the flagstone floor.

As Vangen circled the desk a large flagstone began to groan as it slid into a hidden channel, revealing a spiral staircase that led down into darkness. He entered the opening and began descending as the green light followed him downward, clinging to the rock wall and tracing paths in the mortar joints.

At the bottom of the long, winding stairs, Vangen stopped and snapped his fingers again. The green light intensified to reveal a large barrel vaulted chamber so high it stretched up into the darkness, beyond the limits of the spell. Along the walls were thousands of large niches carved in the bedrock.

Vangen approached one of the niches and pulled heavily on a thick wool blanket that covered a large shapeless mass. Two bodies rolled out of the alcove and thumped onto the damp stone floor. Vangen crouched next to the sprawled out bodies and covered his face from the stench of the decaying flesh. "I can tolerate the cold and damp down here, but there is never any fresh air this far under the castle," he said taking his glove off his other hand.

Using a small knife Vangen pricked his finger and drew a symbol on each of the cadaver's chests. He then slid his fingers down the length of his sword's missing blade and watched the black flame spring to life from the gaping maw carved in the hilt. He plunged the burning blade into each rune he had drawn and bit his tongue to silence the scream of pain that grew within him.

Taking a few deep breaths and wiping the sweat from his brow he stood up and watched the bodies on the floor begin to writhe. A few moments later the lifeless corpses stood on shaking legs before him, mouths agape and staring with milky eyes at their summoner.

Vangen pulled the book from his cloak and wiped a streak of blood on each corpse's forehead. "You hunt the man whose blood was on this book, my reavers. Go. Find him. Kill him and those with him."

Vangen smiled as he watched the corpses turn down the dark hallway, drop to all fours and begin to change into wolves. He turned to head back up the spiral stairs, hearing their nails scrape against the stone floor as they ran into the darkness.

Back in his study as he sat in his desk amidst the clutter he heard the faint howling of wolves in the distance and smiled. "Good hunting my reavers."

Chapter 12: Over the Mountains

"A few more minutes of daylight. Let's finish our descent and make camp in the lowlands," Aran said over his shoulder to the other three behind him. The sun, which had warmed their backs most of the day as they climbed and nearly blinded them as they descended, had finally settled below the horizon thirty minutes ago.

"He probably won't let us even make a decent fire," Gron grumbled as he half slid down the last few feet of the talus cone. "I was hoping to roast something tonight."

"If you had focused more on your feet and less on stomach while we climbed we could have finished this descent and made camp an hour ago," Ceredyn shouted up as the three waited at the bottom of the hill for Gron.

"It's not my fault you crows of Corvus make these mountain passes so thin that only a sparrow can squeeze through," Gron said dusting off his legs as he joined the others.

"We break the *staminis* spell and make camp here for the night. We don't have time for hunting game, and I won't risk a fire anyway," Draegan said looking out over the windswept marshes that lay ahead for tomorrow's journey. "Ceredyn, seal this area. Hide our presence and make the magic barriers outside of our camp easily passable by any person so we know if we're being pursued. Gron, make camp. Aran, use the last few minutes of light to scout a path through the marshes. I'll take first watch. We're up before dawn men. Rest well."

***

Aran stirred in his bedroll. Looking at the stars he saw it was well past midnight and Draegan hadn't awakened him to switch shifts. He turned and saw him sitting on a low boulder reading a book in the moonlight.

"You forgot to wake me," Aran said walking over to the rock.

"Couldn't sleep, no sense making you lose sleep too." Draegan closed the book and slid off the boulder into the wet mossy ground. "I can't help but wonder what evil Vangen is planning. It's been a full day and we've seen nothing. The Night Watch should have been at our heels in the mountains."

"I don't think he'd spare them to hunt the four of us. You've seen him these past few months. He's become more paranoid. He sees dissent and plots everywhere. He'll keep them close to home to do his dirty work now that we're gone. He needs to keep the threat of Iss alive and he needs skilled hands to do it." Aran watched Draegan slip the book back into his pack. "If he's as powerful as you claim, then I'd rather not try to predict what dire plans he has in store for us."

"You always give wise council. I should focus on what we do know. Getting into the archives will be no small feat."

Aran saw how worn Draegan looked. "Here chew this. It'll help you get some rest," he said handing him a dried root from his satchel. "I'll take the watch now."

If Draegan dreamed he didn't remember. He woke in the false dawn feeling heavy and slow, but with a deep breath of crisp air his body was shocked awake. His wound felt better as he rolled his shoulder to loosen it up. Packing up his gear he saw the other three standing nearby pointing in different directions. Gron was gesturing emphatically.

Ceredyn broke from the group and approached Draegan. "Gron wants to turn south and make for the coast as swiftly as possible. He thinks we can take a boat through the harbor of Skeldus and reach the island of Vatn faster. I know this land and think we can make the western coast as swiftly by foot as through the harbor, which is bound to be patrolled." Ceredyn looked back at Gron, still gesturing wildly, and turned to Draegan. "What would you council?"

"I have little love for the wetlands you call home, Ceredyn. To make the journey by foot as swiftly as by sea would require the use of the *staminis* spell every day. We'd reach the coast broken, with little left for the journey to the Isle of Vatn. I'll risk the harbor as it's harder to track us than if we went by land."

"But we're easy targets in a boat, Draegan," Ceredyn said. I know this land is hostile to outsiders, but as hard as it is to navigate even for me, it makes it that much harder for our pursuers.

"We don't know who or what if anything is pursuing us and I don't want to find out. I want speed. We go by sea. We'll skirt the coast and break for land if there is trouble," Draegan said looking at Ceredyn, "though there shouldn't be too much if your magic seals are put to good use. Tell the others."

"It just makes more sense this way," Gron explained loudly as the four broke from the camp site. Ceredyn sulked a few paces behind the others, pulling his black cloak tighter around his slight frame.

Gron looked over his shoulder. "Does it ever stop raining here? The ground's wet, the rocks are wet, the air's wet. I've swallowed so much water I bet I'll sprout gills before I even make it to sea," he said. It had started to drizzle during Aran's watch and now at first light it was coming down heavier.

"You'll get less of it in you if you keep your mouth shut," Ceredyn snapped.

Draegan pulled his cloak tighter against the cold wind that had picked up with the rain. "Aran, I need your eyes in the lead. Ceredyn I want you pulling up the guard, making sure we leave no trace. Gron, you're with me."

Like a fox Aran began finding solid ground as he quickly put distance between himself and the others. Ceredyn had begun dismantling the spells that sealed their camp. "The sooner, the better," Gron said looking at Draegan.

"I have an uneasy feeling, but I can't place it. Let's move," Draegan said following Aran's footsteps through the soggy ground. "Keep up, Gron. I don't want you in the rear slowing Ceredyn down with small talk," he said, a slight smile on the edge of his lips.

It was a little after sunset when Ceredyn ran up to Draegan from the rear. They had been making slow progress through the fens and were soaked to the bone from the driving rains. "Call Aran back from the front. I'd like his eyes on something."

"Might as well make camp here then," Draegan said. After a few minutes Aran returned to the group and backtracked a mile with Ceredyn. Gron and Draegan began to make camp. When Aran and Ceredyn returned they found Draegan and Gron huddled around a small fire burning in the shelter of a rock outcropping.

"What do you know of wolves coming this far south, Gron?" Aran asked.

"I've rarely heard of them crossing the Iron Mountains, and the few times they have they picked better sport than this sponge of a country."

"Then we have a problem," Ceredyn said. "We have two wolves tracking us."

"Two wolves aren't problem," Gron said laughing. "They're dinner."

Ceredyn didn't laugh with the others. "I've been placing barriers and removing all traces of our movement. Wolves shouldn't be able to track us if they don't have a scent to follow," Ceredyn said.

"Maybe you're just not that good of a mage," Gron replied, stretching his hands over the fire.

"I think these are something more than wolves, Draegan," Aran said crouching down near the rock to get out of the rain. "At the rate they're going they'll be here in an hour."

"Well then I'll eat in an hour," Gron said leaning back against the rock while trying to find a spot that wasn't wet.

Ceredyn was the first to notice when the wolves broke the outermost of his seals. "No animal should be able to do that," he said pointing off in the distance. Two yellow eyes flickered in the light of the fire. A moment later they were joined by another pair.

"Ceredyn, stay here and put up a seal behind them to cut off their retreat. I want lights on them when I give the command. If you can pin them with a spell, do it," Draegan whispered. "Aran, cover Ceredyn with your bow. Use the arrows with the glyphs. If you can put an arrow in each one, Ceredyn can track them through spells if we lose sight of them. If Ceredyn can't pin with them with his enchantments then keep them boxed in with your arrows. Gron, we'll head out and flank them."

Ceredyn squatted by the boulder and began drawing symbols and chanting. Aran knocked two arrows and drew his black bow.

The wolves paced back and forth in the distance, staying close to the edge of the seal they had just penetrated. "Ready when you are," Aran said.

"Count ten after we leave, then fire." Draegan looked at Gron who nodded in agreement. He was breathing heavily in the damp air and anxiously squeezing the grips of his hatchets. "Now," Draegan yelled.

Draegan and Gron each sprinted out from opposite sides of the boulder and ran toward the wolves. As they closed the distance two white bolts flew over their shoulders at the wolves who continued to pace back and forth, tongues lolling out of their mouths. As the arrows sped toward their quarry, Ceredyn shouted and the shafts burst into flame. Each arrow found its mark behind the wolves' shoulder blades. Draegan and Gron stopped in their tracks thirty feet from the wolves.

Each wolf had a burning white arrow piercing its body, yet they both continued to pace back and forth. Ceredyn yelled from behind the boulder.

"I can't pin them. Something's not right. I don't think they're alive."

"They look plenty alive to me," Gron said, looking at Draegan.

Suddenly the wolves fell to the spongy earth and began writhing. Their forms twisted and bent with audible snaps and cracks. In the light of the burning arrows the four watched in horror as two human bodies began to rise from the ground.

"Shapeshifters?" Gron said. "I've got something for that." He charged the rest of the distance and sunk his hatchet up to the handle into the closest human's neck. The pallid body shot out its arm with blinding speed and locked on to Gron's wrist as he tried to prise his hatchet from the corpse.

"It's like iron," Gron yelled. Draegan rushed over and brought his blade down in a savage arc, severing the arm at the elbow. The appendage released Gron and both he and Draegan ran back to the boulder. Arrows whistled over their heads and stuck ineffectually in the cold, pale bodies that were shambling closer to the group's position.

"I think they're already dead. Corpses. You can't kill them," Ceredyn said scratching runes on the boulder with a burnt stick. There's nothing left to kill,"

Aran stopped firing arrows. "Ceredyn, what can we do?"

"I'm not sure," Ceredyn replied.

"Well fire isn't working, we can't pin them, and our weapons can't kill what's already dead," Aran said climbing down from the top of the boulder. "Think quickly Ceredyn. They'll be here soon."

"He has my hatchet stuck in him," Gron said between breaths. "I want it back."

"It'll have to wait Gron. We make for the coast as quickly as possible. *Staminis* spell. They seem slower in their human form. Let's hope they can't change back with those arrows in them," Draegan said.

"I can't cast as well while using the *staminis* spell. Right now we really don't know what they're capable of. There's no point using up all our energy running away, only to find them right on our heels when we collapse," Ceredyn said slapping his hands on the boulder and muttering incantations. "I set up a stronger barrier spell and a way to track them."

"Then let's go. We'll have to come up with something while we move. I'd rather not have them following us to sea," Draegan said pulling his hood over his head and stepping into the rain. He turned to look at the creatures behind him. "They seem to be struggling with the barrier. Good. More time. Let's move. It's going to be a long night."

The first rays of dawn had broken the overcast sky when Ceredyn yelled at the group. They had been running all night, constantly pushed by the two reavers, without opportunity to rest.

"They've stopped," Ceredyn said turning to look behind him. "The last seal has held."

"Thank the Sages," Gron said, leaning over to catch his breath on one of the many small boulders that dotted the marsh.

"Do we keep moving or go back and find out why they stopped?" Draegan asked.

Ceredyn looked at the sky and thought for a moment. "Sunrise? Maybe they don't move in the light? But where would they shelter out here? The fens offer little protection."

"We still don't know enough about them," Aran said, putting a hand on Draegan's shoulder. "I don't have many arrows left and we have no solutions if we have to fight them again. I'd like to put some sea between myself and them while we think."

"Wise council. Let's make the coast today," Draegan said looking at the clouds breaking in the east. "I want to get ahead of the storm that's coming."

***

It was evening when they began to smell the salt water in the air. An hour later they were at a small port talking with a boatswain as he inspected the rigging.

"We can't take one more person, let alone four," he said while looking up at the mainsail. "No room and no provisions. We have all the men we need, thank you."

Draegan reached his hand into his pack and produced a fistful of gold. "Put us in the cargo hold. Two days out we'll take a life boat and be gone. We will cause you no trouble."

The boatswain looked at the seal of Skeldus on the gold pieces and back at the four bedraggled men with their muddy boots, and wet clothing. "Fine, but keep silent in the cargo hold. One word and the whole crew will dump you overboard. They might get ideas that you're stealing our merchandise." He led them down to the dark, musty cargo hold where they cleared a space to rest.

As the hatch slammed shut Draegan cast a small illumination spell and looked around. "Ceredyn, if you would please." Ceredyn made the marks for a barrier and slumped against a barrel. He was asleep instantly.

Gron muttered something about a hatchet and passed out on a sack of flour. "I guess I'll take first watch again," Draegan said smiling. "Get some sleep Aran. This journey has only just begun."

***

Miles from shore, as the sun sank into the sea and the last rays of light were swallowed by the dark water, two of the many hundreds of small boulders that dotted the fen began to tremble. In the growing darkness the rocks distorted. Arms and legs appeared and within moments the small boulders were now two men, standing in the marsh, mouths hanging slack, dead eyes looking to the south and west as their prey slipped out of the dock and into the black waters.

Together, they began walking west.

Chapter 13: A Night at Sea

Aran was on watch when he heard Ceredyn stir in his sleep. "The seal," was all Ceredyn managed to say before the hatch above the cargo hold creaked open. Draegan snapped awake and saw the boatswain walking down the stairs with a torch held in front of his face. His wide grin showed his mouth had more metal than teeth.

"Been thinking," the boatswain said as he stepped into the cargo hold and looked around. "The crew and I appreciate the token gesture you fine gentlemen from Skeldus have made, but as we're fifteen hard working men, and you've only given us seven pieces of gold, well it makes it very difficult to divide fairly. I'm sure you understand our predicament, and would be more than willing to help."

Gron, who had been sleeping, woke up enough to ask, "What are we dividing?"

"We're about to divide this boatswain," Draegan said reaching for his sword.

"No need for any of that now. Don't want to make trouble. We only need eight more pieces and you fine men look like you could easily find two pieces each between the four of you," the boatswain said looking from man to man. "Fine boots too, once you look past the mud. Those could fetch a fair price if you'd rather keep your gold. Just trying to be fair."

As the boatswain talked a small door behind the water barrels creaked open and several dark figures slipped into the room. Several more men came down the stairs and stood behind the boatswain.

"How many?" Draegan asked, keeping his eyes locked on the figure in front of him.

"Fourteen," Ceredyn said backing against Aran. Gron joined Draegan. "Block the rear, we're going up the stairs," Draegan said.

"Gentlemen this would go so much easier if you'd just look within your generous hearts," the boatswain said. "A mere eight more pieces of gold for your fifteen humble servants." The boatswain stepped closer, and held the torch over his head. "I'll say it again. Fifteen humble servants, serving four honored guests. Please don't be rash."

"I'd rather get a look at your generous heart, friend," Draegan said leaping at the boatswain and cutting him down in one motion. Instantly Ceredyn raised his hands, wove his fingers together and breathed into them. A blue fire erupted between the companions and the ten men who were charging from the rear of the cargo hold. They stumbled back as Gron leapt toward the three sailors at the front of the hold and buried a hatchet in a sailor's skull. Aran sunk two bolts in the remaining attacker's throats.

"Up the stairs and bolt the hatch," Draegan said.

Once they were topside, they quickly began lowering the boat's dinghy into the dark water. Below they heard the men yelling.

"We better hurry before this ship catches fire," Gron said looking over his shoulder.

"The fire was an illusion, though that boatswain's torch was real enough," Ceredyn said.

The small boat landed with a splash and Aran leapt over the rail and landed softly toward the rear. The three hurriedly threw packs down to Aran and climbed down the rope into the boat. Draegan was the last to enter and pushed off the ship with a paddle.

"Row toward the Tear of Helian," Draegan said. "It's going to be another long night."

"We should go back and save some of them," Gron said wistfully looking at the ship.

"Save them? Those filthy sea dogs tried to kill us. And what would we do with them in this tiny boat?" Ceredyn asked.

"No no. The salted pork barrels from the cargo hold."

Chapter 14: The Isle of Vatn

It was two days of hard rowing and as many sleepless nights before they put their feet on dry land again. Aran read the wind and guided them during the day while Ceredyn had quickened the pace by calming the waves. The four of them drank greedily from a small stream that emptied into the bay a few hundred feet from where they put ashore. They dragged the boat into some brush and hid their tracks.

Filling their water skins, Aran was the first to speak. "How far to the White Temple?"

"And just how exactly will you get them to spread wide their gates for four enemies of the Empire?" Ceredyn asked.

"A day's journey north and east. As to entering, usually I would favor a direct approach. I am known to many of the acolytes and priests. I trained here for some time in my youth." Draegan paused before continuing. "I also have familial ties that would gain me entrance."

Looking upstream through the dense forest he said, "Though if Vangen has done his duty and made us official enemies of the Empire, then such an approach will surely be futile. I don't think it's worth the risk." He turned to face the company. "There are other ways into the archives. Vangen used them to steal in and out of the library with his books. There are air shafts in the bedrock of the White Temple, used to ventilate the archives. With skill we should be able to slip in through them."

"I can't imagine what protections the priests have erected on this island, let alone what they would do to guard Athar's most famous store of knowledge," Aran said.

"I'm sure they already know we're on the island," Ceredyn said.

"Then we should make this quick," Draegan answered.

It was near midnight when they stopped to make camp next to the stream. They had been following it upstream all day making good progress through the dappled shade of the forest. The White Temple was built in the center of the island on the only mountain, shortly after Sage Vatn broke from the failed Council of Dullahan. She and her followers had terraced the mountain and built lush gardens that encompassed the entirety of the slope and spilled down to the lowlands. The warm ocean air kept the island in a perpetual spring. All rivers and streams flowed outward from the mountain spring and through the temple gardens where they continued downhill and poured gently into the sea.

"Can we risk a fire, Draegan?" Gron asked. "A real fire with real food would do us good."

Ceredyn spoke up. "I haven't sensed anything all day. I put up a few basic seals and met with no resistance. It makes me worried that it's so easy, but I can assure you we're not being watched."

"Start your fire Gron," Draegan said. He turned to Aran who was busy fletching an arrow and asked, "Why would they have no protections set up here?"

"They are a peaceful people. They suffered only one attack during the thousands of years the five kingdoms warred. Perhaps they leave their fate to Helian, like all things."

"Or perhaps they don't care about the island as much as they care about the Temple. Maybe that's where we'll run into trouble," Draegan wondered aloud.

Gron had begun roasting a piece of meat over the fire and pulled a pack of cards from his pack. "I need one more for a quick game of Six Sages. I promise to go easy on you."

Ceredyn looked at the worn cards and laughed. "You brought cards? Of all the things. Extra rope? Extra clothes? At the very least I would have thought that pack stuffed with nothing but bacon."

"He did say it would be a long journey. You never know," Gron said sheepishly.

"Well I think I still remember how to play that ancient game. I call Blades," Ceredyn said clearing a space near the fire and sitting down. "Do the Iron Mountains prevent everything new from making it to the Clans?"

"Its age doesn't prevent it from being a good game. A true classic," Aran said finishing up his arrow and checking it in the flickering fire light. "I used to play it with your father in the war," he said looking at Draegan.

Draegan smiled briefly and turned to the fire. "Infinite strategies, though my father only ever used one. The most direct." Recalling something he turned to Ceredyn. "You used to be a Raven, yes?"

Ceredyn froze, then looked up at Draegan. "You know more of me than perhaps you should."

"What I don't know is our plan for tomorrow," Draegan said. "We'll arrive near the White Temple, but we don't yet have a solid strategy for getting inside." He paused. "I suggest we walk in the main gate. Well, more precisely you should," Draegan said looking at Ceredyn.

"But you just said if Vangen has made us known it would be unwise to knock on their front door."

"You will not go as yourself. Since the founding of the Kingdoms, the Ravens of Corvus have occasionally come to Vatn to train and make use of the archives. I suggest you present yourself as a fledgling of the Rookery. Ieros is the keeper of the library. He's been there since before I was born and will probably still be there long after I die. He knows my face from the year Vangen and I trained here in our youth, but you should be able to pass by him with no trouble. Once inside the library, find a dark corner and wait for me," Draegan said handing a piece of parchment to Ceredyn. "Don't lose it, it's important."

"What do you hope to find in there?" Ceredyn asked.

"Answers to the riddle of where the Dark Artifacts are kept. The history books make no mention of them after the failed council. It is if they all disappeared, and yet here I am wearing the Shadow Walker of Dalken Tor, while Vangen wields Carnis Fornax, the black sword of Fet Reth," Draegan said. "The other four must have also survived the Sundering of Athar."

Aran began working on another arrow. "That leaves us hunting the remaining four. The World Render, the axe of Arkon Fell. The Black Horn of Malthier the Hideous. The Dark Ichor, the poisonous bow of Talus Sen. And finally the Burning Chains of Pyr the Red Scourge. This will be a dire hunt indeed."

"So you're going in there to look for books or maps or scrolls? And what of the rest of us? Would you like us to mill about the gardens?" Gron asked between mouthfuls of mostly burnt meat.

"Yes you and Aran will wait nearby. Ceredyn will leave once I'm safely inside, and then the three of you can make your way back to the boat. You'll most likely make it there before me, so push off and wait a few hundred yards off the coast. I shouldn't be more than a day behind you."

"So we're going to babysit a boat and leave you walking about the White Temple?" Gron said, trying to move his card on the makeshift board while Ceredyn looked at the paper Draegan gave him.

"This is the shadow walking rune," Ceredyn said looking up from the paper. "And don't think I didn't see that, Gron. Move it back, cheat." Gron looked up at the night sky and moved his card, grumbling under his breath.

"That's why I want a dark corner. I have some memory of the layout of the archives, but I have no idea what books I'm looking for. I'll need time."

"You'll need me. We have no idea what seals and barriers they've set up in there but I guarantee that they have been spun by experienced hands. You'll need someone with skill to unweave them," Ceredyn said.

"This cloak has certain properties, for which I've become very grateful." Draegan touched the brooch at his neck and looked into the fire. "I can pass through most barriers undetected. If I can first get inside, my cloak will help me the rest of the way."

"Well you've got a plan. Now you just need to execute it," Aran said as he reclined against a gnarled tree root and shut his eyes.

Draegan had to force Gron and Ceredyn to stop playing and take rest, as their matches became more heated when Ceredyn came to the realization that Gron was actually the superior player.

At dawn the group arose surprisingly well rested. "I hope it goes this well for the rest of the trip," Gron said stretching his enormous frame.

"I wish I shared your optimism. Getting into the White Temple will be a challenge, even with luck and skill on our side,"

Draegan said as he finished packing the book he was reading. "Break camp and leave no trace. Ceredyn and I are off. Wait for me one day after he returns. If I take longer, leave without me."

"Ha," Gron chuckled as he grabbed Aran's pack and added it to his own. "Let's get to that boat. You first, and clear a path wide enough for a healthy sized man."

"Be cautious, both of you," Aran said heading down the stream bank.

Ceredyn and Draegan made easy work of the remainder of the journey upstream to the White Temple. As the forest thinned the ground began to rise up sharply. In the distance they saw the alabaster minarets and grand dome of the White Temple. Great birds wheeled slowly above the High Altar as the sun set, turning the sky a fiery orange. The marble stairs poured down the granite mountain the Temple sat atop and spilled into the meticulously maintained terraced gardens where acolytes walked slowly, lost in contemplation, or sat in quiet meditation.

"Ten thousand steps for the ten thousand years the Sages fought the Blades of Darkness," Draegan whispered as he pulled Ceredyn behind an ancient tree whose trunk was large enough to hide them both. "Go up halfway and turn either direction. The platform will circle around to the library entrance. You'll need to hurry to reach the top of the steps before the sun sets and everyone leaves to return to the Cloister gallery. Make yourself known to Ieros, enter and find a secluded spot. Place the parchment on the ground and leave as quickly as you can."

"Understood," Ceredyn said placing the parchment into his sleeve. He drew a black mark on the back of his hand and a duplicate one on Draegan's. "These marks are linked. When it fades from your hand, I will have done as you asked." In another moment he was off and moving swiftly through the garden and up the marble stairs.

Draegan watched Ceredyn's slim form become smaller as he ascended the stairs, the lone figure in black moving against the sea of white that flowed downward as the acolytes exited the Temple. "This will probably go well," Draegan said, trying to summon some of Gron's optimism.

The sun had just dipped below the horizon and the entire Temple grounds had become serenely still. Draegan anxiously watched the mark on his hand, but he saw no signs of it fading. "This is taking too long." Draegan had begun considering alternate plans, fearing Ceredyn had been detained and questioned, when the mark was absorbed by his skin. "Well done, raven," he whispered.

Draegan took the small knife from his boot and pricked his forearm. "Just enough to cover the scar," he said as the blood trickled down and pooled in his hand. He pressed his palm into the trunk of the ancient beech tree, mumbled a few words and watched the world bend and fade in the swirling black mist that swept in from the edges of his vision.

Ceredyn exited the main library, past Ieros who looked up from a dusty tome and smiled briefly through his thick white beard. Once at the main doorway Ceredyn looked over his shoulder to the far corner of the room where he saw a shadow slide around the corner into the connecting hallway and watched the small cloud of black mist evaporate into the hazy red light that filtered in through the clerestory windows. "He's grown in skill," Ceredyn said as he hurried down the stairs and into the darkening garden.

Draegan sped down the empty hallway, sticking close to the wall and moving in shadow. His cloak darkened to match the already deepening shadows of the evening to further obscure him. Ahead he knew there was a staircase that led down into the vaults. Whatever he was looking for must surely be down there.

Turning the corner he saw that the staircase was protected by a massive iron door that barred his passage. Draegan checked the door for seals and barriers. Nothing. "Well then this should prove simple," he said taking a small slip of parchment from his pack. Drawing the shadow walking rune on the parchment he slid it under the door and opened the scab that was forming on his arm. "I may lose a pint before I get off this island."

Placing his palm on the stones near the door he once again felt the world spin and contract. Moments later, as his vision steadied he saw a staircase descending into the darkness below him. Enough light slipped in under the iron door for him to grab his marked parchment and destroy it. He could make out the first few steps and saw they curved downward. "Do I risk a light?" Draegan paused for a moment and traced a symbol on the wall. Once finished he blew on it and watched a soft green light shoot out from the mark and trace the mortar paths down the stairs. In the dying light he saw the way was clear.

After what felt like an eternity of walking down twisting stairs he arrived at the bottom landing. The air felt much cooler than above. "Must be in the bedrock of the Temple. Then this should be it. Don't want to risk a light here." The darkness was nearly complete and Draegan could see little. He sat and thought for a moment then remembered a spell Aran had taught him. Feeling in his pack for a small pouch of powder he put a pinch in each eye and held back the tears. Choking out a few words as he eyes began swell he noticed thick iron bars in front of him. "It must be working already."

In a few moments he could see his position dimly. Iron bars in front of him blocked a long arched tunnel that disappeared into the distance. Along the length of the tunnel smaller barred doorways led to what appeared to small cells. "Those must be the store rooms, but how will I know which one has what I seek?"

Sliding through the large vertical bars of the main gate was no problem. The cloak had the ability to make his already lithe form even thinner and the bars of the gate were spaced far enough apart that they would have only been an issue for Gron. But the endless tunnels of locked doors posed a problem. Draegan walked slowly down the tunnel inspecting each door for some sign of its contents. After ten minutes of walking he noticed a slight disruption in the uniformity of the rock wall near one of the doors. His eyes picked up the variance but there wasn't enough light even with his vision spell to discern if it was just a defect in the rock or something else. He ran his hand over the spot and his blood froze. It was a carving of the shadow walking rune. "Vangen has been here."

Taking another sheet of parchment from his pack he hastily drew the familiar symbol and slid it under the door. Taking a deep breath he took his knife and opened another spot on his forearm. Once he had enough blood he traced the mark on the wall and clenched his teeth.

As the mist cleared he looked around and saw an impossibly large vault stacked from floor to ceiling with books of every size and shape. His heart sank. "There must be tens of thousands of them here." Draegan reeled as he took in the enormity of his task. "I can't possibly finish before they leave without me."

Pacing by the tomes, he thought for a moment. "Ceredyn would have some trick to sort through these. Aran would probably be able to sniff it out. And Gron…can he even read? He'd most likely just burn this place down."

Draegan began walking to the back of the vault. "I'll just have to do this the hard way."

Draegan walked to the far corner to begin his task of sorting each book by hand. As he passed among the countless stacks of tomes and loose sheaves of parchment, he noticed a small glimmer of light near a stack of books. It was a pile of weapons and armor strewn carelessly on the floor. He moved closer for a better look and saw that in the center of the pile lay a closed sarcophagus. "This must be someone of little note to be buried so unceremoniously."

Wiping the dust from the stone he felt the engraved markings and gasped, "Islak? It can't be. One of the greatest chroniclers of Vatn, buried here? He should have a place of honor in the High Temple." Draegan checked the sarcophagus for barriers. "Nothing. Why?"

Draegan set his feet, shoved his shoulder into the slab and pushed. The stone ground slowly as it moved and then slammed to the floor. The ground shook as dust fell from the ceiling. Draegan paused to listen. Hearing nothing, he reached into this pack and fumbled blindly for a small tin of paste. Dabbing some on his fingers he said a word and his hand gave enough of a glow for him to see more clearly. With the soft glow and the aid of Aran's powder he could discern the details of the coffin's contents.

A simple white shroud barely covered the decayed remains inside. Islak's hands were clasped over a small leather bound book on his chest. "This must be what Vangen was searching for," Draegan said slowing reaching over the side toward the small volume. Turning toward what remained of the revered historian Draegan said, "I apologize Islak, but this is for the good of the Empire." Then he noticed a reflection in the corpse's eye. Looking closer he saw that though all of the flesh had rotted from the bones, his left eye remained in perfect condition. "It's glass."

Dark shapes and clouds of smoke swirled in the lidless glass eye. Draegan stared, hypnotized as the shadows moving in the eye took form and then dissipated. Snapping himself out of his daze he reached for the book and gently removed it from Islak's hands. Flipping through, he saw the pages were blank, except for the last page which was inscribed with the words, "I have seen enough to know."

"The eye." Draegan placed the book gently on the ground and carefully removed the eye from its socket. "It is not the book, but the eye that must contain Islak's visions." He looked closer at the eye now that he held it in his hands but could make nothing of the shapes that formed and broke like storm clouds. "Ceredyn will have to figure something out," he said gingerly placing the eye in his pack.

His vision was beginning to fade and the room began to appear darker. "I've got to move," Draegan said reaching once again for his knife. He made a cut and felt the warm blood gather in the palm of his scarred hand. Smacking his hand on the side of the sarcophagus he took a deep breath of the musty air and felt the world close in on him.

An instant later he heard the chirping of crickets and felt the cool night air stir the black mist that surrounded him. He stood up near the ancient beech tree he had waited behind earlier and took in the cool air while looking around. He saw a flash in the undergrowth as a hissing white bolt sunk into the bark near his face, sending him diving for cover in the brush.

"He's over here," a voice shouted in the darkness. "Keep him pinned down," came the reply as several more bolts whistled through the air in response.

"I should have made a mark on the boat. Although with my luck Gron would probably be sitting on it," Draegan said trying to look into the darkness to see how many men had him surrounded. "Five guards. This could prove difficult. Luckily I still have some blood," Draegan said and traced the *staminis* mark on his throat.

Taking a sharp breath of air he rushed from his cover with blinding speed and drove his blade deep into an unsuspecting acolyte's chest. Draegan caught the crossbow as it fell and spun on his heel. He fired a bolt into another white robed acolyte as he began to shout in alarm. Quarrels flew over Draegan's head as he sprinted through the brambles and plunged into the forest. He heard the other three crashing through the dense undergrowth after him, but knew they'd never be able to reach him at his current speed. He just needed to intersect the stream and follow it to the shore. Twelve hours of running at most.

***

The sun was beating down on the sand as Draegan burst from the forest onto the beach. He skidded to a halt to let his eyes adjust to the brightness. Raising his arm to shield his eyes he saw a dark shape rocking on the horizon. He grabbed a dry branch and with a few words it ignited. Throwing it into the air the fire consumed the wood and exploded in a shower of sparks. He moved back into the undergrowth and slaked his thirst at the stream as he watched the boat move closer.

"How'd they treat you?" Gron asked as he hauled a dripping Draegan over the side with one arm and deposited him on the floor of their leaky craft.

"Like an old friend. That you owe money. Put out as quickly as you can," Draegan said between gulps of air. "I put some distance between us with the *staminis* spell but I doubt they called off the hunt."

Aran and Gron began pulling hard on the oars. "Ceredyn, take a look at this," Draegan said as he pulled the eye from his pack. Ceredyn gasped.

"You crows and your shiny baubles," Gron said between strokes. "But why take some poor old fellow's glass eye? I thought we were coming here for books. The place is supposed to be lousy with them."

"How did you…? Where did you find…?" Ceredyn started and stopped half a dozen questions before Draegan silenced him.

"Just tell me how it works," Draegan began, turning the eye in the sunlight and finding it revealed little more than same clouds and smoke as before.

"The eye of Islak," Ceredyn said, staring at the piece of glass as Draegan turned it in the light. "Well to put it simply," Ceredyn said, pulling himself out of his admiration of the orb, "you need to make a trade. An eye for an eye." Draegan lowered his hand and looked at Ceredyn. He looked at the eye and back at Ceredyn before taking a deep breath.

Rubbing his throat he said, "Will it work? Does it actually function as an eye?"

"Not in the traditional way," Ceredyn said. "It pierces darkness, or rather the darkness of the unknown, and reveals to its wearer bits of the future. Of course the future is mired in shadow and is constantly changing so what pieces it reveals may mean nothing, or they may mean everything, and always they are murky."

Aran and Gron had stopped rowing to listen. "Keep pulling, the both of you. I want us to be nothing but a memory for them by sunset," Draegan said.

"They say it drove Islak mad toward the end," Ceredyn said, staring at the glass eye. "That's why he wrote so much. He became obsessed with recording what the eye showed him, but it was always changing, contradicting what it had revealed moments before."

Ceredyn gestured for the eye, but Draegan closed his hand around it. "Does it show the past?"

"Only Islak's. The rumor is that in his final years, before he went mad, he figured out a way to put both his memories and wisdom into the eye. Although this didn't save him in the end."

Draegan turned from the others. Opening his hand, he stared at the sphere resting in his palm, smoky shapes shifting within. He turned back around with sudden decision.

"Take out my eye and put this in its place," he said.

"You can't be serious," Gron said, ceasing his rowing again and leaning forward.

It would be ill advised," Aran said as he too stopped rowing. "It drove Islak mad, and told him nothing of value. If Islak was unable to read its wisdom, what hope do you have?"

"I hold no great hope for myself, but rather for Fyrian and its people. Doing nothing won't lead us to the Artifacts of Darkness. Vangen will find them or burn Fyrian to the ground trying. This eye may reveal nothing, it's true. But there is also a chance that it may reveal something that will aid us in our quest, and while that chance exists, I must take it."

There was a long pause while Draegan's companions considered his words. Ceredyn finally spoke. "I can keep the bleeding to a minimum. You won't die, but I don't have everything I'd need to make it painless."

Aran shook his head and began rowing.

"I can't believe you're going to do it," Gron said, picking up his oars.

Draegan positioned himself on the bottom of the boat with his pack under his head. Ceredyn pulled several jars of salves and sachets of powder out of his pack and sat on Draegan's chest. "This will hurt," he said pulling out his small curved knife.

"Give me a moment and let me take one last good look at the sky," Draegan said as he settled back into his pack and tried to make himself as comfortable as possible on the floorboards of the rocking boat. He looked up and watched the white clouds drift lazily across the azure sky. He felt the sun warm his face as the boat rocked gently in the waves. He drew in a deep breath of warm salty air, closed his eyes and thought of Issa. He opened both eyes together for the last time.

Several miles away in the forest of Vatn, three acolytes following a trail of broken branches toward the sea paused as they heard a blood curdling scream.

Chapter 15: The Last Watch

"I have no need of them," Vangen said as he paced behind his chair in the council chamber. His footsteps echoed in the stillness.

Maluk spoke. "The Night Watch has a celebrated history. Only the best and the brightest are chosen to serve the king. The title carries great honor."

"I do not dispute that, I simply have no use for a cadre of soldiers who once served under the command of a traitor to the Empire." Vangen came to a stop and looked around the cavernous room, glowing white in the morning sun. "Is it always so bright in here? How is one to see anything?"

"It tends to be bright during the day," Baledin offered. "With all our clandestine midnight meetings I'm sure you forgot."

"One hundred loyal, good men. These are elite soldiers, proven in battle," Tysta said. "The Tribe of Docga would gladly pay for them. Our numbers are still reduced from our contributions during the War for unity."

"They should be disbanded and return to their own kingdoms," Maluk said. "After loyally risking their lives to protect the Empire it's only fair to let them return home."

"If they are planning insurrection as you suggest you can't simply disband them and release them into the Empire," Arius croaked, staring at the others with his beady eyes as his withered frame sunk into his feathered gray robes.

"Thank you for your input, councilors," Vangen said, raising his hand. "Truthfully they are my men, not part of the Empire's standing army. They are mine to do with as I please," Vangen said.

"This meeting was not called to ask for your suggestions, I was merely extending you the courtesy of knowing the Night Watch will be no more and you will no longer enjoy their services which I have so graciously extended to you four."

The council members stared at Vangen, who had now resumed pacing behind his chair. "I know Draegan. I am certain he planted seeds of sedition against me and the Empire among his men. It is my task to find those in whom these seeds took root. Traitors will be brought to justice; the rest will be free to join the standing army of Fyrian."

Vangen dismissed the council members and left the chamber as quickly as possible. Once in his study he let his eyes adjust to the dim light and took a seat at his desk. He rifled through a pile of scrolls until he found a small piece of paper on which he had scribbled a few hasty notes.

"One hundred Night Watchmen. One hundred more reavers." Vangen leaned back in his chair. "This will be a needed addition. But I still require more. I have nearly exhausted my supply in the catacombs, so I'll need to start looking elsewhere." Vangen turned to the myriad charts hanging on the wall behind him.

"I think it is high time for Baledin to become a staunch believer in the threat of Iss," Vangen said looking at the vast expanse of land above the Iron Mountains.

Chapter 16: The Highlands

Draegan awoke moments before the boat struck ground. "The Frozen Maw," was all he said before he passed out.

The other three hauled the boat ashore and carried Draegan to a small outcropping of rock that offered shelter from the wind. Aran scouted for game while Ceredyn went back to the boat to retrieve supplies. Gron set up camp and watched over Draegan.

Draegan stirred in the wool blanket. His head throbbed. Sitting up he opened his eyes and saw Gron's massive frame squatting over the fire while he idly poked at it and looked out over the white capped ocean waves. The steel gray sky blended with the dark gray water as he got his bearings. He also saw a mass of black clouds in the periphery of his vision. Shadows moved through them. He blinked and saw a black tower rising through a snowstorm. The image faded as quickly as it had come, leaving a surge of pain in its wake. Draegan yelled and brought his hand up to his glass eye.

"You're back," Gron said looking over his shoulder. Standing up and brushing off his thighs he walked over to where Draegan lay and sat down beside him. He leaned close to get a good look at Draegan's eye. "How do you like the new addition? Ceredyn had a rough time of it out there," he said pointing to the choppy gray waves. "The wind never stopped. We're on the shores of the Clan of the Iron Mountains now. You can only row so hard against that wind, and Ceredyn was too busy with you to be any help to us."

"We need to find a black tower. North of the Frozen Maw Mountains. The remnant land of Iss," Draegan said between labored breaths.

"Still hurts, huh? Figures. Rough business, popping out an eye. Never heard a man scream like that before." Gron leaned back against the rock and put his hands behind his head. "Frozen Maw? My uncle made it over the Frozen Maw. Only person to have made it back too. He came back so beat up he wasn't of any use to us so they sent him off to Dullahan as the War Chief. Sits in a big chair on the Council now."

"Baledin Stormhelm is your uncle?" Ceredyn asked struggling under the weight of the packs from the boat. He dumped them near the fire and joined the other two near the rock. "Ah, now I see the family resemblance. Too dumb to know better and too ignorant to die," Ceredyn said. Gron laughed and slapped him on the back, nearly knocking him over.

"So he has seen Iss. Did he say anything of his journey over the Frozen Maw that would be of use to us?" Draegan asked.

"He didn't like to talk about it, but from what I gathered, he said it was just mostly snow. A blizzard that never stopped. Never said much more than that. He walked north for a few days and just figured it kept going, so he turned around and came back."

Aran slid down the rock and landed silently by the three. "Slim pickings," he said as he placed an emaciated rabbit on a spit and began turning it over the fire. "Draegan, you take it. You haven't eaten in days."

"I couldn't eat it if I wanted to. This thing is giving me a serious headache," he said rubbing his forehead.

"I'm sorry I couldn't have done a better job. I don't have the proper tools," Ceredyn said . "And those waves didn't help."

"No, it's the visions. Or vision I should say. It burns long after it's faded."

"Incredible," Ceredyn said, peering into the eye. "The same vision? Islak was driven mad by the changing visions." Ceredyn paused and thought a moment. "It must be your purpose. You must be of one mind to see so clearly."

"I would not have plucked out my own eye if it were not so. We hunt the four remaining Dark Artifacts, and the eye tells me one of them lives in the land of Iss over the Frozen Maw Mountains in a great black tower," Draegan said pulling his cloak around him as another gust of wind howled over the beach, whipping up wet sand. "The eye has been clear. Painfully so."

"Then we head for the Maw. A storm is coming through tonight. We might as well bed down here and wait it out," Aran said. "All I saw out there was a windswept expanse of lichen covered rocks. This is the best cover we have."

"Welcome to the highlands," Gron chuckled. "Ah, it's good to be home. It gets better as we move off the coast. The Frozen Maw is on the other side of the kingdom, so we've got some hiking to do. It'll turn to pine as we move inland, then once we get past Brahne, we reach the northwestern sweep of the Iron Mountains which makes passing through pretty tight near the White Lake. But it'll be winter by the time we get there so we can walk over the ice. Then it's up over the jagged teeth of the Maw."

"We're months away from winter, so how will the lake be frozen?" Aran asked.

"Winter starts a few months earlier up here. We pretty much skip fall, no use for it. The wolves like it better that way. They can come down out of the mountains sooner and hunt."

"So when you say it gets better, you mean it gets worse," Ceredyn said. Gron grinned and punched Ceredyn on the arm.

"I'll take watch tonight," Draegan said. "I don't think this thing will let me get much sleep anyway."

"Watch? On a night like this?" Gron said between mouthfuls of the rabbit. "Enjoy the storm. Smells like a good one."

"How quickly you forget our friends that stalked us in the fen. Something about them reeks of Vangen. We will all need to stand watch. Ceredyn, I want the same seals you used back in Corvus. If anything breaks through it, I want to know."

None of them slept well that night. The storm was relentless and a cold wind blowing from the highlands kept them huddled under the rocks while their small fire sputtered and hissed in the driving rain. Draegan took all four watches. The eye kept him up and in constant pain, sending him the same vision over and over.

An hour after sunrise the storm was far enough at sea that the group could break camp and move inland.

"A day's walk and we'll run into a few pine trees. It's a good place to camp with plenty of wood. More game, too" Gron said as he buried the fire pit.

"Then let's move and get off these windswept rocks," Draegan said grabbing his pack and heading up the bank.

"At that rate we'll be carrying him," Ceredyn said pointing at Draegan. "He hasn't slept." Ceredyn shouldered his bag and followed after him.

They kept a quick pace and made good progress, stopping only to fill their skins at a small tarn. The wind abated as they moved inland over the moss covered rocks, though there was a cold dampness in the air. The clouds were thick and the sky was a steel gray. The sun began to set and the light faded quickly.

"Is that it?" Draegan asked as he crested a small hillock and pointed into the distance.

"A few pine trees?" Ceredyn said as he saw the mass of green-black foliage in front of him. "Why it's a wall of pine trees. I can't even see where it ends."

"Yep. Good wind break. You'll sleep like a baby tonight," Gron said taking off down the hill, his big form moving with surprising ease.

Aran watched the three head down the hill to the edge of the forest and turned to look behind him. He sniffed the air but the wind was too heavy with the scent of pine to allow any other scent through. He lingered for a moment longer and looked back across the empty expanse they had just crossed. He'd heard no birds all day nor seen any sign of animal life. "And they'll still want me to bring them dinner," he said as he made his way down the hillside to the camp.

"Something bothering you?" Draegan asked.

"All day. I don't like that I can't smell anything and I haven't heard anything but the wind. But there's something else I can't quite figure out," Aran said stringing his bow. "I'll go see what game I can find," he said nodding his head toward the forest. "A deer would be nice."

Gron looked expectantly at Aran as he disappeared into the forest.

It was an hour after sun down when Aran returned with two small rabbits tied to his waist. "I practically had to run them down. It's hard to get a shot off in there. We have thick undergrowth back home, but it's pitch black in there and quiet as a tomb."

They had barely finished dinner when Ceredyn stood up. "Over there," he said pointing to the hill they had come down.

"It's those two, isn't it?" Draegan asked. "Put the fire out. Same as before. I want a light on them. Try to pin them."

Ceredyn drew a large circle on the ground and sat in the middle of it. He knitted his fingers together and shut his eyes as he breathed a few words. With a shout he opened his eyes and a flare of white light shot into the sky, illuminating the small depression they camped in as well as a few hundred feet in every direction. Coming down the hillside they saw two pale white bodies.

"Shouldn't one of them be missing an arm?" Aran asked.

"I'll make him pay if he's left my hatchet back in that swamp," Gron said through clenched teeth.

"It seems they can heal themselves," Ceredyn said rummaging through his pack and pulling out an old piece of leather marked with hundreds of tiny runes. "It's a strop. Run your blades over it. Draegan managed to take an arm off last time, but his blade is blessed by a priestess of Vatn. This'll have to do for now."

Gron ran his broadsword and hatchet on the strop and joined Draegan. Aran ran a few arrows across the leather and knocked them in his bow.

"When you're ready, light them like before," Draegan said. Seconds later two white arrows sped through the air and with a shout from Ceredyn burst into flame as they sunk into their target's chests. The figures slowed momentarily, then kept lumbering toward the campsite.

"Our turn yet?" Gron asked looking at Draegan.

Draegan set his jaw and nodded. The pair rushed the reavers just as they reached level ground. Closing the distance far faster than his size would suggest Gron brought his two-handed broadsword down with vicious strength and nearly sheared the first reaver in half from its collar bone through to its rib cage. The reaver hissed and spat black blood from his mouth as he grabbed the blade and began moving it back up the length of the cut.

"Stronger than I thought," Gron said straining to keep the sword firmly lodged in his victim.

Draegan was right behind him and slid between Gron's legs while bringing his blade up, jointing the reaver at the knee. The sudden loss of a limb caused the reaver to fall backward, allowing Gron to lean on his sword and pin the corpse to the ground.

"This one's mine," Gron said taking his hatchet off his belt. He began hacking at the creature's limbs severing every flailing appendage. "You can't follow us without feet. You can't catch us without hands," he shouted as he went about his work.

Draegan met the second reaver who proved more nimble than the first. He dodged Draegan's first swing and jumped back out of range, circling him cautiously while making a low hissing noise. Black foam frothed on his mouth and flecks of the liquid sputtered out onto its chin.

Draegan feinted and pressed his attack as the reaver moved back. Driving his sword down in a large arc, the corpse caught the blade in its bare hands. The force of the blow severed a few of its fingers and the blade lodged in the creature's forearm. Draegan used his forward momentum to shove the reaver backward until it stumbled and fell. Gron was at his side an instant later and they both began dismantling the body.

Arrows shot over their heads as they finished their grisly work. Gron stood up and looked back at the camp. "What're you doing?" he yelled. Ceredyn yelled something incomprehensible and several more arrows whistled by Gron's cheek.

Draegan grabbed Gron and spun him around. "There," he said pointing to the top of the hill. The sky was barely distinguishable from the ground in the darkness, but they could make out movement on the ridge. Pausing in their work, they saw myriad yellow eyes reflecting the dying light of Ceredyn's illumination spell.

"More wolves?" Gron asked.

"Back to camp," Draegan said with urgency.

Gron put his immense boot on the reaver's still twitching mouth and yanked his broadsword from its body. "Well at least you won't be chasing after us," he said before running back to camp.

"I count eight," Aran said as Gron came panting back to the others.

"Well let's dig in," Gron said between breaths.

"Let's not," Draegan replied. "We don't know how quickly they heal themselves, so it may be ten before you know it. I'd rather have them struggle with the barriers as we push through the forest," Draegan said. Keeping his eye on the hill he asked, "Ceredyn can you mark them so we can keep track of their progress? I'd rather not have them flank us."

"If Aran puts an arrow in them with my marks I can keep track of them," Ceredyn said.

Aran took a few arrows and began carving marks on them with his hunting knife. "I don't think I can get all eight at once. I'll do what I can, and then hit the rest as we move."

Five burning quarrels streaked through the night and disappeared into the darkness. "Four out of five. Not bad," Ceredyn said. "I'm putting up seals now," he said carving a rune in the nearest pine tree and smearing a paste over it.

"Another long night?" Gron said looking at the towering pines in front of him.

"Builds character," Draegan said.

They had been running for hours through the black pine forest. The wolves kept their distance but always pushed the group whenever the companions slowed to catch their breath.

"It's almost like they're herding us," Draegan shouted to the others. "Where does this forest lead?"

"Onto the plains, then the tundra," Gron said.

They ran on in silence, crunching the dry pine needles under their feet and trying not to stumble over the exposed, twisting roots. Aran stayed in the front and had put arrows in two more wolves since they had entered the forest. Ceredyn was in the rear putting up barriers whenever they paused longer than a few seconds. The wolves continued to find them despite every spell he wove.

"I fail to see how they can know where we are. My spells should at least stop them, but they don't even deter them. They push us easily as sheep," Ceredyn said while carving a symbol in the tree bark.

"They must be driven by some dark magic," Draegan said. "No doubt it's Vangen's work."

Aran came running through the low hanging branches, covered in pine needles and wiping sap from his face. "I've marked the last two," he said. Ceredyn closed his eyes, took a breath and nodded in agreement.

"So what's our plan?" Gron asked as he tried to peer into the impenetrably dark forest.

"They seem to match our pace and stay just out of sight and arrow shot," Draegan said. "Except of course when we pause long enough to catch our breath. I've a mind to see how fast they can move. We'll use the *staminis* spell and push for the plain on the eastern edge of the forest." He pulled his hunting knife from his belt. "I'd rather face them out in the open than in here."

"At this rate our bodies will be spent before we even reach the tower," Ceredyn said.

"They leave us little choice," Draegan said, drawing Ceredyn's attention to the limit of the illumination spell.

Several feet away eyes began to flicker at the edge of the dull light Ceredyn kept above the group. A wolf pressed close to the seal he had constructed. Immediately the arrow buried in its shoulder ignited. The wolf slipped silently back into the shadows and joined the rest of the pack, pacing just out of range of the spell.

Once everyone had the *staminis* mark drawn, Draegan and Aran shot off into the forest. Gron followed shortly, while Ceredyn put up one last spell. "I hate all this character building," he said before chasing after them.

The wolves skirted the edge of the barrier and once past it broke into a full run. They matched the pace of the four men, both groups churning through the forest at blinding speed. The men and wolves crashed headlong into the darkness as branches whipped by, cutting their faces. For hours they ran, streaks of cloth and fur slipping through the darkness.

"It should be daybreak by now," Ceredyn said gasping for air. "How much longer?"

"The trees are too dense. It's always night in here," Gron panted. "A few more miles at most.

Minutes later the group careened out of the forest and onto an open plain of heather that stretched to the horizon. The sun shone brightly on a field of purple flowers and the men stopped running to let their eyes adjust to the bright light.

"Break the spell," Draegan said. "They're right on our heels so they should be here any minute. Fan out. We'll take them here." He spoke between gulps of air.

Aran was stringing his bow when they heard the crashing and snapping of branches. Gray, black and white streaks shot out onto the plain and into the light. The wolves splayed their legs to stop their forward progress and howled in pain. The sunlight seemed to burn them as they thrashed on the ground, teeth snapping at the air.

"What's happening?" Gron asked.

As he spoke the wolves' forms contracted violently, with audible cracking, taking on the shape of small boulders.

"The sunlight," Ceredyn said. He crouched down and traced a spell in the dirt with his finger. "They're not dead, if that's the right word, just immobile."

Aran kept his bow drawn and aimed at the gray masses as Gron walked over to the collection of eight new rocks that dotted the fields. He took his hatchet off his belt and gave the nearest stone a quick rap. "Sounds like stone," he yelled to the group.

"So they can hunt only at night," Draegan said.

"Or whenever there isn't sunlight," Aran said following the other two as they walked over to join Gron, who was sitting on one of the rocks, emptying a water skin in his mouth.

"What do you think Ceredyn?" Draegan asked, counting the boulders again. "Wait, what about the other two. The human corpses?"

Ceredyn unrolled a woven mat inscribed with thousands of tiny marks and arcane writings extending radially from a central seal. He laid the mat flat on the heather and sat in the middle, closed his eyes and began whispering.

"There," he said, eyes snapping open as he pointed to the edge of the forest that rose like a green-black curtain straight into the sky and extended for miles into either direction. A few feet behind the forward most pine tree were two more boulders.

"So they still managed to follow us. We've got to figure out a way to stop them," Draegan said. He walked closer to one of the rocks and looked at its base. The heather was wilting. "Ceredyn," he said, pointing.

"It's hard to read signs with Gron's snoring," Ceredyn said.

Gron had stretched out in the shadow of one of the boulders and fallen asleep. Aran walked over to him and kicked him awake. "A man's got to sneak a nap when he can. Especially with this crew," Gron said rolling himself over and standing up. He brushed decayed heather from his cloak. "Hmm, it wasn't dead when I sat down in it."

"Ceredyn?" Draegan asked again.

"I don't know what to make of this. Give me another minute," Ceredyn said rummaging through his pack and producing a small glass vial of luminescent powder. "Gron bring me some of that dead heather."

Crumbling up the withered plant, he sprinkled some powder over it and wove his hands into a sign. "Nothing. It's dead."

"I could have told you that," Gron said, cracking his back and stretching in the sunlight. "Don't need any powder to solve that riddle."

"It's been drained of any life that flowed through it," Ceredyn said trailing off and looking curiously at the rocks. Draegan and Aran walked over to him.

"They do regenerate. They are alive, somewhat, although not in the way we understand it." Ceredyn continued. "They don't eat or drink, and they haven't been killed by any of our weapons nor my magic. But now we know that even they have limits. It seems they can't move in sunlight. They change their form to blend into their surroundings and then drain the life from any living thing they're touching in order to heal," Ceredyn said.

"We're being hunted by creatures that pursue us by night, suck the life from the very earth during the day, and can't be killed." Aran said. "They will push us past our limits before long."

"Is there a way to stop them from gaining strength while they're in this form?" Draegan asked.

"That's what I don't understand. This stone form harbors a soul, but not as you and I inhabit our bodies. They must be alive in some fashion for they drain life from the earth, but I can't fathom why spells or weapons have little effect on them," Ceredyn said getting up from his mat.

"Your spells couldn't pin them when they hunted us, but could you bind them in this state?

"I will try, though I may only be able to bind these stone forms," Ceredyn said waving his hand at the rocks. "At night when they change again the binding may not hold them."

"Do your best," Draegan said gathering the other two and leaving Ceredyn to his work.

Draegan looked out over the gently sloping plains of heather moving calmly in the breeze. On the horizon, clouds cast shadows that sailed gently over the rolling fields. He heard the larks calling in the distance and turned to face the sun.

Aran put his hand on his shoulder. "I stand by my earlier assessment. We need to put distance between those things and us."

"Wise council as always," Draegan said. He turned to Gron. "How far is the nearest town? We're tired, and we need horses."

"It's a good hike," he said pulling at his red beard and looking thoughtfully at the clouds. "Best to find a farm and 'borrow' some ponies." He nodded at his own wisdom.

"I smell a wood fire coming from the east," Aran said.

Ceredyn joined the group and they began their hike eastward over the plains with Aran in the lead.

Chapter 18: Bryhne

They made good time through the gently rolling hills, despite being exhausted. Within an hour they crested a small rise and saw a single farm in the valley.

"I wish I could give you four horses. I'd give you five for that much gold," the old farmer said, stacking bales of hay next to the stable. "Problem is I only got one."

Ceredyn sat in the shadow of the stable while Aran filled his water skin at the rain barrel.

Before Draegan could respond the farmer continued. "Then again I'd pay about that much gold myself to see the four of you on my old plow horse."

"So we can have the nag for free?" Ceredyn said. He turned to Aran. "Can you just put an arrow in his head and we can be off?"

Draegan held up his hand to Ceredyn, hoping the farmer didn't hear. "Sir, we obviously can't travel with one horse. Do you perhaps have a cart or wagon?"

"Course I do. You think I carried each bale here by myself?" he said, waving his hand absent-mindedly at the other bales.

"Could we perhaps buy the wagon in addition to the horse?"

"Well you could, but then I'd be out of a horse and a wagon." The farmer spat on the hard ground and watched it dry in the sun.

Draegan was about to speak when the farmer looked up and continued. "I suppose you could take me in your wagon over to Bryhne and I could just buy another horse and wagon with all that gold once I'm in town."

Ceredyn hung his head and groaned. Aran smiled.

Draegan composed himself and drew a breath. "Sir, would you be kind enough to drive us into Bryhne? We'll pay you two pieces of gold which is more than fair," Draegan said, trying not to lose his temper.

"No I like it the other way. Need a new horse and wagon anyway."

The door of the house creaked opened and Gron came walking out smiling from ear to ear. "Lingonberry pie," he said licking his fingers. "Got some good stuff packed up for later, too. The old lady is real nice."

A stout old farm wife poked her head out of the window and yelled toward the stable, "Just take them into town and be done with it you fool. Three pieces of gold. And we need pigs, not horses."

Gron laughed and pointed his thumb over his shoulder. "Reminds me of mum."

A few minutes later they had the wagon hitched and were on their way. Gron waved toward the farmhouse as the wagon creaked and groaned down the rutted path that led from the farm to the narrow road.

The farmer kept quiet for most of the ride as the four slept in the wagon. Draegan's dreams were filled with shadows and light and he yelled out in his sleep a few times, waking the others.

It was late in the evening when the cart came to a stop. The four sat up and hopped off the back of the wagon. Draegan paid the farmer and thanked him.

"Well if I don't come home tonight there's no use in me coming home ever, so I might as well turn around now. But if you fellas need a drink," he said pointing to a dilapidated building, "try the tavern. It's called 'The Tavern'."

"Ah, I get it," Gron said, nudging Ceredyn in the ribs.

"I understand Gron so much more now," Ceredyn said.

"We need horses. Are there stables around here?" Draegan asked.

"Well now that I think about it, no. Well yes, but they closed down a while ago," the farmer said turning his horse around.

"Can we kill him and at least have one horse?' Ceredyn asked.

They watched the old man, the old horse and the old cart head back up the dusty road. "Well we might as well have a drink while we think," Gron said walking over to the tavern. The others followed.

Though the sun was just dipping below the horizon, the air was already becoming cold. Inside the tavern was a lively crowd of farmers, miners, woodsmen, and trappers gathered in groups at small tables. Smoke clung to the rough hewn rafters of the low ceiling. A few flickering lanterns cast dancing shadows on pine benches and low tables. A fireplace opposite the entrance warmed a large black pot hanging from an iron hook. The men paused in their conversations and looked up at the newcomers. Gron strode directly over to the fireplace and took a seat at an unoccupied table.

"Smells like mutton stew," he said, rubbing his hands together.

The others followed him and sat down. Once the conversation of the patrons had resumed its normal volume, Gron threw his pack on the table and opened it up.

"Hardtack," he said spreading the pack's contents out for everyone to see. "And shortening and bacon and jerky and cheese," he said glowing with pride. "We owe that farmer's wife a favor or two when we get back from this black tower business."

"Do you think we're on a camping trip?" Ceredyn said. "When are we going to prepare this feast? Before the wolves find us or after? What we need are horses."

"If you were half as decent a mage as you think you are, you could turn this into a horse," Gron said slumping into his chair.

"Let's eat what we can now. I don't want you carrying all this across the tundra," Draegan said picking up the cheese and sniffing it. He laid it back down. "In the meantime Aran is right. We need to put distance between us and the creatures that hunt us and we need horses to do it. On foot they'll easily run us down."

"How many do you need?" came a voice from a corner booth.

"Four," Draegan said before anyone could respond. A stout man came over to the group carrying a large flagon which he set in the middle of their table. He wiped his hands on his apron and extended one to Draegan.

"Taur," he said crushing Draegan's hand in his vice-like grip. "This is my place."

"Well met," Draegan said extracting his hand and forcing a smile. "Can you get us four decent horses, and quickly?"

"As quickly as you can pay," he answered, gesturing to a door near the staircase. "Wait back there. I don't need this crew watching. It's hard enough getting them to pay for what I serve. If they saw where I kept it all I'd be out of business by sunrise."

The door was banded with iron and locked in three places. Taur fumbled under his belt and produced a ring of keys. Turning to the four behind him as he searched for the right key he said, "Keep the good stuff back here. Extra food too. Can't be too sure with this crowd."

The door swung open and the five stepped into the small room. It smelled of garlic and vinegar. Near the back was a small table with two chairs. Taur took one and Draegan sat in the other.

"Now I see you're in a predicament," Taur began. "Pretty far north for the King's men. How is old Leon doing these days?"

The four looked at each other. "How do you get your news?" Ceredyn asked.

"From my wife. She's quite the gossip. But back to business. Four horses is no small feat in this country. I can do it, for King and country of course, but I want two gold pieces per beast."

"Done," Draegan said. Taur stood and extended his hand again, grinning from ear to ear. Draegan reluctantly accepted another crushing squeeze.

"I'll return in short order. Don't eat anything," he said pointing at Gron and left the room. They heard the locks click.

"I feel like I'm in the cargo hold of a boat once again," Aran said looking at Draegan. "How do we continue to end up like this?"

"I don't think he'll stick us like that, though it can't hurt to make ready," Draegan said. "Ceredyn, would you be so kind?"

Ceredyn was weaving symbols with his hands when Aran said, "I smell fresh air. And horses." He looked around the room and stopped on a large shelf of dry goods. "Gron, can you help?"

The two grabbed the shelf and slid it across the floorboards. In the wall a small crack let in the red rays of the setting sun. "A door," Draegan said as it opened outward. Standing in the door way was Taur who froze for a moment.

"Going to run off before you paid me?" he asked holding out one of his giant hands. Draegan put the eight pieces of gold in his palm and Taur motioned for them to follow him outside. The door exited into a narrow alley between the tavern and an outbuilding.

"There they are," Taur said pointing to four black horses, saddled and tethered to a rail. The group walked up to them and began securing their packs.

"How did you manage to get four horses so quickly?" Draegan asked as he climbed into the saddle. He turned when he heard heavy boot steps coming around the corner. Taur slipped back into the doorway. "Enjoy," he said locking the door behind him.

"Thieves," a man shouted, pointing at the group as they mounted the horses. Several more men came around the corner brandishing swords and axes.

"That's how," Ceredyn said. "These aren't his horses to sell."

"I see we won't be given a chance to explain ourselves," Draegan said as an arrow whistled over his head. "I imagine they'll make Taur pay them well once they figure things out."

"Ride," Aran yelled, snapping the reins as he dug his heels into the beast, driving the horse down the alley. The men dove and scattered as the group charged through them. Arrows flew by them as they rode into the night.

Chapter 19: Tun's

They pushed through the night, never stopping. By dawn the horses were exhausted, foam flecks streaking down their jaws and splattering on their chests. The men were saddle sore and weary. During the night they followed a road that lead continually upward through the rolling hills. In the breaking daylight they saw that the fields of heather had given way to moss and lichen covered rocks. The road continued to gain elevation and the pine trees became fewer and more skeletal. A cold wind had been blowing steadily for the last few hours.

The group dismounted near a stream and followed it to a clear tarn where they watered their horses. Aran strung his bow and perched on a rock overhanging the pool, looking for fish. Draegan pulled his cloak tighter against the wind and sat behind the rock, watching the clouds swim through the clear water and rubbing his head.

Gron took a deep breath of the cold air and exhaled forcefully, slapping his chest. "That'll wake you up. Another day and we'll be on the tundra. Nice and cold."

"We've put some distance between us," Draegan said, rising to his feet and walking over to the lake's edge. "But I think we should keep moving. They rest during the day so we can push further."

"You may not need to rest Draegan, but the horses do," Aran said loosing an arrow at a small trout.

"I'm still trying to figure out how they can track us through all the barriers I've put up," Ceredyn said. "I'm blocking all traces of our passing. Unless…" he trailed off and took a book out of his pack.

"Unless what?" Draegan asked walking over to him.

"Unless they have a connection with you, something beyond the ordinary senses." Ceredyn snapped his book shut and looked at Draegan. "You claim these things are Vangen's work. You two are brothers and share the same blood, yes?"

"No, I'm adopted," Draegan said, then paused for a moment. "Wait. The book." Draegan looked thoughtful for a moment. "When we fought I used my blood to shadow walk out from his study. I left a bloody handprint on a book," he said staring at the scar in the palm of his hand. "Vangen has my blood after all and now I see he's clever enough to make good use of it."

"He must have done so. If he created these things with the dark sorcery of Iss and added your blood, they would be bound to you beyond the limits of my magic. This is indeed grave."

"Curse him," Draegan said, narrowing his eyes. "So they will forever hunt us. Unless we figure out a way to stop them. We can't continue to run both day and night, as they've proven that they can match our speed, even under aid of the *staminis* spell."

Aran returned from the tarn with five trout strung on his line. "We should eat before we move on," he said as he squatted down to gut them at the lake's edge. Looking around at the sparsely wooded land he added, "We have little in the way of wood for a fire so they won't be well-done."

"You can burn the heath," Gron said as he joined Aran at the water's edge. He ripped up a few handfuls from the rocks and blew into the mass of vegetation. Thick white smoke poured from his hands and within seconds the heath burst into flame. He placed it gently on the ground. "I know some magic too."

"You are a man of hidden depths," Aran said nodding approvingly at the fire. Ceredyn squinted at Gron with disbelief.

"The trick is keeping the wind off it," he said moving some rocks to form a windbreak. "Now let's get those fish frying."

Aran and Gron hunched near the fire and fried the fish with the shortening in a large skillet Gron had produced from the bowels of his mammoth pack.

"Did you leave anything in that poor old woman's kitchen?" Ceredyn asked.

"The plates. I figured we could just eat out of the skillet," Gron said expertly flipping the fish. "It'll be ready soon."

"The man's a walking larder," Ceredyn muttered under his breath as he returned to reading his book.

Draegan walked to his pack near the horses and took out a small worn volume. "I want you to learn as much as you can about the workings of Iss," he said handing the book to Ceredyn. "If they are bound to me then there is nowhere we can hide. We must find a way to kill them."

"How can we kill what's already dead?" Ceredyn asked. He and Draegan sat behind a rock outcropping near the fire and pulled their cloaks tighter against the frigid wind. "Vangen couldn't possibly control them over this distance. They must be animated by some force within them. If we could draw this force out of them, we might weaken or even 'kill' them."

"How would you do that?" Draegan asked.

"I have no idea, but your book is a good place to start. If you have any more I would like to take a look," Ceredyn said looking at

Draegan. "I would have given my left eye to be in the vaults of Vatn. You must have armfuls of treasures."

Draegan's hand moved to his eye. "Let's not speak of it. It was all I took and I still don't know if it was worth the price. The other books I brought are 'gifts' from Vangen."

"These fish aren't going to eat themselves," Gron yelled.

After the four had eaten they packed up and mounted the horses. They took a small rocky footpath that led upward to a ridge of small hills. On the other side the path connected to a road. The horses moved more easily along the dirt road. Shortly after noon Ceredyn rode up next to Draegan.

"There is one possible explanation that might account for the inhuman nature of the creatures that hunt us. Vangen must have put souls into dead bodies to animate them. When I tried to pin them they seemed hollow, empty. The body and the soul inside didn't match. Of course, I don't know how one gets unbound souls, but I think that's our answer," Ceredyn said.

Draegan slowed his horse down to match Ceredyn's pace and scowled. "I know where he got them. But how can we use that information to aid us?"

"If a soul can be transferred in, it follows that it could be pulled out and put into something else. A simple *ferian* spell should suffice. The Council of Rune was trying something similar at the Rookery before I left."

Draegan eyed Ceredyn. "How would it work?"

"I know little of what these things are and even less of the ways of Iss, so what I say is speculation." He paused and rubbed his face, eyes drifting to the leaden sky. "We would need to attach a runic mark to the corpse. When they're in human form and whole, not as wolves and not with pieces amputated. Then I'd need time to make the transfer. I've never moved something of that magnitude before. It could take seconds or it could take hours. I won't know until I try."

"We don't have hours when we're under attack," Draegan said. "I haven't found anything in these books to help us, but perhaps you can. Here, read these and see if you can come up with something less time intensive. I feel you're on the right track, but there has to be a better solution." Draegan reached in his pack and handed the rest of his books to Ceredyn.

It was mid afternoon when the four crested a hill and saw a small clapboard cabin next to a stream. Smoke rose from the chimney but was swept down into the valley by the harsh wind before it could rise more than a few feet above the roof line.

"Let's check it out," Draegan said taking his horse down the footpath that broke from the road they'd been following.

The four left their horses near the frozen stream and knocked on the door. When no answer came Gron tried the handle and pushed the door open. They filed into the cramped space. Within the cabin they had to stand shoulder to shoulder to fit in the tiny space in front of the counter. A wiry old man looked up from his rocking chair and smiled.

"First customers of the day," he said as he tried to stand up and quickly decided seated was the best way to conduct business. "Well, first customers ever. Buy something," he said gesturing all around him.

The four looked around the tiny room and saw every open space and shelf was crammed with food and dry goods. The counter split the room in half. On the shopkeeper's side there was a small path cleared between barrels of oil and sacks of flour for him to exit and enter through the back door. Lanterns and garlic and rope and snowshoes hung from the rafters, hitting Gron on the head as he tried to move into a more comfortable position. A pot bellied stove popped and smoked near the shopkeeper's chair.

"Why is there a store in the middle of nowhere?" Ceredyn asked.

"Tun's General Store," the old man said from his seat. "Don't have the sign yet, but I'm getting around to it."

"But why?" Ceredyn pressed. Draegan and Aran looked around in amazement.

"Haven't heard? The war's over. The kingdoms are united. Soon tourists will be coming by the hundreds to see the tundra. In summer of course. Two weeks a year you can see the ptarmigan chicks hatch. A real sight. This place'll be a gold mine."

"You look well prepared," Draegan offered as he scanned the panoply of objects crammed into the shelves.

"Why yes sir, I am. I have a hunter friend who lives in the Iron Mountains. He goes to Dullahan once a year and packs me out these supplies. Tells me the news, too."

The old shopkeeper leaned back in his chair and began rocking. He pointed into the distance over Gron's shoulder and said, "Troubles are brewing though. Told me that just last week, a village was burned by the reavers of Iss." He nodded to himself and continued. "He said four of the King's own men deserted and joined the army of Iss. Night Watchmen like yourselves. We're to turn them in at first sight." The four looked at each other. Aran moved his hand slowly to the hunting knife in his belt.

"You four must be up here hunting them traitors down. Well I can't give you any help so don't ask. Never seen them in my life.

Haven't seen anybody in fact. No one comes this way. Horrible place really, except for those two weeks in summer."

Draegan relaxed and Aran folded his arms across his chest.

"I'll take as much paper as you have. And ink," Ceredyn said. The shopkeeper blinked. Ceredyn tried again. "Parchment? Papyrus? Anything to write on or with."

"I have limited space young man, I can't afford to waste it." He thought and rocked for a while and said, "I have some canvas and leather. Oilcloth too. You could write on that I suppose."

"I'll take it," Ceredyn said reaching in his pack for payment. The other three shuffled around him as he tried to approach the counter. The old man struggled to get up from his chair.

"We'll wait outside," Aran said as he pushed his way past Gron and stumbled through the doorway into the open air. A biting wind had picked up and the horses had grouped together near the shack's chimney.

"The reavers of Iss?" Aran asked. "Are we to believe the words of that old man?"

"Normally I would laugh it off, but from what I've seen pursuing us then I fear he may be right," Draegan said as he tightened his pack to his horse. "Vangen has truly fallen."

"Are you going to tell us what you and Ceredyn have been whispering about?" Gron asked. "You're getting pretty cozy with that crow."

"He's our best mage and thus our best hope to stop these reavers. As you've seen, our weapons have been of little use." Draegan watched a gust of wind take the smoke from the chimney and whip it down the valley floor. "We think Vangen has found a way to put human souls into corpses. These unholy creatures are the reavers that hunt us. They can change from man to beast and have the power to regenerate lost limbs. He's marked them with my blood which makes Ceredyn's seals useless since they are blood bound to me."

"And how does Ceredyn plan to stop them?" Aran asked.

"If a soul can be transferred once, it can be done again. He thinks we can transfer the soul out of the corpse and into something less menacing. I imagine that's why he wanted the paper. It's a theory, and the only way to test it is in battle."

Draegan was explaining the details when the door of the cabin banged open and Ceredyn staggered out with an armful of oilcloth. "Where did everyone go?"

"Back here, out of the wind," Draegan yelled. As Ceredyn came around the corner Draegan said, "I've told them what we suspect."

"Good. Now I need some time to make the glyphs," Ceredyn said dumping his spoils on the ground. "This looks like the only place in the valley that's out of the wind, so I might as well do it here. Keep an eye out for that old man." The others stood and watched as Ceredyn sat down and laid out several instruments from his pack. He rolled up his sleeves, revealing forearms covered in intricate tattoos that obscured every inch of exposed skin and climbed up his arms, disappearing under the bunched cloth at his elbows. Gron stared, dumbfounded.

"What are those markings?" Draegan asked.

"You've never seen a Raven of Corvus this close? We're all marked, though some more than others. They cover my whole body."

Aran took a step back, eyeing the mage warily. Ceredyn smiled. "Draegan steals his books one way. I steal them another way."

"So you write the spells onto your skin? Is this why you were anathematized by the Council of Rune?" Draegan asked as Ceredyn began inscribing marks on the oilcloth.

Ceredyn shrugged. "Maybe I left first, and then they wrote me out of the Gray Book to save face. I don't pretend to remember the details. The instructors at the Rookery have ways of toying with one's mind."

"Vultures," Gron said, turning his back and looking out over the hills.

The sunlight was fading by the time Ceredyn finished writing. He stood up and looked down at his work. The oilcloth sheet had been covered in thousands of glyphs, repeating patterns of sigils and arcane symbols.

"How does it work?" Draegan asked. Ceredyn opened his mouth to speak, wobbled, and fell to one knee. Aran and Draegan rushed in and helped him back up.

"Are you hurt?" Aran asked.

Draegan saw drops of blood running down Ceredyn's arms and dripping off his fingers.

"He didn't have any ink," Ceredyn said with a weak smile. "My blood should make the spell stronger. Since I can't simply move a soul into a rock or paper or even this oilcloth, the blood should act as a temporary host. There are several markings that will hold information about the nature of our pursuers. Once the *ferian* spell is complete and I've read the sigils, we can burn the cloth."

"You look to be in no condition to cast any spell," Aran said. "I have some herbs in my pack that may help."

"Going to be a cold one tonight," Gron said, exhaling and watching the vapor from his breath dissipate above his head. "Clouds are high."

Aran brought over a gnarled red root and shaved a bit into his hand with his knife. "Put this under your tongue," he said handing it to Ceredyn. "You'll sleep like the dead for hours. We have to keep moving though, so we'll tie you to your horse, and tie your horse to mine."

By the time Ceredyn was secured he was already dozing. The other three walked their horses next to the stream and down the valley where they picked up another footpath that eventually connected with a small road. The Tear of Helian had begun flickering faintly above the horizon when they were able to mount their horses and push at a faster pace. Aran held Ceredyn's reins as they cantered down the road. The crunching of small rocks in the horse's shoes and the sudden gusts of wind where the only noises that disturbed the night.

A few hours after midnight Draegan, who had fallen asleep in the saddle, started up and gripped his eye. He took a sharp breath between his clenched teeth and exhaled painfully.

Riding up to Aran with Ceredyn in tow he said, "Can you wake him? They're coming."

"It's a little soon. He may be groggy when he comes out," Aran said as the four came to a stop and dismounted. They untied Ceredyn and laid him in his cloak on the road. Aran pushed his fingers into two places on Ceredyn's neck and stood up. Moments later Ceredyn's hands shot up as if he was defending himself from an attack. He took a large gulp of air and coughed.

"Time to go to work," Gron said, grabbing him under the shoulder and lifting him up as if he were a child. It took a few seconds for Ceredyn to find his legs.

"The reavers are coming. I saw them by Tun's. You never told us how this is going to work," Draegan said.

Ceredyn rubbed his eyes. "I never told you because I don't know how it works either." He went to his pack and pulled out the oilcloth. He unrolled it on the ground and used an illumination spell to light the area.

"The target needs to be bound in this cloth, and then hit here and here," he said pointing to two large circular marks that stood out from the other writing.

"In the midst of battle we need to find a way to wrap the enemy in this sheet, and then strike it in specific marks?" Gron asked in disbelief.

"It's a chance to improve your swordplay," Draegan said, fingering the hilt of his blade.

"And I need you to keep it pinned while I draw out the soul into this shroud. Then I'll burn the cloth."

"So it can only be used once?" Aran asked. "What should we do about the other nine reavers that hunt us?

"Distract them." Ceredyn replied. "I don't even know if this will work. If it does though, I'll learn more and hopefully the next time I can offer a better solution."

"I appreciate your optimism," Draegan said. "I hope there is a next time too."

"We'll find out soon. They approach," Aran said pointing down the road.

A break in the clouds let enough moonlight slip through to reveal eight wolves loping down the road toward them, followed by two reavers, their bodies glowing white.

"Aran, mark as many wolves as you can. Keep them off us while we focus on the corpses," Draegan said. Motioning for Gron to join him at the front he said, "We'll hack the first one to bits, and try to bind the second one in this cloth."

Two arrows flew over their shoulders and sunk with a thud in the lead wolves. The arrows burst into flame and the other wolves scattered left and right. More shafts whistled through the air and bursts of light lit the road as Gron and Draegan charged the nearest reaver. Gron took its head off with one blow and black liquid bubbled from its neck. Draegan ducked as its arms flailed blindly at him and cleanly removed the left leg. The reaver collapsed and began dragging itself off the road.

Two wolves circled back toward Gron and Draegan. "Keep the last reaver whole," Draegan yelled as he turned his back to Gron who faced the remaining reaver. "I'll handle the wolves." Gray fur and white fangs snapped at Draegan's throat as he darted away from the wolf's deadly maw and buried his blade down the animal's gullet. The beast began shaking violently, thrashing from side to side, knocking Draegan off balance as the second wolf leapt at him from his right. Draegan released his sword and deftly pulled his hunting knife from his belt. With one swift motion he buried it in the beast's neck. The wolf hit the dirt with a thud and Draegan kicked him off the blade and watched the body tumble down the hill.

Draegan spun and ran to help Gron who was taking wild swings at the reaver. The creature stayed just out of range and hissed at him, its fingers pulled back into menacing claws. Draegan pulled the oilcloth from under his cloak and charged the reaver. "Hold him," he said, unfurling it.

"The best I can do is knock him down." Gron rolled his wrists as he took a ferocious swing and smacked the reaver across its skull with the flat of his blade. The creature stumbled backward as Draegan rushed in and slammed it in the chest with his shoulder. He took his hunting knife and pinned the oilcloth to the reaver's chest in the center of the first mark.

"Now Gron!" Draegan yelled as he nimbly kept out of the way of the reaver's raking grasp. Gron's massive blade skewered the beast through the second mark on the cloth with such force both of them tumbled to the ground.

"Ceredyn, it's done," Draegan yelled.

Ceredyn hunched over in the middle of the road and began chanting. Gron and Draegan were rushing back to his side when a wolf sprang from the roadside and blocked their path. The wolf growled and gnashed its teeth on the hilt of a sword that protruded from its mouth.

"I thank you for returning that to me," Draegan said circling the wolf. The beast backed up, violently shaking its head in a vain attempt to dislodge the weapon from its throat.

"You've got to put it the whole way through," Gron said and barreled straight into the wolf. He grabbed the protruding hilt of Draegan's blade and drove it through the length of the creature, pinning it to the ground. The wolf squirmed and thrashed futilely as Gron brought all his considerable weight to bear on the beast's neck. He pulled Draegan's sword out, tossed it to him, and then hacked the wolf to bits with his hatchet.

Draegan cleaned the black slime from his blade and ran to Ceredyn, who was rocking back and forth.

"How much longer?" Draegan asked. Ceredyn didn't respond. His eyes shone white as his chanting became louder.

"The horses," Aran yelled. He loosed shafts with blinding speed into the night. Audible thuds confirmed that the arrows found their marks, keeping the wolves at bay for the moment. The horses had bunched together on the road. Their eyes rolled in their sockets as they stamped the ground and champed at their bits.

Draegan rushed past the horses and dove into the mass of wolves that encircled them, his blade catching the moonlight as it tore into his prey in a fury of flashing violence.

Gron was soon by his side, his hatchet scattering and felling wolves with primal savagery. Aran's arrows flew into the churning mass of man and beasts, finding their mark with expert skill.

A moment later Ceredyn screamed and scrambled backward on his hands and feet, kicking rocks and dust into the air. The other three ran to his side. Behind them the reaver burst into flames.

"It tried to supplant my body," Ceredyn said between gulps of air as he grasped at his chest. Gron lifted him from the ground and onto his horse in one motion.

Draegan ran toward the burning reaver where it flailed on the ground. He placed his boot on the corpse and ripped Gron's broadsword from its chest. The creature grasped at the air and the black liquid in its mouth boiled as it coughed and sputtered at him. He kicked out his hunting knife, picked it up from the roadside and ran back to the horses, listening to the reaver crackle in the consuming fire.

"The wolves are down, let's ride," Aran said spurring his horse into the darkness. "We can make the tundra by dawn."

The others followed him into the night.

Chapter 20: The Tundra

The wind blew unrelentingly through the night so that by morning the four were chilled to the bone and frozen to their saddles. The terrain had leveled and all traces of trees were gone. The heath, lichen and moss that covered the rocks were the only signs of life in their new environs. Cirrus clouds feathered the ice blue sky, stuck in place as if frozen. All traces of the road had disappeared hours ago and the horses stepped gingerly through the rocks, picking their way carefully.

"Is it always this windy?" Ceredyn asked, pulling himself deeper into his cloak.

Gron smiled. "Winter's coming. It always gets windy right before winter."

"Then the wind will die down?" Ceredyn asked, hopefully.

"Then it'll get even windier, but at least it'll start snowing."

Draegan slowed his horse to allow Ceredyn and Gron to catch up with him. "I want to know what happened last night. Did you learn anything?" he said flexing his stiff fingers.

"A lot less than what I'd hoped to. I didn't want to burn the whole shroud because I used part of it to store information from the spell, but I panicked when the soul jumped and tried to supplant mine," Ceredyn said looking at the heath and grasping his cloak near his heart.

"That's what you said last night. What do you mean?"

"I used a *ferian* spell to move the soul into the ink on the oilcloth. But because the spell was written in my blood, the soul used this as a bridge to enter my body instead, as if it was searching. I panicked and burnt the shroud unfortunately losing all the information the spell had stored before I had a chance to read it. Thankfully the soul was lost with the oilcloth," Ceredyn said.

"Well then at least we got one of them. That's a start. What will you do differently when we try again?" Draegan asked. "You'll have nine more chances tonight."

"I hope we make it to tonight," Aran said. "We're tired and hungry. We need to rest, at least for a few hours. The horses too." Aran pointed to a lone hill in the distance and spurred his horse ahead.

"Well I won't use my blood next time," Ceredyn said as they followed Aran. "It appears the soul is weakly connected to the corpse, and as soon as I loose it from the reaver, it looks for a new host. Blood seems to be a perfect conduit. I need to find another creature whose blood is less precious to me than my own."

"You won't find many living things in these parts," Gron said, watching the tundra stretch out to the horizon as the rising sun began to melt the hoar frost.

"I agree. We're moving north of Brahne, then southeast to the White Lake. We won't be encountering much life. We need another solution, something less involved because we're closing in on the Frozen Maw. We'll be trapped there if we can't figure something out," Draegan said and pulled ahead of the two, following Aran to the hill.

An hour of riding brought them to the base of a small hill that provided a break from the wind. They dismounted and made camp. Gron brought out a large piece of hardtack and broke it in his skillet.

"This'll fix you up. Maybe some bacon too," he said, placing four frozen strips in the pan. They sat in silence and listened to the grease sizzling as the wind whipped around the hill.

"We can assume the wolves and the reaver are regenerating," Draegan said, breaking the silence. "I believe what Ceredyn said about the other reaver being destroyed, but we should be prepared for the worst." He stood up and walked to the horses, which were a few feet upwind of the fire. Returning to the fire he unfolded a map and handed it to Aran.

"We may rest for a few more hours, but then we need to press on. You and Gron can decide where, as long as we stay off major roads and away from large populations. You know our destination is the Frozen Maw and then the Black Tower beyond, so choose wisely."

"Aren't you going to rest?" Gron asked.

"I'm going to climb this hill and take a look around. I don't get much quiet time anyway," he said pointing to his eye. "Maybe it'll show me something useful this time."

"He barely eats and rarely sleeps," Aran said to Gron as Draegan wrapped his cloak about him and started up the hill. "The eye takes a heavy toll." They watched him grow smaller as he ascended the hill, becoming nothing more than an inky black dot at the crest.

Aran and Gron studied the map for a few minutes discussing possible routes as Ceredyn poured through the books Draegan had loaned him. Shortly after finishing their spare breakfast all three were asleep.

Three hours later the group was awakened by the horses snorting and stamping their hooves. Aran sat up and saw Draegan coming down the hill.

"Northeast. A village has been burnt and raided by the reavers."

"How did they get ahead of us? I put seals up that should have warned us of their approach," Ceredyn said, pushing himself out of his blanket.

"Not our reavers, another group. The eye showed me. It was a few nights ago in a small village. The same tactics we used as Graywalkers, but what they lack in magic they made up in brutal ferocity." Draegan mounted his horse. "Vangen must be creating more reavers to continue his charade and lend credence to his claim that Iss is a threat to the Empire."

"Are you sure they aren't looking for us," Aran asked.

"If they were they should have found us by now. They attacked the village days ago and could have moved west to pinch us between the other group of reavers we encountered last night."

"He doesn't have any more of your blood, does he?" Ceredyn asked. Draegan shook his head. "Then if they decide to hunt us it won't be for long. My barriers should stop them." The others began packing and saddling up their mounts.

It was well past noon when Aran reined in his horse. "I smell burnt wood. And blood." He looked around and tried to smell the air, but the gusts of wind whipped the scents away too quickly. He reached into a bag on his belt and began rubbing a fine powder between his fingers. He watched the wind carry it up above his head where it turned blue and shot off like a bolt into the wind. "This way," he said and rode northeast.

The others followed behind him and slowed when they saw him stop. "There it is," he said pointing in the distance. On the horizon they saw a black patch of ground amid the gray rocks and moss.

"Ceredyn," Draegan said, "can you detect any sign of them?"

"No reavers, just a mass of bodies. The dead villagers and livestock."

They approached cautiously and circled around the edge of the village. A few stone foundations, turned black from the smoke, were all that remained along with charred timbers that rose haphazardly like the bones of a decayed carcass. Bodies were strewn in what could be considered the center of the tiny village, bloated and frozen in contorted poses of horror.

"This looks all too familiar," Gron said, dismounting and walking through the wreckage. "It sickens me to think we used to do this."

"Our past is our burden to carry. I can only hope to make some small amends by doing some good in the present," Aran said looking around at the devastation. "This truly is a wholesale butchering."

"They can't use magic, so they resort to coarser methods," Ceredyn said joining the others on foot as they left their horses by the remains of an outbuilding and walked through the carnage. Ceredyn bent over a dead body slumped against a foundation wall. "Frozen stiff."

Draegan stopped and turned to face him. "You found your volunteers. Take what you need from the dead and be quick. And respectful as possible given the nature of what you're doing."

Ceredyn nodded and turned back to the horses to retrieve implements from his pack. The three continued sifting through the chaos when they heard Ceredyn scream. Racing back to the horses they saw an impossibly large man squatting over Ceredyn raising a massive axe over his head.

"Got you, you dog. Or is it crow? I'll take your head back to the council." The man looked up and saw the other three circling him. Aran had his bow drawn and aimed at the behemoth's face. The man grinned through his shaggy beard and twin braids, though his face was partially obscured by his fur-lined hood.

"Release him," Draegan said as he gripped the hilt of his sword, "and you won't be harmed, friend. We weren't the ones who burnt your village."

The large man turned to look at Draegan. "You're right. A sewing needle like that won't do more than make me angry." He shifted his weight and Ceredyn's chest cracked. Ceredyn tried to inhale but instead passed out. "Ha. Bird bones. I've eaten chickens with more grit than you." He raised his axe higher. Aran made ready to put his arrow through the man's eye.

Gron shouldered past Aran, sending his shot wide and rushed at the man. He swung his hatchet at the falling axe with such force it sent both him and the man sprawling on the ground. They began wrestling and grunting as Draegan and Aran rushed over and pulled them apart.

"No way to treat your nephew," Gron said.

"He's not my nephew," the strange man said, spitting at Ceredyn, as he freed himself easily from Aran's grasp. He began straightening his garments. "Now help me find my axe or I'll just have to kill you three bare handed."

"I'm your nephew, uncle," Gron said pointing at himself wildly while trying to look the old man in the eyes.

"Baledin?" Draegan said.

Baledin threw back his hood and grabbed Aran by the arm, shoving him effortlessly over to the other two. "Let me get a good look at you." He squinted for a moment then stood up straight. "So it is you, Gron. Sorry to say you don't keep good company these days." Baledin walked up to the three to examine them more closely. "Draegan, you don't look like yourself. I barely recognize you even as I'm staring at your bony face. You're thin boy. Thinner than normal. And paler too," he said poking his giant finger into Draegan's chest, causing him to wince. He exhaled a cloud of frozen breath in Aran's face. "Don't know you and don't want to."

He turned and looked at Ceredyn who was still passed out in the dirt. "Well I'm bringing you four back to the Council. You're wanted men. You can come alive or I can hack you up," he said picking up his axe. "I came up here to see the devastation first hand. They said you traitors were here killing people in my kingdom and here I find you gutting the bodies of those who can't speak against you. I hate to think that Vangen was right, but it's worse to see you boys falling from the light. And why my kingdom? Gron this is the land of your father and your ancestors. Why would you do this to your own kin? You're father would be ashamed if he were still around. Maybe it's better he isn't."

Draegan stepped forward. "Baledin please. Let me explain. This isn't our work. Vangen is lying. These are his foul deeds," he said gesturing at the corpses at their feet.

"Vangen doesn't have the strength to buckle his belt, let alone butcher a village. He's a wisp of a man, and a coward at that. Always in his study anyway, daydreaming of assassination plots. No time to commit genocide." He shouldered his axe and pointed at the group. "Face your crimes like men. Follow me to Dullahan."

"Baledin you knew my father and you know me," Draegan said fingering the clasp at his neck. Baledin looked at the clasp and met Draegan's eyes. "Vangen is the true threat to the Empire. He is the real Iss. He uses dark arts to raise the dead, then commands them to raze villages. He kills his own people to keep you and the Council occupied with an imagined foe so he can search for the Dark Artifacts. He is the one who has fallen"

Baledin snorted. A large plume of white steam clung to his beard and then dissipated in a gust of air. "Well, I can't say you're not brothers. You're both paranoid, conniving cowards."

Gron stepped forward with his hands outstretched. "Uncle let me explain. Draegan makes things more complicated than they need to be."

Gron explained the past few weeks to Baledin with sweeping hand gestures and no fewer than five diagrams drawn with his finger in the ashes and dirt. Baledin squatted and nodded earnestly as he studied the drawings. Gron continued to elucidate the proceedings of the past year, missing a few key points and adding several events that never occurred. As they talked, Ceredyn began to stir and rose to his hands and knees.

"Never would have guessed it, but you speak sense." Baledin said as he put his hand on Gron's shoulder and stood up. "My nephew tells me you make for the Frozen Maw" he said, turning to Draegan. "I can't tell you much about what lies beyond it though. That's one place I'll never go back to. I'd rather be in the council chamber. It may be filled with traitors and imbeciles, but the seats are warm."

Aran walked over to Ceredyn and gave him a drink from his water skin. Aran felt Ceredyn's ribcage as his friend winced slightly. "You'll be fine," he said, popping a rib back in place. Ceredyn's eyes began to water.

Baledin turned and began walking south to the Iron Mountains. "This will be strange news to deliver to the Council, though I don't know if I can keep it straight in my head by the time I get back there. It would be easier if I could just kill Vangen and then explain everything to the rest of them. I'll have to think of something while I hike back to Dullahan."

Baledin walked past Ceredyn who was leaning on Aran. "Wipe up your tears, no need to cry my boy. Sorry for the mix up," he said slapping Ceredyn on the shoulder with his colossal hand. Ceredyn lost his balance, fell forward and bloodied his lip as he hit the dirt once again.

They watched Baledin's silhouette get smaller as he walked away, giant axe over his shoulder, still talking to himself.

Chapter 21: The White Lake

Ceredyn had finished his gruesome work in the village by evening. They decided to spend the night in the remains of the village, as the remnants of the stone walls provided shelter from the winds. Aran made a fire and the four ate the last of Gron's bacon.

"You three rest. I'll take watch. We leave in a few hours and will head northeast around Brahne. It makes more sense to follow Aran's path to the Frozen Maw Mountains although it'll be slower going as we need to stay off the roads," Draegan said.

"Will we ever get more than a few hours sleep?" Gron asked.

"The reavers will hunt tonight. I don't want to be curled up by the coals when they get here," Draegan said as he wrapped himself in his cloak and leaned against a stone wall.

"No need to stand watch. My seals will tell us of the reavers," Ceredyn said.

"But they did not warm us of Baledin. If he can slip past us and catch you unawares, I wonder how many others who hunt us will do the same," Draegan said, turning to the group sitting at the fire. "Vangen has truly made us hated if Baledin has to be convinced of our innocence. Even that old man in the store is aware of us," he said gesturing over his shoulder.

A gust of wind carried embers into the night sky. Gron clapped his hands together and began pulling stones from the fire. "Keep a few in your bedroll. Makes for warm company," he said handing them to Aran and Ceredyn.

Draegan looked out over the vast frozen tundra. Patches of moonlight showed the heath was already turning silver white as the frost spread over the ground.

"When we encounter the reavers again what's our plan?" Draegan asked of Ceredyn.

"It will be more difficult than before. The corpses were burnt so I could get little blood and no flesh." Gron looked at Ceredyn with disgust and muttered under his breath.

"Vultures, all of you. Why would you need my kinsman's flesh?" Gron said staring at Ceredyn.

"Draegan's paper is lifeless," Ceredyn replied. Gron stared at him suspiciously. "I mean no disrespect to your countrymen when I took their blood and bones. I'll make glyphs in the bones, and then infuse them with their blood. Once they've cured you can stab them into the mark to seal the soul," Ceredyn said looking at Gron who narrowed his eyes at the tiny mage. Ceredyn waved his hands and continued. "The mark that would have been draw on your kinsmen's skin but as I have none you'll need to carve it yourself on each reaver we bind."

"So that's the difficult part. This gets worse night by night," Draegan said as he walked back to the fire.

"Luckily you're the best swordsman in the whole of Athar, so it should be child's play. The *ferian* symbol is quite straightforward to craft," Ceredyn said describing it with three simple strokes in the dirt near the fire. "Put the mark on the reaver and then plunge this into the center of it," he said handing a thin white sliver of bone to Draegan. Draegan took it from Ceredyn and turned it in the fire light. Numerous etched symbols and marks came to life along the bone's length.

"This is light. Can it be shot like an arrow?" he asked looking at Aran.

"I can try, though it's a bit short and thicker than my arrows. I'd need to fletch it to give it a better chance of finding its mark." Aran held out his hand and Draegan gave him the bone. Looking at Ceredyn, Aran asked, "Am I able to make my spells on this without interfering with yours?"

"As long as you don't obscure my marks," Ceredyn said.

Aran spat on the tip and dipped the sharpened end in the bag of powder that hung from his belt. He held it in the flame of the fire and turned it slowly, listening to the powder sizzle as it liquefied.

He looked down its length. "I should true it, but it'll be serviceable at short distances," Aran said.

"Good, then we have a plan. We'll have a chance to test it soon enough. You should sleep now," Draegan said returning to the crumbling stone wall of the outbuilding and leaning against it. He watched the Tear of Helian rise in the west.

It was shortly after midnight when Draegan roused the group from their sleep. "We need to move."

"They haven't even broken the seal," Ceredyn said pushing himself up from his bedroll.

Draegan tapped his temple near his glass eye. "They aren't coming right for us. They're flanking us, trying to cut us off. If we don't push out now they'll get ahead of us," he said tying up his pack and saddling his horse.

Within a few minutes the others were mounted. The wind whipped at their faces as they rode off across the tundra, the horses hooves crunching the frozen moss. After an hour of riding they came to a dirt trail.

"We can move faster on this for tonight just to get out ahead of them, but we need to be off the trail before dawn," Draegan said, spurring his horse. The others followed, riding low to avoid the wind.

By daybreak the four had made good time and moved off the trail, back onto the frozen tundra. They turned south and east and rode until mid morning when they began to see the Iron Mountains appear on the horizon. Hundreds of small lakes covered in sheet ice dotted the expanse in front of them, reflecting the rising sun.

"How far to the White Lake?" Draegan asked, stopping his horse and scanning the horizon.

"We should make it today," Gron said. "Though I don't know if it'll be frozen just yet. Been unseasonably warm these past few days."

Aran looked at Gron in amazement. Ceredyn buried his face in his horse's mane and groaned.

"Our plan hinges on crossing the White Lake," Draegan said. We've passed Brahne and need to cross the lake to head for the Frozen Maw. If it's not frozen we'll have to turn back and cross the western sweep of the Iron Mountains. That will delays us by a week at least and push us right into the reavers on our trail.

"We've got horses," Aran offered. "We could pass it to the north."

"That route is too long and indirect. And exposed," Draegan said. "This land is impossibly flat. Four men riding high on four horses can be spotted miles away."

"It'll be mostly frozen," Gron said. No one looked at him. Gron crossed his arms. "This warm weather isn't my fault."

"Mostly?" Ceredyn asked. "How much is 'mostly'? I know some techniques for freezing water. I can teach you three and better our chances," he said.

"That will have to suffice," Draegan said.

The group saw the first sign of the White Lake by late afternoon. It appeared on the horizon as a sea of glass, skirting the edge of the Iron Mountains and fading away as it stretched close to the Frozen Maw.

They rode for another hour, watching the lake grow larger as their shadows lengthened. The ground began to slope gently downward and became rockier as they approached. Dismounting, they continued on foot.

"The horses won't do well on the ice," Aran said. "I'm sure you have a plan."

"Yes. Food. Hopefully they can fill our bellies a few times in the coming days," Draegan yelled over a gust of wind. Gron looked at him questioningly. "We'd be too slow walking these things over the ice and if it's not completely frozen we'd have to set them loose. So we might as well eat and pack up some extra meat. They've served us well. We'll give them a better end then they'll get from the wolves. This is as good a spot as any." Gron hung his head and patted his mount.

The four began their bloody work in the shadow of a lichen covered boulder. The ground was frozen solid and the heath was still covered in morning frost. When they were done the small violet and blue flowers of the heath were stained red and the ground was steaming from the heat of the carcasses.

Gron hefted his pack and found a good balance on his back. "That's going to be a fair amount of good eating."

"Now we'll have every wolf in the Iron Mountains on our trail as well as those reavers," Aran said, wiping his blade on a patch of moss.

Ceredyn showed them a sigil for turning water to ice while they cleaned up. "It's not much, but it will help. The one I use is a bit more complicated though it takes more time to master."

"Time we don't have," Draegan said. "Sun's going down. I want to be halfway across that lake by midnight." They walked the rest of the distance to the edge of the lake.

Gron stopped them as they reached the shore. "You'll thank me for this," he said grabbing a handful of white sand from the frozen shore. He sat down and spat on his boot heels and rubbed the sand in. "Traction," he said looking up and grinning.

The others followed suit, although Aran modified the procedure with a thick paste he pulled from his pack. "A bit more secure than spit," he said.

The ice at the shore was thick and cloudy. Delicate frost patterns were etched in the surface. The setting sun turned the sky a fiery red as the group began crossing the lake. The wind howled across the ice and blew a fine mist of frost into the air, obscuring their vision and stinging the exposed skin of their faces.

"Due east, as fast and as steady as you can," Draegan said above the roar of the biting wind.

"What's that?" Gron asked from the rear of the column.

"Another long night," Ceredyn yelled over his shoulder. Gron laughed and leaned into the wind.

***

By midnight the wind had died down. The four had made good progress and covered more distance than expected. Draegan called the group to a halt.

"Ceredyn, can you test the ice?" Draegan asked.

"No need," Aran said pointing straight ahead. In the distance they saw the reflection of the moon bobbing lazily on the surface of the lake. "There's your answer."

"Let's get as close as we safely can, then we'll start," Ceredyn said, moving forward more cautiously. The group moved slowly, listening for any signs of failure in the ice. Gron stopped when he heard the ice crack beneath his feet.

"You should take some of this," he said tip-toeing as gingerly toward the group as his large frame allowed, the ice creaking and popping with every step. He pulled a small pewter flask from his cloak and unscrewing the cap, took a quick sip. He coughed and wiped a black liquid from his red beard. His teeth were a slimy black as he grinned and handed the flask to Draegan.

"It'll keep you warm if we should happen to go in," he said pointing at the open water ahead. "Good stuff really, just don't ask any questions about what comes out when you relieve yourself. Terrifying."

Draegan took a pull from the flask and coughed half of it out onto the ice as he handed it to Aran, who did likewise. Ceredyn took a whiff from the flask and refused.

"I've got my own method. Now let's get to work," he said taking off his gloves and placing his palms flat on the ice. His cloak spread out around him making him appear as a black rock on the white ice. Slowly a blue light began to glow underneath him, deep within the ice. It spread slowly at first and then moved along imperceptible cracks and faults in the ice. A grinding noise along with cracks and pops emanated from the blue light as they watched delicate ice crystals grow where the light had once been, forming first as frost then ice.

"Any time you want to help," Ceredyn said, looking up at the other three.

The three began to bend down on the ice when Ceredyn shouted. Turning, they saw the reflection of eyes moving toward them from the direction they had come. Aran strung his bow as Draegan and Gron circled Ceredyn.

"Focus on the ice, Ceredyn. We need a way to get across should they prove too much," Draegan said, unsheathing his sword. Clouds passed in front of the moon, darkening the lake. Ceredyn began chanting. The wolves stopped a few yards beyond the range of Aran's bow and paced back and forth. For what seemed an eternity the three waited for either the wolves to attack or Ceredyn to finish his work.

A gust of wind whipped up loose frost from the surface of the ice and blocked their vision for a few seconds. When the wind died down they saw the wolves had parted. A pale white figure walked between them.

"The other reaver is back. We need that bone arrow Ceredyn," Draegan yelled over his shoulder as he watched the figure move ever closer. "Any time you're ready."

"Make the mark first, buy me some time," Ceredyn said in a strained voice as he tried to speed up the spell.

Draegan looked at Aran. "Stay close, watch him. If those wolves break, keep them off Ceredyn."

Gron and Draegan circled left and right of the reaver who kept moving straight for Ceredyn. They closed the distance and charged the creature while the wolves stayed out of range and continued to pace warily.

Draegan lunged at the reaver who jumped back and directly into Gron's oncoming hatchet. Gron sunk the bit of his blade deep into the corpse's back. The reaver hissed and flailed trying to turn around, but Gron had buried the blade up to the shoulder of the handle.

"He's not going anywhere," Gron yelled, trying to stay out of the way of the reaver as it swung its arms wildly behind its head.

Draegan rushed in, pulled his hunting knife from his belt and made three deft strokes across the reaver's chest. The corpse hissed and spat black liquid at him. Draegan jumped back and shouted, "It's done. The arrow."

Ceredyn pulled his hands from the ice and tossed the sliver of bone to Aran who caught it and knocked it in his bow in one swift movement. Aran ran toward the reaver to close the distance as Ceredyn returned to his chanting.

Aran fired and missed. A gust of wind took the arrow wide and it fell to the ice and skidded some feet toward the wolves. Gron released his grip on the hatchet and dove across the ice snatching it from the snapping jaws of a wolf who had charged in after it. Gron threw the etched bone to Draegan and with his other hand grabbed the wolf by the throat, stood, and hurled the beast at the other wolves that were racing at him.

The wolves scattered as Draegan caught the bone and drove it into the reaver's chest.

"It's in," Draegan shouted, diving out of the way of the reaver. He and Gron ran toward Ceredyn as Aran fired shots into the charging wolves. Ceredyn stood and blew on his frozen hands. "Can't weave the sign with these numb fingers," he said shaking off the cold.

The wolves had reached the reaver who was beginning to stand when Ceredyn clapped his hands together, wove the sign and shouted. The reaver burst into flame and fell onto the ice, arms and legs writhing in a ball of red orange fire. The creature hissed and clawed at the ice, trying to drag its body closer to the group.

The intense heat of the fire cracked the ice. In a clap of thunder the reaver plunged through the ice and into the frigid water. The wolves scattered left and right. Draegan watched the ball of fire continue to burn underwater as the reaver sank out of sight.

"Let's move," Aran said, pointing at the wolves. The beasts had skirted the newly formed hole in the ice and were now trying to gain speed as they pressed closer to the group.

"Will the ice support us?" Draegan asked as he turned and ran with the others.

"I hope so," Ceredyn said.

The group ran at full speed as the wolves struggled to find purchase on the ice. They had just lost sight of their pursuers when they heard unnerving creaks beneath their feet. Ceredyn took a knee and began to remove his gloves.

"No time to finish the spell," Draegan said grabbing Ceredyn by the scruff of his cloak and hoisting him to his feet. We're going to get wet. Keep moving."

A hundred feet farther the ice gave way completely with a deafening crack and the four plunged into the icy water. Draegan came to the surface gasping and clawing at broken sheets of ice. He took in a mouthful of water, yet it felt warm to him. The black liquid Gron had given him worked.

Several feet away Aran rose to the surface. The two swam together and threw their packs onto a large slab of ice. They began looking for Gron and Ceredyn. Nearby in the darkness they heard Ceredyn alternately gasping and gulping air. Gron rose beside him and grabbed him by the neck. Gron swam over to Draegan with Ceredyn in tow, flailing wildly. When they had placed their packs on the ice the four began swimming and pushing the ice across the remaining expanse of unfrozen water.

Draegan looked over his shoulder. "I think they're going to try to catch us," he said to the others. The wolves had made it to the edge of the ice and were sniffing and pacing nervously. After a moment's hesitation they plunged into the water and began paddling after them.

"About four hundred yards behind us," Aran said. "They're better swimmers than we are."

"Then we better get to the shore soon," Draegan said. "How much further?"

Ceredyn raised a hand over his head and nearly went under. Gron grabbed him by the cloak and threw him up onto the ice. Ceredyn raised his hand again and a ball of white light congealed above his head. He lowered his hand swiftly and the orb of light shot up into the sky and intensified before it burnt out.

"Looks like three hundred yards," Ceredyn said, slipping back into the water to help push the ice block toward the shore.

"Then let's swim like our lives depend upon it," Draegan said.

The sheet of ice rammed into the edge of the frozen side of the lake, cracking and crushing the thin ice before grinding to a stop. Aran slid effortlessly up onto the sheet and threw the packs farther toward the shore. Gron and Draegan were already out and running to grab the packs when the wolves were a few hundred feet away. Aran pulled Ceredyn out and began running to catch up with the others.

"Where's Ceredyn?" Draegan asked as he put on his pack and looked around.

The three turned and saw Ceredyn bent over the edge of the ice, both hands thrust into the water up to his elbows.

"Ceredyn, don't. They're too close," Draegan yelled running back toward him. The wolves were paddling furiously, already snapping their slathering jaws in anticipation. A blue light began to form within the water under Ceredyn. When the lead wolf was within a few feet of Ceredyn, glowing tendrils of light shot out into the dark water, turning it from black to white and freezing the wolves in place. The nearest wolf was caught with his jaws open, eyes wide and white, inches from Ceredyn's face. Ceredyn collapsed on the ice.

Chapter 22: The Frozen Maw

"You gave us a scare," Gron said as Ceredyn sat up in his wool blanket. The other three sat shoulder to shoulder to shield a small fire they had burning as wind whipped heavy flakes of snow through their makeshift camp. Ceredyn looked confused.

"We hit the shoreline an hour ago, through we never knew it," Draegan said leaning in toward the sputtering fire. "This storm swept in right after you passed out. Couldn't see a thing."

"Did it work? The wolves?" Ceredyn asked extracting himself from his blanket and joining the others.

"If it hadn't you'd have much less skin on your face," Gron said as he handed his flask to Ceredyn. "This works better than your magic though. You were about frozen stiff once you passed out."

"He's right. This fire is for your sake, not ours. Drink it. It leaves a vile taste but it works," Draegan said. "Then we need to be moving."

"Through this storm?" Aran said. "Two reavers are dead and the wolves are trapped in the ice. We should use this opportunity to rest, at least until the storm abates. We can't see more than twenty feet."

Draegan looked at his companions. Their clothes were worn and tattered, their faces drawn and covered in cuts and scrapes. He hung his head. "I wish we could, but Vangen does not rest. While we sleep he sends his reavers to burn villages. He incites war, he kills his subjects, and he hunts us. And all the time he also seeks the Dark Artifacts. Every moment we wait he closes his grip more tightly around the Empire."

Aran sighed. "Ceredyn is weakened from his casting. He needs time to regain his strength. Gron and I are exhausted. And it pains me to watch you go night after night without sleep and day after day where you eat less than a bird. We all have limits. You do as well, and I fear they will catch up with you before long."

Draegan touched the clasp at his neck. "You are here voluntarily. We're about to cross over the Frozen Maw into uncharted land, from which only one man has ever returned to tell the tale. If a snowstorm and a few nights of lost sleep have you on edge, then break from this quest now. I will respect your decision."

Gron turned to Draegan. "Aran speaks the truth. The Frozen Maw is a dangerous mountain range. Passing over it is no small feat. Ceredyn is weakened. You've not slept in days, and you barely eat. The ice on the lake will stay frozen through the night, holding the wolves." Gron laid his hand on Draegan's shoulder and said, "Not to mention that I lost my other hatchet to those reavers. I'm in a foul mood."

Draegan looked at Gron and then the others. "As you wish. You may have your rest. I will take watch." He pulled his cloak tighter. "And I will eat if you make something palatable," he said smiling wanly at Gron.

Gron laughed and brought out the skillet and a few strips of horse meat. They ate heartily and slept until nightfall. Draegan took first watch.

Shortly before midnight the storm died down. The clouds broke and moonlight brightened the desolate landscape. Draegan saw the foreboding silhouettes of the Frozen Maw glimmering faintly against the sky. "If old Baledin can make it over that range, we can as well."

A flash of light shot through his skull, followed by pain. Draegan gripped his head and rocked back and forth, breathing heavily until the pain subsided. Looking up at the Frozen Maw he saw the white capped peaks shift and twist in a cloud of black smoke. As the haze cleared he saw the black tower he'd seen so many nights before, only this time the image was unambiguous. He could feel the presence of the Artifact inside the tower.

Draegan roused the others a few hours after daybreak. "The storm's passed," he said smothering the coals in the fire pit. "Time to move."

They broke camp and shouldered their packs as they headed northeast from the shore of the White Lake. The vegetation they'd been walking through on the tundra became sparser as the ground began to rise. The frozen mosses and lichen changed to ice covered rocks as they made their way slowly to the base of the Frozen Maw range.

Progress was slow. Though the storm had passed, the wind never relented. By midday they had covered far fewer miles than Draegan had hoped.

"Does this wind ever stop?" Ceredyn asked. "Every way I turn it finds a way to blow directly in my face."

"You'll get less of it in you if you keep your mouth shut," Gron said as he smiled and trudged past him.

They began to gain elevation for the next few hours until they reached the large black rocks of a talus slope.

"This'll be a bit tougher than the scramble up the Spire of Heaven," Gron said dumping his pack on a rock and stretching his shoulders. "Good spot to eat. We'll be out of the wind until we summit," he said sitting down next to his pack and rummaging through it for some hardtack. "The storm on the other side rages night and day. They say it's lasted a thousand years and shows no signs of letting up. When the wind hits these mountains it pushes up and comes down hard on the lake. That's what keeps it frozen most of the year."

Gron shoved a handful of hardtack into his mouth followed by his water skin. Wiping his mouth he continued, "This close to the Frozen Maw though, there isn't any wind. The old folks say there was a time when my people would come here to bury their dead," he said offering some frozen hardtack to Draegan who refused. "Though now most of the barrows have been pillaged and the standing stones overturned."

"So what do you do with the dead now?" Ceredyn asked.

"These days it's a little hard to dig a decent grave up here," Gron said scuffing the ground with his boot, "so we mostly just burn them." Ceredyn winced. "Well it sure beats being dumped in a peat bog like you crows do."

"Ceredyn, have the reavers moved?" Draegan asked looking at the magnitude of the task that lay before them. Half a mile up the talus slope of large boulders, the base of the Frozen Maw shot straight up and rose into the roiling clouds. Wind howled at the peaks, promising a terrible reward for any brave enough to scale its sheer granite walls.

Draegan stared at the cliff face trying to find any sign of a path, or any easier route than scaling a frozen barricade of granite. Aran approached him. "Looks like the only way up, is up."

"Well then I suppose it's time for another *staminis* spell," Draegan said walking over to his pack. Ceredyn groaned. "Here's rope, and plenty of it. Take a few lengths. Though it sure would be nice to have a hatchet to drive spikes," Draegan said throwing down a few hundred feet of coiled cord.

"Don't remind me," Gron said.

Draegan pulled his hunting knife from its sheath and sat on a rock. He was about to draw some blood for his *staminis* spell when his eye sent a bolt of pain through his head. The knife slipped from his gloved hand and clattered down among the rocks. Draegan cursed to himself and slid off the rock, rubbing his forehead.

"Keep prepping the rope while I find my knife," Draegan said as he moved between the wagon sized black rocks. He was less than a hundred feet below the others when he saw the silver blade glint among the rocks a few feet farther below him. He jumped off the boulder and landed squarely next to his knife. He picked it up and sheathed it, then noticed the small bits of scree near his boot sinking inward, toward the mountain.

He kicked the toe of his boot into the gravel and a hole opened up. "I think I found one of your ancestor's barrows," Draegan yelled up the hill to the group. A cold wind escaped from the hole, making a hollow noise and displacing the small pebbles near its mouth. He stared in amazement then yelled up to the others. "I think you better come see this."

When the other three were standing next to him he removed his glove and placed his hand over the small entrance. "It's cold."

"Everything's cold around here," Gron replied.

Aran took off his glove and tested the air. "It may be from the other side. There's no wind here. It could go the whole way under the range."

"Those mountains are near impossible to scale. If this is another way, we need to test it out before we commit to climbing."

Draegan looked at Gron. "Can you make this entrance big enough for us to fit through?"

"Even if we do get in, there's no guarantee that the passage is big enough for us the entire way. It would have to be clear for at least a few miles. Wind can fit through smaller cracks than we can," Ceredyn said.

"Can you find out?" Draegan asked.

"I could send an illumination orb into the tunnel, track it with a *topos* spell and follow it on my chart to see if it comes out on the other side. That should tell us if the tunnel extends to the other side of the range, but it's still no guarantee that we'll all fit."

"If we can't we can always turn around and climb over. I don't see these mountains going anywhere anytime soon. But I want to exhaust all other possibilities before we risk our lives going straight up that frozen cliff," Draegan said, scrambling back up the rocks to gather their packs.

Draegan returned with the group's belongings and saw Ceredyn concentrating on the hole with his arms stretched out to either side. His eyes snapped open. "It's no barrow. I tracked the orb to the other side."

Draegan smiled. "Good thing I dropped my knife."

"Just because a ball of light the size of Gron's head made the journey, does not prove we can," Ceredyn said as he stood up and brushed the dust from his sleeves. Draegan was unmoved. "But I guess you'll want to find out for yourself."

By nightfall they had cleared enough debris to allow them to enter.

"Ceredyn, place a seal behind us. If the reavers come I'd like to know," Draegan said before turning to the others. "Keep your rope at the ready. Ceredyn said it's not a steep decline, but I'd rather be safe than sorry."

Draegan cinched his belt tighter and peered into the hole. He raised his hand over his head and slapped the other onto the gravel. A bluish white light coalesced in the air above his outstretched palm. He gently lowered his hand and brought the orb in front of him, illuminating the mouth of the entrance. He slipped into the hole and slid gently downward for a few feet. He hit the bottom and looked around.

Ahead of him lay a neatly carved tunnel, not tall enough to allow him to stand but high enough that he didn't have to crawl. He yelled up for the others to join him.

When they were all bunched at the foot of the slope Draegan's illumination spell flickered and died out. "Not enough natural light down here to support it," he said. "Let your eyes adjust and we'll proceed single file."

Gron was barely able to fit and complained about bringing up the rear. "I can't even turn around, let alone draw my blade. Ceredyn should be back here. I can't stand being boxed in like this. Makes me nervous."

Draegan silenced his objection. Gron cursed under his breath and slammed his fist into the wall. A low rumbling was followed by a rainstorm of pebbles, small rocks and dust that poured through the opening they had just crawled through. Draegan craned his neck and watched a boulder slide over the entrance, plunging them into complete darkness.

"We only have one option now," Draegan said over the obscenities that came gushing from Ceredyn. "Forward."

"At least the wolves won't be following us this way," Gron said, trying to sound hopeful. Ceredyn spat on the ground and shuffled after Aran.

Chapter 23: The Wastes

Ceredyn's *topos* spell indicated they had only a few miles to travel, but the pace was excruciatingly slow. With no ambient light to fuel an illumination spell they had to move through the constricted tunnel in complete darkness. Every step forward was preceded with utmost caution as they couldn't be sure of drop-offs, turns or unknown obstacles. They traveled through the night and into the next day. The darkness was so complete they remained in constant contact for fear of the ground dropping suddenly. Draegan warned against a fire spell for fear of burning out their air and igniting subterranean gasses, which further limited their ability to travel quickly.

"Three miles in a day is torture," Gron shouted from the rear. "I'd rather have gone over this hill than under it at the speed we're moving."

"You're welcome to try," Ceredyn said.

"The air stopped flowing shortly after we began this trek," Aran said. "I fear we'll come to an impasse soon.

As if on cue Draegan stumbled into a solid barrier. He put up his hands and began feeling in front of his face. In the complete darkness he could see nothing, but removing a glove he felt cold metal in front of him. "A door? It doesn't feel like the rough hewn walls. It's cold and metallic, very different than the tunnel. Ceredyn?"

Ceredyn fumbled blindly in his pack and retrieved a small glass vial. He took the topper out and carefully placed drops in his eyes. Wiping away the tears with his sleeve he wove his fingers together into an arcane sign and looked around the tunnel. "Ahead of you is a thick metal door, very ancient. When we stepped into the tunnel it must have triggered. That explains why the air currents stopped when we entered. I don't know whose work this is, but the mage was accomplished."

"Any ideas on how to get past it?" Draegan asked.

"It's sealed completely from this side, blocking all air and access to the other side. That explains why it was beginning to smell so putrid in here. However I see traces of the triggering magic on the other side. It was clearly meant to keep people from Fyrian out."

"So if I can get to the other side, I could unlock it?" Draegan asked.

"Possibly. Or we could turn around, dig out of the tunnel and climb over the mountains," Ceredyn said.

"We'll use that course of action if this one fails. Gron can you get up here and chisel a hole big enough to slide a piece of paper through? I need to Shadow Walk to the other side."

After what seemed an hour's worth of shuffling, grunting, clanging, and cursing Gron had made his way past the other three and began chipping away at the rock near the door.

"Good thing I brought this skillet," he yelled between strikes. "Fries up bacon and saves ours."

Another hour of toil and Aran smiled as he felt a slight breeze trickle in through the hole. "He's through," Aran said, pressing himself against the tunnel wall. Draegan took a sheet of paper, marked it with the shadow walking rune, then slid it through the tiny hole. Cutting his forearm he wet his palm with blood and pressed it to the cold surface of the door.

With one word he felt himself tumbling in the darkness. As quickly as it began it ended and Draegan was on the other side of the door. "What am I looking for?" he yelled through the small opening Gron had made.

"There's a mark in the middle of the door. Find it and trace it," Ceredyn yelled back.

Draegan did as he was instructed and after a moment of silence the door began to glow from within. The light spread from the sigil and consumed the entire piece of metal. After so long in the dark the four shielded their eyes from the intense light. As the flash died out and their eyes readjusted to the dark, they saw the door had vanished.

Cool air rushed through the tunnel. "If there aren't any more surprises, let's keep moving," Draegan said.

The air progressively cooled as they scraped their way through the narrow tunnel. Soon the ground began to slope upward. They could hear the wind howling above ground.

"Must be close," Aran said.

"I can hear the storm," Gron replied.

Draegan reached the end of the tunnel and began shoveling handfuls of loose rock behind him. "Careful where you're slinging that," Aran said, wiping dust from his face. "We're still back here."

"Looks like it's sealed with ice. A pretty large crack but nothing any of us can squeeze through." Draegan turned over his shoulder and said, "Any trick for this Ceredyn?"

"Fire," Ceredyn answered.

"I was hoping for something more elegant." Draegan took off his gloves and placed his hands on the sheet of ice. "No sense making you squirm up here. I'll do it myself." Draegan began chanting as the ice reddened. Soon rivulets of water ran down his arms. The ice cracked and shattered into thousands of tiny fragments, raining down into the tunnel. The wind howled in, whipping in ice and hail and loose stone.

The four extricated themselves from the tunnel. They were a few hundred yards from the base of the Frozen Maw. The land that stretched before them was flat, barren of all life, and completely covered in snow. The sky was a deep blue black and an unrelenting wind blasted ice and snow directly into their faces.

"So this is it?" Gron said hooking his thumbs in his belt. He took a deep breath and exhaled. Ice began forming on his beard. "This is the leftover land of Iss? Doesn't seem so bad."

The other three were trying to figure out which way to turn to put their back to the wind. "Comes from all directions at once up here. Might as well learn live with it," Gron said. "Now which way are we going?"

"North," Draegan yelled over the howling wind. "Always north, though I don't know how far. We seek the Black tower."

"It could be anywhere," Ceredyn shouted. "We can't see more than a few hundred yards in this squall."

"Then we should spread out and increase our chances of seeing something," Draegan said. We'll tie ourselves together with rope so we don't drift apart in the storm."

They lashed themselves together and began marching north. The wind tore at their faces, watering their eyes. Gron's beard had gone from red to white in a matter of minutes. The snow was knee deep and the pace was slow.

After a few hours of trudging through the snow, Aran yelled, "Shouldn't the sun be up by now?"

"Not for another couple of months," Gron answered. "This far north it sets for the season."

"So now it's permanent night. Perfect conditions for the reavers," Draegan said. "Ceredyn any sign of them?"

"None. I would guess they're still trapped in the ice. And even if the spell broke and they're free I don't see how they'll get over the Frozen Maw," Ceredyn said.

"There may be more than one of those tunnels," Draegan said. "We should still be cautious. We have no idea what those things are capable of."

The company kept pushing north for another few miles before Draegan spoke again. "We'll keep going until it would be nightfall and then we'll make camp. I want you to craft more of those bone stakes, Ceredyn. Something tells me we'll need them."

There was no indication in the sky that it was nearing midnight when the group stumbled to a stop in the snow. They had been marching against the wind in knee deep snow for hours and were completely exhausted. Their faces were wind burned and red, eyes half frozen shut when they tried to make camp.

"There's no shelter out here," Draegan said. "No game, no vegetation, and no life, save us."

"We can make a shelter," Gron suggested gathering armfuls of snow and piling it in a semi circle. The other's joined in the effort and within minutes they had a passable wall to huddle behind.

With nothing to burn the companions made do eating frozen hardtack and horse jerky under an illumination spell that cast an eerie bluish white light on the snow. Gron passed his flask of black bile around and everyone took a mouthful.

"Hope we get to your tower soon, Draegan," Gron said taking his flask back and feeling its reduced weight. "I don't have much more."

"Then we'll only sleep for a few hours and get moving," Draegan said. "I don't want us turning to ice up here."

Despite the howling wind and freezing temperatures they all slept, including Draegan.

***

Draegan sat bolt upright just as Aran leaned over to rouse him. "The Black Tower," he yelled seeing a large object in the distance.

"No, that's just Gron," Aran said. "You've slept for five hours. It's time to move."

Draegan sat up and rubbed his face, watching the image of the tower dissolve into the form of Gron, who was securing his pack.

The group lashed themselves together again and continued their journey north. Every step was hard won as they labored through the snow. The wind tore at them mercilessly, blurring their vision with tears that quickly froze on their cheeks.

They walked all day, eating on the move. The absent sun, incessant storm, and unchanging terrain gave the group the feeling of having made no progress as time and distance were impossible to mark. Ceredyn used the *topos* incantation to keep the four of them moving due north.

By what should have been midnight, Ceredyn shouted for the others to stop. Using the rope as a guide the three made their way to the mage.

"Have you found the tower?" Draegan asked.

"The reavers," Ceredyn said. "They've passed the seal I placed when we exited the tunnel." Ceredyn turned and tried to keep the wind from blowing in his face.

"How many?" Aran asked. "And how did they make it so quickly?"

"All I know is that they didn't come through our tunnel, but I can't say beyond that," Ceredyn said pulling the hood of his cloak tighter. "I count all eight."

"Have you made any more of your bone stakes?" Draegan asked. "It seems we'll need them before too long."

"I've managed to finish two more," Ceredyn said, "in between doing everything else. Though we have more time than you think. They seem to be moving as slowly as we are."

"There's some good news at least," Gron said, struggling to pull his hood over his large head.

"They must have come over the mountains the way we intended. They have used no true sorcery in any of our encounters, so I would guess they shifted from their wolf form to human in order to scale the cliff face," Draegan said. "This is indeed good news. Now we have another opportunity to make use of Ceredyn's arts."

Draegan turned to Ceredyn. "How quickly can you make more arrows and stakes?"

"I have enough bones, but the blood is frozen. If each of you take a vial and carry it close to your skin it should thaw quickly. Then I can do my work, though we'll need to stop."

"We have a day's lead on them," Aran said. "I think we should take the opportunity to arm ourselves in case they can close the distance faster than we anticipated."

"Agreed," Draegan said. "Give us the vials and let's press on."

After distributing the vials the companions continued their arduous plodding northward. After several hours Aran felt a tug on the rope and stopped the others.

"I think Ceredyn's strength is waning," he shouted over the gale. "I've felt him lagging behind for some time." The three built a snow wall and huddled together around him. Aran pulled an ampoule of oil from his belt and handed it to Draegan.

"It will burn without fuel. Pour a few drops on the snow and use it as you would tinder or branches," he said. "It comes from a flower in the south of my country. Now seems like a time when we need a real fire," he said pointing to Ceredyn.

Draegan did as instructed and once the small flame caught on the surface of the hard packed snow he used incantations to amplify the miniscule flame until he had created a roaring fire.

Ceredyn opened his eyes and flinched when he saw how close he was to the fire.

"This fire should help. Are you well enough to do your work?" Draegan asked.

Ceredyn propped himself up on his elbows and coughed. "It will take some time."

"You have until they get here," Draegan said, smiling wryly.

Ceredyn labored by the fire through what should have been daybreak, morning and afternoon. Aran and Gron slept while Draegan intermittently watched Ceredyn and drifted off into his mind, watching the visions in Islak's eye. Amidst the roiling darkness and blinding light the eye showed him, the Black Tower always rose from the chaos. Without being aware, several times Draegan shouted in pain, causing Ceredyn to start, ruining his work.

Several hours after he began, Ceredyn indicated to the others that he had finished his work. "Now they need time to cure. Another day perhaps. I don't know how the cold will affect the process."

Draegan sighed and watched his breath disappear into the darkness. "The fire is pleasant, but I don't want to wait for them here," he said standing up and feeling the pounding of the wind and ice against his cloak as he moved from the protection of the windbreak. "Let's get moving."

Lashing themselves together again the four once again set off due north. They continued their punishing march through the rest of the day and into the night. Ceredyn kept them aware of the direction of their travel.

"How far have we come since the tunnel," Gron asked.

"Thirty miles," Ceredyn yelled in response. "Though it feels like three hundred."

"How much further to your tower?" Gron shouted.

The rope went slack. The others shouted but Draegan gave no response. They pulled themselves along the line toward the middle and found him curled up on the snow, his black cloak whipping around his writhing body.

"Don't touch him," Ceredyn said. "And stay out of reach of his blade."

Draegan shouted in agony and thrashed desperately. The storm seemed to intensify with his suffering so they could barely see him though they were only a few feet away.

"We have to do something," Aran said moving toward him. Gron held him by the shoulder.

"There," Draegan shouted. Curled on the ground he shot his arm out in an impossible angle and gestured toward a nondescript patch of blackness in the squall. He put his hand down and pushed himself up to his knees.

"It's close," he said, his chest heaving as he tried to gather himself.

He stumbled as he tried to stand. Aran stepped in and steadied him. "Are you well enough to continue?" he asked.

"I want to make it to the tower before those reavers get here," he said, pushing off Aran and tightening the cord on his belt. "It looked like only a few more miles."

Draegan led the company in single file and moved with decided purpose. The storm increased in intensity tearing at every bit of exposed skin with shards of ice and hail as if it was trying to drive them back.

After an hour of slogging through the tempest, Draegan stopped and allowed the others to catch up. One by one they followed in his footsteps until all four stood shoulder to shoulder in awed silence beneath the massive Black Tower that rose into the sky before them.

Chapter 24: The Valediction

"It certainly is odd to be summoned to a council meeting that is occurring without my knowledge," Vangen said, seating himself in his chair and glancing around the council chamber. "To what do I owe the pleasure?" He crossed his feet upon the great obsidian table.

"It's been over a week and you've not mentioned one word of your work with the Night Watch," Arius said.

"I am sure your Ravens have whispered of my comings and goings, Arius. No need to pretend you do not know." Vangen smiled and placed his fingers together.

"I know one hundred Night Watchmen are gone," Arius said in low tones, staring at Vangen.

Vangen squinted, and then smiled. "It is as I told you. Draegan planted seeds of sedition and I brought to justice those of whom in which it took root. I am under no obligation to tell you the details of what I do with my personal guard, just as I choose not to pry into the unnatural work you do in your Rookery." Arius bowed his head.

"Then it is safe to assume all one hundred were brought to your justice," Maluk said.

"Say what you will, that is what the council chamber is for. Your words might never leave this room, but your actions do. Or rather, do not do, since you have done little enough to help find Draegan and his followers. Therefore if you are all finished prying, I will return to running an Empire, and you may all continue your gossiping and speculations."

"You're not done yet," Baledin said glaring at Vangen.

"Ah, the Great War Chief speaks. What news from the north?" Vangen said. "I trust your trip was enlightening."

"It was. I learned the truth. I know who you are and what you've done to my kingdom."

Vangen placed his hands behind his head. "Oh please continue. Council chatter is always so dull, but you continually manage to find ways to interject your bad comedy, Baledin."

"I met Draegan and his companions in the ruins of a village you had destroyed."

Vangen laughed as the other council members looked at Baledin in shock. Baledin reached out a massive hand and slapped Vangen's feet off the table and back onto the ground. Vangen sat forward to steady himself and placed his hands on the table.

"You strike the Emperor of Fyrian?" Vangen said, his temper rising. "You had better explain your actions and quickly."

"I swat at a child who thinks himself a king," Baledin growled. "A false shadow of his father."

"You encountered Draegan and his traitors?" Tysta asked. "Why have you not brought them here? If you let them go you are at great fault, Baledin."

"They're not the enemy of Fyrian that Vangen claims," Baledin said, jabbing his finger toward Vangen. "It's Vangen who has orchestrated the entire threat of Iss, when in truth Vangen himself is Iss." The rest of the council stared at Baledin, dumbfounded.

"Vangen seeks to disband the council and rule Fyrian uncontested. He uses the dark arts of Iss to create unliving beings. These are the creatures that ravage our lands. His unholy servants.

He seeks the Dark Artifacts to aid him and he seeks power above all else," Baledin said pointing a finger at Vangen while addressing the other council members.

"You have had your fun, old man. I wager you have had enough to drink as well. I ask that you leave and sleep it off. Tomorrow I will deal with your subversive speech personally." Vangen rose and pointed at the door. "Your deteriorating mind need not bother the council any longer."

"Hold Vangen," Arius said raising his hand. "Quite often Baledin has come before the council with less than sound logic and inflammatory speech, but never before with such imagination." Arius looked at Vangen. "Beings from beyond the grave? Dark magic. Plots to rule the Empire? I would hear more."

"I would have evidence," Tysta said, her usually soft voice rising over the outburst of voices. "Accusations can be made with little effort but something tangible would lend credence to his theory."

"I have no evidence beyond the chaos I saw with my own eyes," Baledin said. Stabbing his giant finger at Vangen, he continued, "He burns the villages to the ground. He leaves no trace of his misdeed. But I assure you with every fiber of my being this man is wicked, loathsome, and corrupt."

"Without any proof, your claims are baseless," Maluk said, returning to his seat.

Baledin ground his teeth and slammed his fists into the monolithic table. The blow echoed in the enormous chamber. "You'll have your proof," he said through clenched teeth and lunged across the table at Vangen with animal ferocity.

The council members scattered as Vangen moved with surprising speed and dodged Baledin's grasp. In one swift movement Vangen reached into his cloak and pulled out the hilt of Carnis Fornax and slid his hand down the length of the missing blade. Black fire sprung from the yawning mouth carved in the guard.

Baledin caught himself and sprung again at Vangen. Both of his massive hands closed like a vice around Vangen's neck. Baledin drove them both toward one of the thick marble columns. Vangen backpedaled as his eyes bulged in pain. An instant later a blade of black fire erupted from Baledin's shoulder blades. Vangen took a step back and Baledin's mammoth body collapsed in a heap on the white marble floor, his blood pooling and running in rivulets toward Vangen's chair.

The council members stood frozen as Vangen casually moved the chair away from the blood on the floor. He walked to the table and thrust the burning blade into the great crack in the black stone. The council members recoiled as tendrils of flame reached across the obsidian mass, frantically searching for signs of life. He wiped his hands on his cloak and rolled his head from side to side, cracking his shoulders. Red marks flared on his white skin showing where Baledin's hands had nearly snapped his neck.

"There lays your proof," Vangen said, pointing to the sword driven into the table. Its blade of fire danced on the table top, searching for any signs of life in the obsidian.

"How did you bring a sword past the doors of the chamber?" Maluk gasped. "This room has seals and protections made by the Sages themselves.

"A sword?" Vangen snapped. "This is Carnis Fornax, the celebrated weapon of the greatest Blade of Darkness to walk in Athar. Fet Reth, the Eater of Souls, wielded this sword in the ten thousand year War for Athar." Vangen sat in his chair and stared into the flaming blade. "And now it is mine."

Arius ran to the doors and banged on them, announcing his name. "They will only open for me, Arius," Vangen shouted across the chamber, his voice echoing. "In fact I removed all your names and privileges from the Council Book before I entered and placed myself in charge of this room. The magic that protects us here now only protects me. You have nowhere to run, so please, come join us in talk," he said gesturing at the empty seat at the table. Arius slowly returned and cautiously slipped into his chair.

The three council members alternately stared at the body of Baledin, the blade in the table and Vangen. No one spoke.

"Baledin was right," Vangen said after a few moments of silence. "Well not quite, but he had the right idea." Vangen stood and pulled the sword from the table. He ran his hand down the length of the blade toward the hilt and the flame evaporated. "I am Iss and I am Fyrian. I am also the Light of Athar. From this day forward your kingdoms and your power over them are in name only," he said placing the hilt back into his cloak.

Walking around the table he continued, "Your continued existence is a mark of my beneficence. You see, what Baledin had wrong was his accusation that I seek power. It is peace I seek. I wish the Empire and the work of my father to continue. In order for this to happen the people require a strong leader. A council comprised of bitter enemies cannot give them the stability they desire. A council cannot act with the speed necessary to assuage their fears. A council will eventually lead to deception and dissension, which will bring us back to war. A war that will last another thousand years. Only I can stop the inevitable failure of this council."

Maluk stood. "Are we to meet the same fate as Baledin?"

"Do not misunderstand me. The council is still necessary, but only as a show for the people. The council will continue, albeit without any teeth," Vangen smiled. "Athar has a new light, a powerful ruler who will ensure continued stability and prosperity."

Vangen moved toward the sealed doors of the chamber. "Your fate now depends entirely upon your actions. Should you follow the path of Baledin and Draegan, you will meet the same fate. And you have now seen I am in command of powerful magic. Wielding an Artifact of Darkness is no trivial matter, let alone in this hallowed hall. I alone have mastered its use."

Vangen walked over to the body of Baledin and shoved the mammoth shoulder with his boot. "Draegan did not understand my vision. Nor did he understand the extent of my power. What Baledin said was correct. I can give life to the dead. I have plumbed the depths of the knowledge of Iss and command its power beyond the might of any of the six Blades of Darkness. I have surpassed even the power of the six Sages themselves."

Sitting down, Vangen continued. "Understand that if you choose to return to your kingdoms and raise arms against me then you, your people, and your kingdom will be overrun in short order by my army. You have seen what a handful of my reavers can do to an entire village. Know that I command thousands."

"The Night Watch?" Arius asked.

"They serve me in a new capacity," Vangen said. "And so do thousands of others. They cannot be killed. Not even magic can stop them. They are my willing, loyal and unstoppable army. It would be folly to engage me in a war."

"The people will not stand for this," Maluk said.

"The people will not know," Vangen replied. He shrugged. "And if they do know what of it? I offer them what they want. Peace."

"The Freehold of Stanrocc will not be ruled by an abomination such as you," Maluk said, rising to his feet.

"The Freehold has a long tradition of autonomy. The very mention conjures images of self-reliance and independence. As the Red Hand of Stanrocc you are free to decide the fate of your fellow countrymen. It is the right given to you by them when they elected you as their representative."

Vangen waved his hand dismissively. "Return to them. Tell them what you saw. Feed their rancor, incite them to arms and meet me in battle." Vangen clenched his fists and set his jaw. "And I assure you that if you do I will level your Freehold. I will rip your children from their mothers. Every heart that beats will stop. Every mouth that screams will be silenced. Every drop of blood that flows will be spilt upon your soil. I will obliterate every trace of life and wipe your country from the maps. The Freehold of Stanrocc will be nothing more than a memory. Nothing more than a tale told to keep children from misbehaving." Maluk sat down. "As always I leave the choice to your good judgment."

"Will no one else stand against this monster?" Maluk asked, waving at Vangen. "We watched him murder Baledin. He wields a weapon of dark magic and claims to know the ways of Iss. He admits to killing his own people. Our people." Maluk pointed at the other council members. "Will you be complicit in this madness?"

Vangen smiled. "No need for such histrionics, Maluk. Arius and his Ravens are mine for the asking. I believe it was Baledin himself who claimed that 'the crows of Corvus can be bought.'" Vangen looked over his shoulder at the mountain of a corpse sprawled on the floor. "He was wiser than I gave him credit for."

Maluk looked at Arius and spat. "And what of you Tysta? Which master will the hounds of Docga choose?"

Tysta looked at the table and exhaled with a sigh. "Our kingdom aided Skeldus in the War for Unity. Many of our finest warriors fought and died for the ideals of peace and unity proposed by Leon. Few returned when the war ended. The Tribe of Docga is in no position to fight another war." Tysta shook her head and looked at Maluk. "Peace is what matters; the means to achieve it, secure it, and protect it do not. The Tribe of Docga will stand with Skeldus, for the Empire."

"Well considered. A sensible decision, Tysta," Vangen said.

"You are no better than the crows of Corvus, Tysta," Maluk said. "You join Vangen from a position of weakness, afraid to stand and fight for what you know is right. Vangen's peace is not the peace of Leon. Peace through threats and coercion is not true peace."

Maluk stood and glared at the council members before turning to face the door. "I will take my leave Vangen, or you may murder me as you have Baledin." He turned and pointed his finger at Vangen. "Know that Stanrocc will fight you tooth and nail to the last man, woman, and child, and the Clan of the Iron Mountains will join us when they hear of your detestable misconduct," he said and then turned and walked to the door.

"So you would consign your people to the fire? If you leave this chamber, you slaughter your people and those of the Iron Mountains." Vangen said. Maluk stood unmoved. Vangen waved his hand. "As you wish, but their blood will be on your hands."

The great doors parted silently, allowing the white light of the council chamber to spill into the darkened hallway. Maluk turned and looked the three remaining council members in the eye, spat on the floor, cursed them all and exited the chamber. The doors closed behind him with a resounding thud.

The council members sat in silence and watched Vangen carefully. Moments later they heard a muffled scream through the heavy doors of the chamber.

Vangen smiled. "So too will you share his fate if you choose to stand against me."

Chapter 25: The Black Tower

Behind the four companions the swirling snow and ice howled and lashed in the darkness. Near the base of the tower where the four now stood the storm subsided, covering the ground in a gentle snowfall.

"The eye of the storm," Draegan said. "Glad to be done with it for now."

The group walked forward cautiously, checking for seals and barriers. In front of them the tower rose into the clouds, a pitch black and perfectly smooth cylinder of obsidian. It was devoid of ornamentation and had no windows or doors, save one cavernous arch at its base.

"Looks like they were expecting us," Gron said, pointing at the open door.

"It worries me that the tower should stand open and unguarded when someone has gone to such great lengths to make sure it's near impossible to get here." Aran said, eyeing the great structure.

"Nothing I can feel," Ceredyn said. "But then again I didn't sense the trap door in the tunnel."

"Aran, send in an arrow and mark it," Draegan said looking up at the black obelisk as it disappeared into the swirling clouds above him. "Ceredyn see what you can read from it. Gron and I are going to take a walk around."

Aran loosed a bolt into the open archway as Ceredyn clapped his hands together causing it to burst into flame. The group heard the arrow clatter to the floor despite the wind raging a few hundred feet behind them. "Hollow," Ceredyn said. "And empty."

Gron and Draegan circled the tower checking for any other means of entry. When they had completed their circumnavigation they confirmed that the open arch was the only way into the tower.

"It's the same the whole way around. I can't tell the front from the back except for this hole," Gron said pointing to the doorway.

"Then there's nothing left to do but go in," Draegan said.

He drew his sword and proceeded toward the tower. The company walked carefully as there was no snow this close to the obelisk, but only ice with hard packed frost covering the ground. As they drew nearer, the enormity of the tower became apparent. What appeared to be a simple archway leading into the tower became gaping jaws that could swallow a legion.

"Put a seal behind us Ceredyn," Draegan said. "I hope to make this quick, but if we have to climb this monstrosity I want to know when the reavers arrive."

Ceredyn did as he was bid and joined up with the others as they stepped through the arch and entered the black tower.

Moments after they crossed the threshold, a colossal slab of obsidian dropped into place behind them, nearly knocking the four to their knees as the entire tower shook. They were enveloped in complete darkness.

"They must have heard that in Dullahan," Gron said, sticking his fingers in his ear in an attempt to reduce the ringing.

"Ceredyn, a light?" Draegan asked.

Instantly the black room blazed to life. From the center of the room a seal carved in the middle of the floor shone as brightly as the sun, then subsided to gently bathe the room in a reddish glow.

The four let their eyes adjust to the dim light after being temporarily blinded.

"That wasn't me," Ceredyn said. "It feels like the same magic as in the tunnel. It's ancient."

"It's hollow," Aran said looking around as his voice echoed through the chamber. "It's just a hollow tube. And there's my arrow." He pointed to the center of the room. "And your Artifact."

The companions saw that Aran was correct. The massive tower was simply a hollow tube large enough in diameter to comfortably hold the market square of Dullahan. The interior walls were as smooth and glassy black as it's outside. In the center of the floor was carved a huge seal of ancient origin that gave off enough light to faintly illuminate the size and shape of the room. In the center of the seal sat a large boulder of obsidian rock. Embedded in the rock was a massive, double-bladed battle axe.

The group approached the center of the seal, keeping an eye on the stone dais. When they were within a few feet of the axe there was enough light to see the weapon more clearly.

"It's the World Render," Draegan said. "Arkon Fell the Reaver carried it in the War for Athar."

The handle of the axe was decorated with twisting bodies and coiled serpents that spread from the end knob to the shoulder. The blade was massive and appeared to be made of smooth black metal. Even half buried in the rock the axe held the promise of ferocious power.

"Well it looks like a fine hatchet to me," Gron said taking another step closer to the dais.

As Gron approached the axe it burst into flame. The four stumbled back away from the dais. The entire axe was engulfed in a black fire that roared with malice.

"What is it Ceredyn?" Draegan asked.

Ceredyn took out a powder and threw it in the fire. "It's pyrrhic fire. There's no way to extinguish it."

"We need to find a way," Draegan said. "Unless of course you can destroy the Artifact."

"The priests of Vatn couldn't destroy the Artifacts, so my spells don't work either. And I know of no way to douse a pyrrhic fire," Ceredyn said. "I am at a loss."

"The Frozen Maw, the endless blizzard, this fire, all these things have been protecting the Artifact for countless years from those who would use it for ill," Aran said. "We should leave it and figure out how to get out of here."

"If we can get here, then so too can Vangen," Draegan said. "We need to get that axe, and quickly. Or did you forget that eight reavers track us?"

"For better or worse, I think we're safe enough sealed in this tomb for the time being," Ceredyn said, motioning at the slab of rock that blocked the arch. "We're still locked in here by some magic with or without the Artifact."

Gron circled the dais, staring at the axe. He completed his circle and stopped, folded his arms across his chest and thought while the others argued.

"While you figure out how to get out, I'll take the axe," he said. Gron took a step toward the obsidian boulder, raising his right hand across his eyes to shield himself from the heat. He plunged his left hand into the fire, gripped the handle and watched in horror as his hand caught fire. He yelled in agony and stumbled backward as the flame changed from black to blood red. As Gron wheeled backward toward the group the flame began to climb from his hand up his arm.

"Gron, no!" Draegan shouted as he rushed to his side. He unsheathed his sword and brought his blade down in a smooth arc, taking Gron's hand off. The hand thudded to the floor. Aran caught Gron as he fell, still screaming in pain. The fire that consumed his newly amputated hand extinguished itself, but Gron's wrist and forearm continued to burn.

Ceredyn grabbed a paste from a pouch on his belt and smeared it on the curved blade of his knife. He pressed the flat of the blade against the open wound and mumbled a few words. Gron's eyes bulged in agony at the sound of his flesh cauterizing. Ceredyn quickly grabbed Gron's forearm and cut a symbol in it as he shouted an incantation. The fire went out and Gron fell to his knees.

"The fire changed as soon as he touched it," Ceredyn said. "I've never seen a flame do that before. It was almost as if it were alive, trying to consume him."

"I've seen that fire before. It was the same color as the flaming blade of Carnis Fornax," Draegan said. "How did you stop it?"

"I didn't stop it on his hand. It must have done that itself," Ceredyn said as he pulled a book and a vial of liquid from his pack. "And I've only contained it on his arm. I need to do a few more things to seal it."

Draegan watched closely as Ceredyn tore a sheet from his book and poured the contents of the vial on the page. He rolled up his sleeve revealing his runic tattoos and used the point of his blade to excise a piece of skin containing a glyph on his upper arm. Ceredyn winced as he cut out the rune and placed it on the sheet of parchment.

"What are you going to do to me?" Gron asked between gasps of breath.

"Draegan saved your life when he removed your hand, I merely stopped the bleeding. Now I have to seal the flame before it spreads to your heart," Ceredyn said carrying the paper and skin closer to Gron. "Most of the fire was cut away with your hand but a small flame managed to get into your forearm. It's still burning in there though you can't see it. Sit still and give me your arm."

Gron moved his stump toward Ceredyn, who took the parchment and wrapped it over the wound. Upon contact with the warm blood the paper and skin dissolved into a fine vapor. Gron bit his lip and watched the mark Ceredyn had carved on his forearm turn from bloody to black.

"There," Ceredyn said as he stood up. "The flame can't spread and consume you. But it will live in that stump," he said pointing at Gron's missing hand, "and continue to burn for as long as you live."

"Pyrrhic fire is a forbidden magic. Who but those of Iss know how to use it?" Aran asked, reaching into his pack. He pulled a roll of gauze from his cloak and wrapped Gron's wrist while applying salve. "This should help with the pain." He looked at Ceredyn grasping his arm. "You too," he said, tossing the salve to Ceredyn. "You Ravens possess some strange magic."

Ceredyn took the tin and applied the salve liberally.

"What pain?" Gron said smiling though he winced as Aran bandaged his wrist. He looked around the room. "Where's my axe?"

"Your axe?" Draegan said. "The Artifact still lies there in the rock, though I can't imagine you'd want to pick it up with your other hand."

Ceredyn studied the burning weapon as it flickered in its bed of stone. The fire had consumed the hand that lay on the floor, leaving not even ash behind. He wove his fingers together and stood in silence.

"Actually Gron is the only one who can touch it now," Ceredyn said after examining the axe further. "The Pyrrhic fire took his blood and flesh, and now it's sealed in him. If any of us were to touch the axe we'd share in his fate."

"Well I gave up two hatchets and a hand so far. I'll take that hunk of metal as payment," Gron said pointing at the axe. He stood up and approached the dais once again.

"How do you propose to get your axe this time?" Draegan asked. "Do you have a more sophisticated plan than shoving your one remaining hand into the fire?"

"Not really. But I have an idea," Gron said rifling clumsily through his pack.

"Should we stand back?" Ceredyn asked. "Gron with an idea is more lethal than that fire."

Gron stood up and grinned from ear to ear. He lofted his iron skillet over his head and approached the obsidian boulder. "It worked in the tunnel," he said pulling the skillet back. "I can get a better swing in here than that cramped space." With an ear-splitting crash the skillet collided with the glass-like rock and both objects cracked and shattered. The tower reverberated and rang as the black boulder broke into thousands of shards that scattered across the dais and seal on the floor. The axe clattered to the ground and the fire extinguished without a trace of smoke.

Gron bent over and picked up the weapon, studying the carvings on the handle and inspecting the blade for damage. "This craftsmanship is exceedingly fine. Not one nick or bit of rust on the thing," he said turning the weapon in the faint light emanating from the seal in the floor.

"It's an immutable Artifact of Darkness, Gron," Draegan said watching him carefully. "The priests and acolytes of Vatn could do nothing to destroy it, though they understood the depths of its evil. Study yourself, and be sure the axe doesn't claim you as the sword has claimed Vangen."

"Not to worry," Gron said. "Pure as the driven snow, I am," he said placing his stump over his heart. The axe was too large to hang from his belt so he swapped places on his back with his broadsword. No sooner had he tightened his belt to secure the axe than the tower began to rumble.

"I don't like the sound of that," Aran said looking around. "We need to figure out how to get out of here."

"Well my skillet is shattered or I'd start working on an exit," Gron said.

"The axe," Draegan shouted as immense fissures began appearing in the walls. "If it was embedded in the rock without losing its bite, it should be able to chip us out of here."

Suddenly the light of the seal went out, plunging them into darkness. Draegan cast an illumination spell and saw great vertical cracks running up and down the length of the tower. "Cut us out of here Gron, and quickly!"

Gron reached behind him and fumbled with the buckle and straps holding his axe. "It's hard to do with one hand," he said. After a few moments of struggling he removed the weapon. Charging the wall he swung viciously and sunk the blade into the black stone. The wall ruptured and exploded outward sending thousands of fragments of sharp black stone into the cold night air. "It's lighter than I thought," Gron said regarding the axe with child-like joy.

"Glad to hear," Aran said. "Now let's put some distance between us and this crumbling tower."

The four hurtled themselves through the opening and plunged into the cold. They ran through the calm eye of the storm at top speed and slowed only when they approached the edge of the storm wall. Aran turned and looked back at the tower.

"It's pulling the storm in," he shouted over the wind.

Behind them the tower trembled and shook violently. The top of the tower which was once lost in the clouds of the storm was now visible and appeared to be sucking the entire storm into itself. In few moments the raging blizzard was silenced and contained within the tower.

Gron smiled. "Well that'll make our trip home more pleasant. I can't wait to…"

With a deafening roar the black tower exploded sending shards of obsidian in every direction. The four fell into the snow and pulled their cloaks about them as the fragments rained down everywhere. When the pelting had subsided Draegan rose to his feet.

"Everyone ok?" he asked.

The other three rose and shook off the pieces of stone. Though their skin was cut in places from the shards, no one was seriously hurt.

"Then let's move," Draegan said. "We've still got eight reavers hunting us."

"I can't wait to introduce them to my new friend," Gron said looking at the blade of his axe for any signs of damage.

The group began marching south at a quicker pace, unhindered by the howling winds and driving snow. Without warning, Draegan collapsed on the ice. He began twisting on the ground raking his face with his gloved hands. The other four rushed to his side, but Draegan kicked at them wildly. He clawed at his eye.

"North," he shouted. "A mountain of fire." He vomited and passed out in the snow.

Draegan awoke in the same spot he had collapsed. Sitting up he saw the others talking nearby. His head pounded and there was a ringing in his ears. He shook it off and stood up.

"How long?" Draegan asked, barely able to choke out the words.

"An hour," Aran answered. "It would be nightfall now, if you're wondering."

"We need to push further north," Draegan said. "The eye showed me the next Artifact." Draegan rubbed his temple and looked at the group. "Flashes of fire. A massive mountain."

"We were discussing those very things," Ceredyn said. "We haven't the supplies to continue north. As it is, I think we'll barely make it back across the Frozen Maw and to the Clan of the Iron Mountains with what we have."

"Ceredyn's right," Aran said. "Unless this mountain of fire is close, we shouldn't risk it. We'll run out of food in a few days and we need rest. This time we escaped with our skins, but it could have just as easily gone wrong for us in there," Aran said pointing to the pile of black rubble that had been lightly dusted with snow behind them.

"I've lost two hatchets, a hand, and a well-seasoned skillet," Gron said, jabbing his bandaged stump at Draegan. "I don't have much left to give."

Draegan looked at each face in turn. "We have two of the six Artifacts. We must find the remaining three before Vangen does or the Empire will descend into darkness. Be that as it may, you are free to leave. I ask only my share of the supplies, the World Render, and the bones you've made for the reavers. They hunt me, not you."

Ceredyn dropped his pack to the ground and opened it up, looking for the bones. "You'll need the spell too, or they're useless," he said handing a book to Draegan. "And here are the other books you loaned me." Draegan took the books and bones and put them in his pack.

"You're not actually going to go back, are you?" Gron asked Ceredyn. "By yourself?"

"I thought we were all going back?" Ceredyn replied as he looked up at the others, confused.

"And leave him alone up here?" Gron said pointing his remaining thumb at Draegan. "He's the Captain of the Night Watch. Commander of the Graywalkers. Our leader." Gron paused. "He wouldn't last one night up here without us."

"Draegan, all we want is some rest, a fire, some food. The reavers are coming and I'd rather face them with a clear head and full belly. Perhaps after that we can discuss your mountain of fire, and our dwindling supplies," Aran said.

"You can have your rest and food and fire. I would like to deal with the reavers once and for all before we continue on anyway," Draegan said.

Ceredyn looked at his half-empty pack. "I guess I'm staying too. You'll need me to save you from the reavers anyway."

They used Aran's oil to make another fire and slept in the shelter of the black tower's rubble. Draegan slept little and watched the night sky while trying to read the book Ceredyn had returned to him. Since the storm had dissipated he could make out the constellation of Arcturus, the great bear of the north, continually marching north no matter the season. Shortly after midnight Draegan's head began to swim. He fell to his knees and waited for the light and pain in his head to pass.

"What were you saying?" Draegan heard Gron's voice. "Something about fire and ice and a mountain split in half?"

Draegan propped himself up on his hands and knees and waited for the world to stop spinning. The constellations had shifted, indicating a passage of time, though the sky was still pitch black.

"I don't know what I said," Draegan replied, "but the eye of Islak keeps showing me the same vision of a mountain split down the middle and fire and ice surrounding it. That's where the next Artifact lies."

"It'll have to wait," Aran said as he pointed behind Draegan.

In the distance they saw shapes emerging from the white horizon and scrambling steadily toward them.

"Took them long enough. They didn't even have to fight the storm as long as we did," Gron said reaching behind him and fingering the intricate carvings on the axe.

"I know you want to try out your new toy," Ceredyn said, "but we need them whole."

"We will draw them out one by one. We can't take all eight at once if we hope to mark them for Ceredyn," Draegan said. "Keep them on one side of this pile of rocks. I don't want them encircling us."

The reavers slowed and fanned out as they approached the limit of Aran's bow range.

"I don't like that formation, Gron," Draegan said. "We need them bunched up so they can't get behind us. You take the one on the far edge and I'll handle the closer one. Try to push them together."

Draegan sprinted to his left and in seconds had closed the distance between himself and the reaver. The creature lashed out at Draegan with surprising speed. He ducked the wild swing and unsheathed his sword in one swift movement, taking off the reaver's leg at the knee. As the reaver pitched forward Draegan sheared off its arm at the shoulder. The limb thudded to the ground and clawed frantically at Draegan as he rushed the next nearest reaver.

Gron had chased down the reaver on the far right and swung furiously with his axe, trying to push the creature toward the others. However the beast proved too nimble and dodged Gron's attempts on its life. The reaver retreated, pulling Gron out of range of Aran's cover. Several reavers closed in behind Gron who had given chase to his initial quarry.

"Gron you've got four on your tail," Draegan yelled, but Gron was already out of earshot. "I've got to do this quickly," he said as he sidestepped a vicious blow. With several powerful strokes of his blade Draegan expertly turned the corpse into a limbless torso that sputtered black fluid on the snow.

"It's just you now," Draegan said as he eyed the other reaver. He sheathed his sword and drew his hunting knife. He feinted at the reaver who dodged the blow and stepped back toward Aran. He did the same thing a few more times until he brought the reaver within Aran's range.

"A few arrows to distract him," Draegan yelled over his shoulder.

Aran had climbed the pile of rubble and had a good vantage point. He loosed two bolts into the reaver who raised its arms in defense as the arrows sunk into its lifeless flesh. Aran fired another bolt into the reaver's knee. The force of the blow knocked the reaver to the ground temporarily giving Draegan enough time to dart in, cut the mark and retreat.

"I've got to help Gron," Draegan said as he tossed one of the bone stakes up to Aran. "No wind today. Make it count," he said and ran off after Gron.

Aran nimbly descended through the pile of obsidian and drew to within a few feet of the reaver. The corpse hissed at him.

"You won't dodge this one," Aran said drawing his bow and taking aim at the oozing black mark Draegan had cut on its chest. He released the string and watched the bolt sink in. "It's done," he yelled to Ceredyn and jumped out of the way of the reaver's grasping claws. Seconds later the corpse combusted and fell to the ice, its body flailing in the flames.

"We should go back up to Draegan and Gron," Aran said to Ceredyn who was sitting near a large black boulder preparing his mat inscribed with arcane symbols.

A few hundred feet away Gron was pulling his axe out of the ice. On either side of the embedded blade the cleaved halves of a reaver clawed futilely at the ground.

"Split you right down the middle with one hand. What are you held together with? I've seen hares with more gristle," Gron said, wiggling the handle of his weapon to loosen its bite in the ice.

Behind him four reavers came into view.

"Friends of yours?" Gron said removing the axe and shouldering it. "I hope Draegan already marked one so I don't have to play nice with you guys."

The reavers fanned out and kept moving toward Gron. He felt the weight of the axe on his shoulder lighten as the reavers closed the distance. A surge of power rushed through him. Gron widened his stance, planted his feet and dropped the head of his axe to the ground. The bit of the blade began to glow red. Gron looked down and saw the serpents carved on the handle begin to writhe. His head swam with rage, blurring his vision.

The reavers were within twenty feet of Gron when he lifted his axe behind his head, the double blade glowing red-hot, and swung with murderous intent at the four reavers who were lunging at him. A semicircle of fire traced the arc that the axe carved through the reavers' bodies. The corpses fell to the ground, their bodies engulfed in flames.

From a hundred yards away Draegan had watched in horror as the four reavers pressed in on Gron who appeared to be standing still, leaning on his axe. "I won't make it in time," he said when he saw a brilliant red-orange swath of fire leap from Gron's axe and tear into the reavers. He sprinted closer and heard the crackling and blistering of the corpses as they hissed in the snow.

"What was that?" Draegan asked when he was within shouting distance of Gron.

"Not sure. I felt the axe get enraged. Or maybe it was me that got hot, and my anger came through the axe," Gron said lifting his axe and inspecting it. The figures in the handle were once again frozen in place and the blades were cool to the touch.

"Let's get back to the others," Draegan said, staring at the four burning reavers. "Maybe Ceredyn knows something."

"Can you do it again?" Ceredyn asked when they had returned to the rubble pile. Aran was retrieving arrows from the still living corpses, being careful to avoid their ineffectual grasping.

"I don't know what came over me," Gron said. He took his axe and made some test swings in the air to no avail. "Maybe I should try on one of the damaged reavers." He walked over to Draegan's first victim and proceeded to lop off the remaining limbs. "No. Nothing."

"I'd have to see it happen to even begin to speculate. I don't think it has anything to do with the pyrrhic fire I sealed in your hand," Ceredyn said.

"That burns my stump constantly," Gron said walking back to the group. "Anything you can do about that?"

"We can change the bandages again and I'll put more salve on it," Aran said unwrapping Gron's wrist. "Hmm, it hasn't healed at all," he said taking off the last wrapping of gauze.

"I don't think the combat helped at all. Do what you can Aran. We need him healed and healthy," Draegan said. "Did you finish the reaver I marked?"

"Yes," Ceredyn said. "And it appears the four Gron incinerated are also gone. That leaves the two here and the one that initially baited Gron away from his position. In this constant darkness they're able to regenerate even as we speak."

"Finish wrapping him up and then let's go," Draegan said. "We're low on supplies so I'd rather make an effort to find the next Artifact than burn through our food waiting here for these three reavers to finish regenerating. A shame your spell only works on whole corpses."

"If I could think of another way to move a soul, I'd do it, but as it stands I need them intact to transfer out the spirit," Ceredyn said as he put the books into his pack.

Without the blizzard and biting wind hampering their progress, the four made good time across the ice. The sky was clear and dark, allowing them to move by sighting the constellations, keeping the Great Bear Arcturus always in front of them.

By nightfall the terrain began to change. They began losing elevation very gradually all through the night until a few hours before dawn when the hard packed snow gave way to a light dusting of frost over thick ice.

"The edge of the world," Gron said. "The northern sea must be frozen up here."

"Can we cross it?" Draegan asked.

"If it isn't completely frozen, I can't do much to help. Freezing a small part of a lake is one thing. Freezing the raging North Sea is an entirely different beast," Ceredyn said. He knelt down and brushed away the dusting of snow and placed his hands on the ice. A minute later he stood up.

"It's frozen solid as far as I could feel. The strange thing is the *topos* spell reads differently two days out in that direction," Ceredyn said pointing northeast. "There's land up there."

"Land?" Gron said. "Impossible. The sea is all that's left. This is the edge of the world. We're the farthest north anyone has ever been."

"Then we're about to go even further," Draegan said. "If there is land up there, it's highly likely that's where the mountain of fire and the Artifact dwell." He pulled his knife from his belt and looked at the others. "*Staminis* spell. I want to get there with some time to spare before they show up," he said motioning behind him.

"At least we won't have time to eat our way out of our supplies," Ceredyn said as he unsheathed his knife.

The four quickly made the symbol and took off across the ice. They ran through the night and next day keeping the Great Bear in front of them. The sea was frozen solid and perfectly flat, aiding them in their progress. By the following night the terrain began to change on the horizon. In the dim starlight it appeared as if black shapes rose from the ice. As they drew closer they could discern a cluster of mountains, lit from behind.

"That must be what you felt," Aran said, pointing to the mass of land growing larger on the horizon. "I feel the air warming as well, though I do not know how that is possible."

As dawn approached the company had come close enough to the black masses to make sense of what they were seeing. They stopped the *staminis* spell and ate and drank as they kept walking, breathing deeply to cool themselves.

"It's a giant island," Draegan said. "Trapped in ice, but burning with fire."

Ahead of them they saw myriad peaks rising from the ice and packed closely in the center of the island. The tallest peak spewed reddish black smoke into the air. Lava rolled down its sides, giving the dark island an ethereal red glow.

"Strange to feel a warm wind in this place," Ceredyn said. "I thought I'd never be warm again."

"It's only going to get warmer," Aran said as he pointed to a flow of lava that seeped slowly down the bare rocks of the shore, hissing and belching steam as it touched the ice and began to cool.

"If you don't sense any danger, let's get off this ice and onto solid ground," Draegan said. "We need to start searching for the Artifact."

The companions clambered up the shore line that jutted out of the ice at harsh angles. Several of the rocks were too hot to touch, forcing them to find alternate routes into the interior of the island. Once they made it past the shoreline, the temperature rose dramatically. Ice and snow still clung to the ground in pockets, and underneath boulders. Elsewhere hot springs bubbled and seethed with thick viscous mud and sickly yellow bile. Sparse patches of moss and heath grew near the less sulfurous springs. A warm wind blew outward from the center of the island, carrying a choking caustic smoke. In the distance a continuous rumble of thunder constantly reminded the four of the presence of the massive, bleeding mountain at the center of the island.

"At least it's not snowing," Gron said and began coughing from the toxic wind. Ceredyn pointed toward the sky. A fine black powder of ash began raining down. "Fine. It is snowing. It's a miserable, hot, smoking island, half on fire and half frozen," Gron said pulling his hood up over his head. "I was just trying to look on the bright side."

Draegan gathered the group close together and spoke over the distant grumbling of the volcano. "I want to get up one of these peaks and have a look around. I think we should find a spot out of the wind and away from any lava flows to make camp. If there's moss growing here, there has to be water," he yelled between breaths, trying to cover his mouth and nose to keep the acrid smoke out.

They followed a yellow-brown hot spring up a small hill to its source, trying to stay out of the way of its splattering liquid. On the leeward side of the hill they made camp near the head water. The yellowish water was boiling hot but clean enough to drink once it cooled and the sediment had settled. Heath and moss provided fuel for fire and Gron took out the last of his horse meat and hardtack.

"Sorry I don't have a proper way to cook this," he said thinking of his shattered skillet.

"Use the flat of your axe," Aran offered. "It's big enough to cook the whole meal at once."

"I'd never treat my hatchet like that," Gron retorted.

"Give it a try," Aran said putting a pinch of powder in the fire.

Gron reluctantly unbuckled his axe and put the head in the fire. He turned it over a few times and after a minute pulled it out and touched the metal. "It's still cool," he said, surprised.

"Let me see," Ceredyn said leaning over and studying the blades. He lightly probed the surface and smiled. "Put it back in," he said and threw another pinch of powder into the fire. The black metal of the axe blades began to turn red. Slowly a symbol revealed itself in the metal.

"The mark of Arkon Fell," Draegan said. "I saw it on the cover of Islak's book in the archives of Vatn."

"The Chronicle of Fire tells how Arkon Fell cleaved mountains with that cursed weapon," Aran said, cautiously looking at the axe. "It became more powerful as Arkon grew more violent, and legend has it that during his final battle Arkon slaughtered five legions of northern warriors before he was subdued and eventually bested by Sage Arcturus. I wonder if the axe draws on its owner's hate to create the fire you saw."

"And here it is being borne by the most jovial man in Fyrian," Draegan said.

"Either way, I'm not eating anything cooked on that wicked thing," Aran said and held his share of meat over the flame with his hunting knife.

Draegan filled his water skin and let it cool in the snow behind a boulder, then climbed the hill that sheltered the camp from the hot wind. As he scrambled the last few feet of bare rock to the crest, the wind began whipping through his cloak filling his eyes and mouth with sulfurous fumes. He raised his arm to shield his eyes and look around.

He came running back into camp pointing behind him. "It's here. The mountain of fire," he said. "The volcano at the center of the island is what the eye has been showing me."

"We should rest a few hours before we head out, Draegan," Aran said. "We used the staminis spell for two days. They need rest," he said motioning to Ceredyn and Gron who were already slumped in the heath, coughing in their sleep.

"Very well," replied Draegan. "You should get some sleep too, Aran. We will all need our strength for the next part of our journey."

Chapter 27: The Mountain of Fire

They awoke at dawn and broke camp. Draegan led them up the hill and showed them where they were headed.

For the remainder of the day they pressed on toward the mountain at the center of the island. Several times they had to retrace their steps and find alternate routes as they encountered unexpected lava flows and deadly hot springs spewing venomous gases.

By evening they arrived at the base of the gigantic volcano. Their cloaks and gloves were in shambles and singed from scrambling over the sharp obsidian boulders. The low rumbling they had heard from their camp at the shore had intensified as they made their way to the interior of the island. The lava flowing from the mountain pounded and rushed like a continual rolling thunder. The landscape seemed to waver in the heat as embers rose from the hissing lava flows while ash descended in a macabre black snow fall.

"So where are we headed?" Gron yelled over the roar of the lava flow.

"Down there," Draegan said pointing from the small hillock he had climbed. He motioned for the others to join him. They climbed the hill and shielded their eyes from the intense heat. Across the valley floor they saw the base of the volcano. It was split cleanly down the middle, cleaved in two as if by some titanic axe and from its wound white hot fire spewed in all directions. Lava oozed out across the black obsidian floor, forming a moat around the base which spilled out into the surrounding valley, creating the flows which had hindered their journey during their ascent.

"Can you see it?" Draegan yelled above the roar of the thundering mountain. "On the plinth." Draegan pointed to a small outcropping of rock near the base of the volcano. There on the black rock that divided the lava flowing from the crack in the mountain was a white marble plinth. On it rested a great red hunting horn.

"No seals or barriers that I can feel, but I've been wrong before," Ceredyn shouted over the roar of the lava. "The rank air is interfering with my breathing. It makes some incantations more difficult."

"Let's get closer and take another look," Draegan said. "The rock it sits on diverts the lava and gives us a place to stand. That should be close enough."

The company descended the small hill and headed into the valley. They wrapped their cloaks around to them to shield themselves from the searing heat. The noxious air burnt their lungs with every breath.

"Anything you can do about the air? I fear we'll choke to death before we get off this burning rock," Draegan said.

"I can't move this much air," Ceredyn said. "But if there was some way to purify it," Ceredyn trailed off, lost in thought as he absently avoided stepping into boiling hot springs of sulfur.

"This may be of some use," Aran said, dropping his pack on the ground and retrieving a small paper-wrapped package. Inside was a thick black tar. "Spread this under your nostrils," he said, offering the package to everyone. Ceredyn weaved a sign and nodded his head in approval.

"This smells worse than the volcano," Gron snorted. "I'd rather be strapped to the wrong end of a sick ox."

"You'll get used to it," Aran said, smiling. "It smells bad, but it's not dissolving your lungs like this air is."

The valley rose gently toward the stone outcropping that held the horn. They made the trip quickly and felt slightly refreshed due to the clean air of Ceredyn's spell and Aran's paste.

"Any danger, Ceredyn?" Draegan asked. "Besides the obvious?"

Ceredyn sat on the bare black rock and spread his cloak around him. He unrolled a leather mat covered in runic symbols in front of him. He traced several of the marks and waited silently.

"No seals, no barriers, and no traps I can sense," Ceredyn said after a few minutes of meditation. Draegan nodded and walked up the incline to the plinth that held the horn. The pounding of the lava, suddenly ceased. The deep channels carved in the rock by the scalding magma dried up as if they had been instantly drained.

A deathly silence fell over the small valley. The four waited apprehensively, expecting something though they were unsure what. In the distance the rumble of the lava began again. Only this time it was more rhythmic. It grew louder and closer.

"No seals, but there is that, of course," Ceredyn said, pointing past the horn and straight at the crevice that split the volcano.

The black rocks of the mountain shifted and moved as if they were about to fall. Peeling itself from the side of the mountain a great black dragon slithered down the mountain face, dislodging boulders that crashed down into the valley where the four stood in frightened awe. Loose rock and debris tumbled down the volcano in its wake, kicking up clouds of dust.

At the base of the now dormant volcano the dragon planted its massive legs and spread its leathery wings. Craning its neck to the sky it and blasted out a deafening roar that shook the valley. The companions fell to the ground and clasped their hands over their ears in pain. Folding its wings and turning its head from side to side the dragon blinked rapidly. The beast was old and battle-hardened as one of its curving horns had broken off and deep gouges covered its scaly hide.

"Look at those cloudy eyes. It can't see us," Gron said. "The tales are true. Famously poor eyesight."

The dragon froze. It blinked twice and snorted a cloud of steam. Opening its gaping mouth it took a massive gulp of air and quickly exhaled a jet of liquid fire at the group. They dove for cover as the searing blast melted the rock in its path. The dragon snapped its jaws shut as globs of burning drool fell from its mouth, hissing as it burned and congealed on the valley floor.

"It can hear us though," Aran mouthed silently and pointed fervently at his ears as he peered at the beast from behind an obsidian boulder.

The dragon raised its head and rolled its milky white eyes in every direction. It took another breath and lowered its great body to the ground. Draegan took a rock, stood and hurled it over the dragon. The stone clattered on the valley floor beyond and in an instant the beast sent another jet of flame in the direction of the sound, liquefying everything in its path. Draegan slumped down with the others behind the boulder.

"We need a plan," he whispered. "Ceredyn or Aran, do you know of anything to make us move silently?"

"I know a spell for stealth," Aran said softly. "We use it for hunting. Unfortunately your boots won't carry it. Made of the wrong material."

"Well then perhaps we should make as much noise as possible," Ceredyn said. "Confuse it." He pulled a small blue stone from his belt and laid it on his leather mat in the center of a ring of runes. He smiled and said, "Cover your ears and get ready to run."

Ceredyn clapped his hands together and watched the stone glow a bright blue. The black runes written on the mat began to turn blue as well, as if they were absorbing the light. The dragon snapped its head in Ceredyn's direction and charged the boulder with its mouth agape. It slid to a stop, pulled its head back and inhaled, about to belch forth another stream of fire, when behind it a thunderous clap tore through the sky. The dragon wheeled and vomited the fire over its shoulder into the dark sky.

Again and again peals of thunder echoed through the valley. The beast sped after each clap, snapping at the air and issuing forth great rivers of fire from its mouth. Draegan, Gron and Aran spread out, trying to avoid being alternately trampled and burnt.

Aran moved silently, trying to gain a clear shot at the beast's weak points. His arrows bounced ineffectually from the dragon's joints and underside. He managed to sink one bolt into the creature's eye and nearly lost his life as the boulder he had fired the shot from dissolved in a blast of fire that was the dragon's reply to his attempt on its life.

Draegan and Gron had no luck trying to wound the beast with their blades. Evading its lashing tail and thunderous footfalls proved hazardous enough. The few strikes they landed were impotent. They regrouped behind the boulder where Ceredyn sat, chanting his spell.

"Nothing works," Gron said, panting. He looked at his axe. "I can't dent that beast."

"Ceredyn, do you have any spells for killing dragons?" Draegan asked.

"None that'd I'd risk stopping the thunder spell for," he said, focusing once again on the stone and mat in front of him. "It's either this, or try something that may not work."

Aran continued to fire arrows at the beast from the top of the boulder. "The horn," Draegan shouted and sprinted out from behind the boulder. He rushed to the outcropping of rock at the edge of the valley and scrambled up to the white plinth.

The red horn lay in front of him. It was twisted and furrowed, capped in a black metal, not unlike Gron's axe. Figures were carved on its surface, intertwined and writhing. Draegan grabbed the horn and turned around.

Below him in the valley he saw Ceredyn chanting behind the boulder while Gron chased erratically after the dragon. Aran moved with purpose, always keeping out of the way of the beast's flailing tail and jets of fire.

"Cover your ears," Draegan shouted and put the horn to his lips.

The thunder stopped as Ceredyn broke his spell to plug his ears. Gron and Aran fell to the ground and clasped their hands to their heads. The dragon wheeled around and charged Draegan, its mouth open, jaws and teeth slathered in flecks of magma.

Draegan closed his eyes and blew on the horn with all his might, emptying his lungs into the mouthpiece. He felt the Artifact crumble in his hands. His eyes snapped open to see the red dust of the horn dissolving through his fingers as the dragon blew a jet of fire at the white plinth.

Draegan rolled out the way as the flames engulfed the plinth and he tumbled down the outcropping to the valley floor. He slammed into the ground and scrambled to his feet just in time to dodge the dragon's tail as it crushed the boulder he was running toward. Draegan turned and sprinted toward the boulder Ceredyn was sitting behind. Ceredyn had begun chanting again, and random thunder claps now filled the valley, diverting the dragon from their resting spot.

"It just fell apart," Draegan said between breaths. He sat and leaned his back against the black rock.

"It's the Black Horn of Malthier the Hideous that we're searching for," Ceredyn said, keeping his eyes locked on the glowing blue stone in front of him. "The Black Horn," he repeated.

"It was red," Draegan said, surprised. "I lost sight of that. Then where? The eye showed me this very mountain."

Ceredyn wove his fingers together and mumbled under his breath. He cursed. "The horn is attached to the dragon," he said and resumed chanting over the blue stone.

Draegan peered over the rock and saw the dragon careening through the valley, jets of angry flame shooting into the night sky. As it turned its head he saw the dragon's only horn framed against the angry red glow of the lava that lit the dark basin.

"That must have been a decoy," he said. He stood on top of the boulder and waved for Gron and Aran to join them. The two arrived out of breath and sweating.

"I can't do this much longer. I'm almost out of arrows, and truthfully I'm doing no harm," Aran said.

Gron nodded. "I can't get it to make the fire," he said turning his axe over in his hand. "And the dragon's scales are harder than rock."

"The dragon's horn is our target," Draegan said. "The other was a fake. The real Artifact is attached to that beast's head."

"We can't hurt the thing, but now we're expected to climb up on its back and rip off its horn?" Gron asked. "Any ideas how?"

"We can't pin it since Aran's arrows won't pierce its hide, but we can try the next best thing," Draegan said. "How many arrows do you have left?"

"Seven," Aran said. "Though I could use the bones in a pinch."

"Don't waste them," Draegan replied. "We'll need them later. Take this rope and tie lengths to each arrow. We'll create a web with Ceredyn's magic. Bind the loose ends to the boulders in this valley." Draegan pulled reams of cord from his pack and began divvying it up among the others. They cut it into lengths while Aran fastened it to his arrows.

"Will this hold it?" Aran asked. "The thing is the size of a barn and formidably powerful. I don't trust these ropes to hold it no matter how imbued with Ceredyn's magic they are."

"We won't be holding it down. We'll just corral it off so I can get at the horn," Draegan said.

"It's a fire drake, so it shouldn't respond well to the ice incantation I'll put on the ropes," Ceredyn said. "I would guess the beast hasn't left the island because it's surrounded by ice. It gains its strength from the heat of the lava."

Ceredyn stopped his spell, rolled up his mat, and placed the stone back in his belt. As the thunder died out the dragon paused at the far end of the valley, twisting its head in every direction and snorting into the acrid air. Ceredyn ran his hands over the rope while chanting slowly. The beast cocked its head and shook the island with a deafening roar. It turned as smoothly as a serpent and came charging toward the boulder behind which the four companions crouched.

"Please hurry," Draegan said.

"Done. Take them," Ceredyn said running his hands over the last length of rope. The other three grabbed their cord and dove from the boulder as a surge of flame poured over the black rock.

Aran rolled to his feet and began lofting arrows at lightning speed. Lengths of cord wove themselves through the valley creating a web of bluish white light. Draegan shouted to distract the creature from Aran who was firing his final shot. The dragon turned and lunged at Draegan who flattened himself on the ground as the massive jaws snapped shut above him, globs of fiery spittle burning his exposed skin in an acid rain.

The beast's momentum carried it forward into one of Aran's threads. A pulse of blue light traveled the length of the rope and in an instant a patchwork of frost formed on the dragon's leg where it made contact with the cord. The giant creature reared backward and shrieked in pain. It fell into another cord and another as it stumbled blindly about, roaring in agony and frustration.

The three ran back to the large overhang of obsidian where Ceredyn hid.

"It knows it's trapped," Draegan whispered. "But it's thrashing too much for me to get the horn."

"I have an idea," Gron said, smiling as he looked at his axe. "I'd hate to break this beauty on that thing's skull but I have a feeling my blade is the stronger of the two." He took off his cloak and folded it into his pack. "Sure wish I still had that skillet."

The other three looked at each other as Gron stripped down and stowed his clothes in his pack. He took off a chain he wore around his neck containing a few bear claws, snapping one off before he tucked the others it into his belt. Placing the claw in his mouth he sat cross-legged on the valley floor and chewed the claw to dust and swallowed the powder.

He coughed, wiped the spit from his beard, smiled and said, "Berserker spell. You'd best not get in front of me." His skin began to redden and perspire as he sat silently with the others under the overhang. His eyes rolled back into his head and he clenched his jaw. When his eyes came back into focus they were flaming red. He grabbed his axe, bellowed and ran straight at the dragon.

The dragon belched a stream of white hot magma as Gron charged forward. Gron turned the flat of his axe to the fire and shielded himself. The flame spilled around him in every direction, swallowing him in a moving inferno as he closed the distance to the creature. Bits of flame sizzled as they flew past the axe and landed on his skin. When the dragon inhaled for another volley, Gron was within inches of the beast's head. He swung his axe upward, straining every fiber in his body. His joints popped and his muscles distended as the World Render made contact with the underside of the dragon's jaw, smashing it shut with such force the creature was lifted off the ground. Both Gron and dragon fell to the ground, limp.

Draegan rushed from the overhang and sped past the limp body of Gron to the dragon. He climbed the beast's head, unsheathed his sword and began hacking away at the horn. It came loose near the base of the dragon's skull amidst the flurry of strokes. He sheathed his sword and put his shoulder to the horn, pushing with all his strength. With a sickening pop, the horn and Draegan came loose and fell to the ground. The others rushed in.

"Is it dead?" Aran asked, his bow drawn and trained on the dragon as he and Ceredyn approached the massive beast warily .

"Is he dead?" Ceredyn asked, "What was it that Gron did?"

Draegan picked himself up from the ground and grabbed the horn. "It's northern magic. Some shamanistic channeling. You can ask him," Draegan said motioning to Gron who was beginning to stir.

"Everything hurts," Gron moaned. He lay perfectly still on the scorched rocks blinking slowly as if waking from a dream. "Did I get it?"

"If you hadn't we wouldn't be having this discussion," Aran said emptying his pack and pouring through its contents for healing balms. He broke the wax seal on a small vial and held it to Gron's mouth. "This is going to hurt even more," he said and poured its contents down Gron's throat. Aran held his mouth shut and watched Gron's blue eyes bulge in pain. A moment later they rolled to the back of his head and he was unconscious.

"Gron can channel shaman magic. I never would have guessed him capable," Ceredyn said looking at Gron's body passed out on the rocks. "I guess I'll have to wait to ask him how he did it."

"Put him on his cloak and let's drag him out of here. I know that the dragon is dead, but I'd still rather be somewhere else while we pack," Draegan said casting an uneasy glance at the lifeless mass of scales and talons.

The three dragged Gron back to the overhang at the edge of the valley. Aran and Ceredyn tended to Gron's wounds while

Draegan held the horn and turned it in the red light. "The Black Horn of Malthier the Hideous," he said quietly as he regarded the Artifact.

"The Chronicle tells how one blast could render an entire army useless, freezing them with fear and causing panic in all who heard it," Aran said while applying a salve to Gron's wounds. During the battle of Talor Den, Malthier walked unassailed to the very doors of the Red Keep of Sage Stanrocc, passing through the trembling armies who dared not raise a hand to attack him. It is a powerful Artifact indeed."

Ceredyn looked at the horn. "Marvelously crafted and bristling with dark magic. It could prove an invaluable tool. I should like to study it," he said reaching for the Artifact. Draegan gripped the horn tightly and stared suspiciously at Ceredyn. After a tense moment he relaxed his grip and held it out to him.

"It was your discovery and your plan," he said. "You should bear it on the journey. If it hadn't been for your insight we'd still be chasing that beast up and down the valley. Or worse."

Ceredyn smiled slightly, said his thanks and placed the horn neatly in his pack before turning back to tend to Gron's burns.

Chapter 28: The Edge of the World

Shortly after dawn the four companions awoke to a low rumbling in the distance.

Gron sat up and flinched at the movement. He held his head in his hands and steadied himself. "Not another one. I can't handle another dragon," he said, rocking slightly.

"This is different," Aran said, looking out across the valley. The corpse of the dragon still lay near the outcropping of rock that held the false horn. Aran turned his gaze toward the massive mountain and saw it flare to life. "The volcano is starting again," he said pointing at the split in the mountain.

Lava began to flow once more down the worn channels in the black rock. The lava hit the outcropping and split into two streams circling the valley. The air quickly turned foul and sulfurous and the four once again smeared Aran's black tar under their nostrils.

"We've got to get back," Draegan said, standing. "We're out of food, low on water and have reavers headed our way. I'd like to meet them on the ice, rather than here." He climbed the small hillock that lead him into the valley and stopped at the brow. Down below he saw that the burning island was melting the sea ice.

He scrambled back down the hill. "We've got a new problem," he shouted over the roar of the flowing lava. "It's not a frozen sea any longer. Huge sheets of ice are grinding together where we crossed onto the shore. It's impassable on foot and the water is too cold and violent to swim back to land. Moving from ice sheet to ice sheet would be folly. One missed step and we're swimming in freezing, churning water between crashing mountains of ice for a hundred miles."

"We need a boat, a raft, anything water tight," Aran said.

They all looked around the desolate landscape. Black obsidian rose from the scorched earth at aggressive angles. No life other than moss and heath grew here. It was a few minutes before Aran spoke again. "The dragon is fire proof, so maybe it's also waterproof," he said looking at the others. "My arrows couldn't pierce it, but now that it's dead maybe it can be cut?"

"It's the only idea we have," Draegan said, grabbing his pack and motioning for the others to follow.

The group headed to the opposite side of the valley with their packs. Gron removed the World Render from the underside of the beast's jaw. He seemed satisfied with its condition and stowed it on his pack.

Ceredyn circled the carcass cautiously. He removed his knife and prodded the side of the fire drake. "It seems whatever magic it possessed in life is now gone. It should part as easily as a cow. A barn sized cow covered in iron shingles."

The four began tearing into the remains. Gron's axe made short work of the massive joints, while Draegan and Aran deftly carved pieces from the beast according to Ceredyn's design. The leather of the wings proved useful in wrapping the ribcage in a watertight shell. With the help of Ceredyn's magic they had a passable raft by late afternoon.

"Let's get it over the hills and to the shore," Draegan said, shaking his head at their hasty and humble creation. Gron was busy cutting strips of meat from the carcass while the other three tugged the raft over the rocks.

"Don't want to be stuck at sea with an empty belly," Gron said, wrapping his cuts and hurrying after the group.

"If it can spit lava, I doubt it's good to eat," Aran said.

"More for me then," Gron said, grabbing a corner of the raft and easily lifting it to his shoulder. "I don't know what was in that stuff you gave me Aran, but I'm usually in bed for days after a stunt like that. My dad would be laid up for weeks, but he usually used a handful of bear claws when he channeled. I never had the guts to try that many. Uncle Baledin refused to learn any of it from Grandpa. Said he had no use for it. He was always an odd bird."

Aran smiled and nodded his head in acknowledgement. "You can thank me by taking my share of the rowing," he said. "I've got some arrows to mend when we put out."

By evening the four had reached the shoreline with their burden. In front of them steam from the melting ice billowed into the dark sky, obscuring the stars. The rumble of the volcano and roar of the flowing magma was lost in the high-pitched hissing of the sea as the lava met the frigid waters. Great sheets of ice cracked and ground against each other, revealing small channels of slushy water suitable for them to travel.

"This is going to prove more difficult than I thought," Draegan said, watching two great sheets of ice crack together and splinter in the distance.

"Steer clear of the big ones. I'll try to keep the smaller ones off us," Ceredyn said trying to look through the steam that came rolling off the sea's surface. Aran tapped him on the shoulder and pointed. "Let's keep southeast until we can't go any further."

They lowered the raft into the water and watched anxiously as the waves beat it against the shore. It stayed afloat. Aran smiled and nodded. The four climbed on and lashed their packs together. Using leather wrapped bones as oars they pushed off and made their way into the grinding ice.

None of them slept that night as they tried desperately to keep their raft from spilling into the glacial sea. Several times massive sheets of ice came close to grinding them underwater, but Gron used his axe to smash them into harmless bits. Ceredyn kept the waves and current in their favor, stopping twice to melt their way through a patch of stubborn ice.

After heading due south for the first part of their journey they turned southeast at daybreak. The ice was less formidable and the journey became smoother. Gron paddled while Aran fletched his arrows and Ceredyn kept the few remaining ice sheets at bay. Draegan, who had drifted off to sleep an hour before, suddenly lurched forward and pointed to the horizon.

"There," he said, one hand jabbing at the southern sky and the other clasped over his eye. On the shoreline in the distance a small mass began moving.

Ceredyn looked up from his spell scroll and closed his eyes, mumbling softly. "Three of them," he said, returning to his scroll. "Trapped on the shore. I guess they can't swim in human form."

"Then we need to get far enough ahead of them when we land so we can rest before we face them again," Draegan said. "They won't stop until we stop them, although they feel like less of a threat with the World Render on our side."

Gron grunted and kept paddling with his one good arm. Draegan fell back into the packs and slept. His dreams were filled with shadowy images of armies marching over desolate terrain, buildings burning, people screaming in terror, and Issa. An hour past midnight he awoke with a start and grabbed his chest.

"He killed her."

Chapter 29: The Inn at the Cliffs

Draegan didn't sleep for the rest of the crossing. The others tried to talk to him but gave up when they got no response. They continued to row and left him to watch the undulating horizon as he sat wrapped in his inky cloak. The ice disappeared as they kept their tack southeast. For two days and nights they pushed through the warming waters. They kept the coastline in sight and by the second day the terrain began to change from flat ice to sheer cliffs. That night Draegan woke the others as they drifted in the dark sea.

"A light," he said pointing to the shore. "We must have passed south beyond the Frozen Maw and White Lake and made it into the kingdom of Stanrocc."

The group paddled their craft to shore and threw their packs on the rocky beach. Draegan looked up and down the cliff face as the others stretched.

"I know this place," Draegan said. "That light must be the Inn at the Cliffs. My father brought me here as a child to go fishing. We'd stay up there." He pointed up the rough steps hewn in the rock face toward the lone lantern that swung in the cold night air.

"Let's get off this beach and warm ourselves by a fire," Gron said.

"We should be cautious," Aran answered. "We're hunted men."

"I'll go first," Draegan said. "He should remember me, because of my father. They were friends during the war." He pulled his cloak tightly around him and headed up the stairs. "I'll come back for you if it goes well. If not we push out again. Keep that raft ready."

Draegan ascended the familiar steps and noticed that they felt smaller. The entire cliff seemed less imposing than he remembered. He approached the Inn from the stables, causing a few horses to wake and snort as he passed. Looking in through the window he saw old Dal with his feet up, eyes half open and mindlessly puffing on his pipe. Behind the bar his wife Eris wiped and hung some glasses above the bar. The place was otherwise empty.

"I'd like a room if you have any," Draegan said shutting the door behind him as the cold night air stirred at the base of his cloak.

Dal choked on his pipe as he got up from chair. "Didn't hear the door," he said, putting out his pipe and brushing ashes from his apron. "It's late but I think we still have some mutton stew that should hold you over until tomorrow." Dal was balder and shorter than Draegan recalled. The years had made him softer as well.

Though he was standing near a lantern, Draegan appeared to be swallowed in shadow. Only his brooch gave any indication of his form. "Step out into the light so I can see you, sir," Dal said as he passed the table on his way to greet the stranger. Draegan took a step forward and Dal saw the emblem on the cloak. He stopped and grasped a chair before regaining his composure. "Eris would you go upstairs and prepare a room and bath for our guest," he said. His hand began to tremble as he gripped the chair back. Once he could hear Eris's footsteps creaking on the floorboards above he whispered, "That's Havek's mark. Take off your hood. Let me see you."

Draegan pulled his hood back and stared at Dal, who nodded slowly. "You look like him now. But thinner, paler. You look stretched, son," Dal said eyeing Draegan in the firelight. "And it's no wonder. Come sit here by the fire," Dal said motioning for him to follow.

"I'll stay here, thank you Dal. I have three more waiting outside who also require room and food. We will pay of course."

"Of course, of course," Dal said. "We know you travel in a group of four. Everyone knows." Dal sat down in the chair by the table and let out a sigh. "I remember you and your father. He was a great man. You were a quiet boy, always watching him. He took such pride in you," Dal said placing his finger in his pipe. A wisp of white smoke rose from the bowl and a soft orange glow lit his face. "I served under his command during the war. Taught me some tricks," he said and smiled as he puffed on his pipe. "Saves me from wasting matches."

"So you know. Then you know what will happen if they find out you aided us," Draegan said taking a step toward Dal.

"Hard to believe you've fallen. You do look terrible, but I have a hard time imagining you and your band of outcasts are the masterminds of the invasion that's terrorizing the country." Dal blew a cloud of smoke and watched it rise to the rafters and dissipate. "You were a smart kid, but not that smart."

Draegan stared blankly at Dal. "As I thought. You don't know. Iss has invaded. Their reavers attack our towns and villages. Stanrocc and the Clan of the Iron Mountains are the hardest hit. Baledin has fallen."

Draegan winced and set his jaw as he looked up at Dal. "We saw Baledin not two weeks ago in a village north of the White Lake. We told him the truth. Knowing him he foolishly brought it to the Council. Vangen must have slain him." Dal leaned back in his chair and eyed Draegan curiously. Draegan told him the story of the past month and the truth behind the murder of his father and King Leon.

"And so you would hunt the Artifacts of Darkness?" Dal asked. Draegan was about to reply when he heard the floorboards above him creak. Dal continued, his voice lower. "If what you say is true, then Vangen needs to be brought to justice. He needs to answer to the people for his crimes. A murder in the dark, behind closed doors will do nothing to undo the evil he's loosed upon our land."

"The people cannot bring him to justice. He is the justice and the law. Nothing is above him or beyond him," Draegan said. "His power is unimaginable. To give life to the dead is beyond even the work of the Sages. If I am to stop him my only chance is to use the Artifacts."

Dal leaned forward and poked his pipe in Draegan's direction. "I thought you hunted the Artifacts to keep him from growing more powerful. Now you want to use them yourself." Dal stood up and pushed the chair under the table. "They can't be used for good. They're poison, no matter the purpose you use them for. Leave them where they lie and bring Vangen to justice another way."

"They're the only hope Fyrian has of peace. You have seen for yourself how he ravages our home kingdom of Stanrocc with his own unholy army. He would kill his own countrymen in order to preserve peace. His peace is fear and obedience. It's not the peace my father fought for, nor you for that matter," Draegan said.

"You would kill your own countrymen for peace as well. You'd kill your own brother." Dal turned and walked behind the bar to the staircase. "Bring your friends. You may stay the night. But tomorrow I want you gone before breakfast." He turned and looked at Draegan. "I do this for the memory of your father. And the memory of who you were as a child. I fear you've grown to be more like Vangen than Havek."

There was a creak on the landing and both Draegan and Dal looked up the staircase. Eris stood there, peering down. "That's Havek's boy. The one who tried to murder the Emperor," she said pointing at Draegan. "Dal, get him out of here. They'll kill us if they find him here."

"It's ok Eris. He's not the enemy that he's made out to be. He and his friends can spend the night, but have to leave by breakfast," Dal said walking over to the landing to try and calm his wife.

Eris looked in horror at her husband. "Vangen's men will kill us, you fool. They'll find out he was here and that we aided him." She stamped her foot and crossed her arms. "No. He leaves now or I turn him in. I'll not risk everything we've worked for to aid a traitor, no matter who his father was."

Draegan locked eyes with Eris and saw how grave was her intent. He heard Dal sigh as his resolve melted and he reluctantly agreed with his wife. Draegan pulled his hood over his head and placed his hand on the hilt of his sword. "I'm so tired, and I'm so sorry," he whispered and drew his blade.

Eris and Dal stood frozen on the stairs. Dal emptied the contents of his pipe into his hand and began an incantation. Draegan sprinted toward the stairs, grabbed a chair as he passed the table and hurled it at Dal. The chair hit him and splintered. Dal and his pipe fell to the ground. Eris screamed and fled up the stairs as Draegan sunk his blade into Dal's unconscious body. In three steps he was up the stairs and cut down Eris from behind as she tried to flee into her bedroom. She fell with a thud to the floor.

Draegan wiped his blade on his cloak and sheathed it. "I'm sorry Issa," he whispered softly to himself. "The finger for the hand. A few villagers for an Empire. It brings me no joy, but it was necessary."

Draegan walked swiftly down to the beach. "Disassemble the raft and sink it. I want no trace of our presence. We have one night's rest," he said as he grabbed his pack and turned back up the cliff to the Inn.

"I guess we're done with our sea travels," Gron said. "I was getting sick of all that sloshing anyway."

Draegan stopped and pointed down the beach. Knocking against the rocks in the high tide, a small group of fishing boats floated in the tidal pool. "We'll take one of those tomorrow, before dawn." Gron shook his head.

***

"Look at that," Gron said as he entered the Inn. "A real fire. About time. Maybe I'll finally dry out," he said throwing his pack on the ground and draping his cloak over the chair by the fire. "Where's the help? I could use some of that stew I smell."

"They're over here," Draegan said moving toward the stairs. "They won't be of much help though. Tomorrow we need to burn this place and the stable to the ground," he said looking at Ceredyn. "Like the old days. It needs to look like the work of the reavers."

Aran froze when he saw the body crumpled at the base of the stairs. "I thought I heard a scream."

"It was bad timing. The wife overheard us and vowed to turn us in," Draegan said, turning to look at the others. "I couldn't risk jeopardizing our mission. Vangen must be stopped at all costs, and unfortunately this is one of them," he said looking at Dal's body. "It was quick at the very least."

Aran folded his arms across his chest. "They were innocent, Draegan. You could have run. We could have taken their boat and disappeared." He glowered at Draegan. "Our fight is with Vangen, and we should keep it that way. Sinking to his level only adds credence to the lies that we are Iss."

"You speak as if your hands are clean, Aran. What of the past year? You were all at my side slaughtering villages and burning other innocent people," Draegan said. "Now you claim to be better?"

Gron and Ceredyn nervously watched the fire.

"We did so at your request, Draegan. We thought it necessary to hold the peace of the Empire," Aran said. "What's done is done. We can't undo our wrongs, but we can stop ourselves from committing more. Now that we know the truth we can work to make amends. That's what makes us better than this. We can't allow ourselves to use such horrible methods to achieve our goals. This is not what your father would have wanted."

A flash of anger passed over Draegan's face. "Don't speak of my father. I know the truth now, the same as you, and as much as it would pain me, I would gladly watch him die a hundred times, if it meant an end to the madness of Vangen." Draegan slid the body of Dal from the landing onto the floor and dragged it behind the bar. "You know what threatens our people, so you know we must use whatever means necessary to achieve our goal. Only the death of Vangen brings a true and lasting peace."

Aran turned away from Draegan and pulled a chair from the table and slouched into it. He took off his boots and stretched his lanky frame. "There will be consequences far beyond your second sight for the path you walk. Vangen must be stopped, yes, but not by any means. Surely you see the folly in your reasoning."

Draegan scowled and went upstairs. He grabbed the body of Eris and dragged it down the stairs placing it next to Dal. He looked at Ceredyn and Gron sitting near the fire. "I leave tomorrow before dawn. I will burn this place to the ground. Take what you will now."

Gron and Ceredyn looked at each other and ran out to the stable. "Meat," was all Gron said as the door slammed closed behind him. Draegan walked over to Aran who was busy stitching his cloak.

"When Vangen is dead I will turn myself over to your justice," he said. "But know that I would die a thousand times to kill Vangen once. I expect the same from you and Gron and Ceredyn. The threat of Vangen is real. Your moral meditations may soothe your conscience but they do nothing to stop him."

Draegan turned and went upstairs to the room Eris had been preparing. He climbed into the cooling bath and stared out the grimy window at the waxing moon. He took a breath and slipped under the water.

Downstairs Gron and Ceredyn returned chatting excitedly about various ways to prepare their meat for long-term storage. Aran sat near the fire and mended his tattered clothes. He said little but watched as Gron and Ceredyn raided the pantry and bar, Gron emptying a gallon of whiskey before moving on to the harder liquors. By midnight the two were passed out on the hearth. Aran shook his head, slouched into Dal's old chair and drifted off.

It was daybreak when Draegan's eyes snapped open at the bottom of the tub. A white flash blinded him and pain shot through his head. He tried to scream and swallowed a mouthful of lukewarm water. Sputtering and coughing he splashed to the surface and shouted. "South. Docga. Black Temple."

Downstairs the three woke up with a start.

"Did you hear any of that?" Ceredyn said, struggling to remove Gron's tree-like arm that pinned him to the hearth.

"Something about a black dog," Gron said rolling to his side and vomiting into the cold ashes of the fire.

"We're going home," Aran said, standing up and clasping his cloak around his neck. "We make for the Tribe of Docga."

Draegan came downstairs moments later to see the three ready to head out. "I'll make the seal," he said. "You head down to the boats and pick one that's sea worthy. I'll join you when my work is done."

Half an hour later Draegan looked back at the cliffs as the four pushed off once more into the sea. He watched the fire consume the Inn and the stable as the sun rose over the water, turning the morning clouds a brilliant orange. Stony faced he grabbed the rudder and faced south.

"To the southern reaches of Docga and the Black Temple," he said and stared out over the water as the others pulled the oars.

They kept close to the shore for two days and two nights. Several times they were spotted by fishermen putting out in the early morning or returning in the evening but they passed silently by, never making contact.

By midnight of the second day at sea, Aran spotted the lights of Sirion on the western shore of Docga. "Now that the leaves are falling you can see the watchfire of Sirion. They keep it burning at all times, awaiting the return of Manath the Hunter. He was one of the greatest woodsmen to ever walk Athar. Some say he rivaled Sage Docga himself."

"What became of him?" Gron asked.

"He went south of the River Sinnas and east of the Lesser Serpion River to the Black Forest. It's so dense and impenetrable that very few of our tribe dare enter it. Those who have rarely return, though they say beyond the Black Forest lie the Wolf's Teeth Mountains. It is said that Manath crossed over them, and our elders still await his return from the hunt."

"Let's keep going past Sirion. A crowded city like that won't be friendly to our cause," Draegan said, wrapping his cloak around himself and staring at the flickering light on the shore.

"We can't make the whole journey by sea," Aran said. "The waters become inhospitable further south. There are also great storms and hurricanes this time of year. We'd be dashed on the rocks." He turned to face Draegan. "I think we should take an overland route through the Vilkas Forest to the River Sinnas and then across it to the Black Forest beyond."

Draegan shrugged. "And from there we'll head south to the Wolf's Teeth," he said and smiled. "I can't see it being worse than the Frozen Maw."

"We've still got those reavers to tend to," Ceredyn said looking up from his rowing. "I'll have to place some seals to be sure, but after what we've seen I doubt they have given up. Although now that we're free from that unending northern night they'll be moving more slowly."

Shortly before dawn they spotted a sandy inlet in an overgrown cove. They slipped the boat to the shore, exited and quietly sunk the craft. Shouldering their packs they headed upstream until they cleared the embankment. An hour later they were on top of a small ridge that dropped down into a wide and shallow valley. As the sun broke on the horizon behind them, they saw the tops of thousands of trees stretching above the mist to catch the morning rays. The forest filled the valley and spread to the western horizon. It seemed to be aflame with the oranges, reds, and yellows of autumn.

"You dogs never get a real winter this far south, do you?" Gron asked.

"We do. It'll be here soon," Aran said, marking the constellations as they faded in the growing morning light. Not as pleasant as your winters I'm afraid. Though further south... well, you'll see." Aran scrambled nimbly down the ridge and into the forest, his footfalls barely disturbing the rocks and leaves as he was swallowed by the foliage.

"Don't let him lose you," Draegan said, tracing Aran's footsteps into the forest. "Looks like the kind of place you can spend a lifetime wandering in." Gron and Ceredyn followed.

At the base of the ridge Aran was busy cutting branches from a low growing bush. "Here," he said handing fistfuls of leaves to the other three. "Break the leaves and spread the liquid on any exposed skin. Keeps the wolves away."

"You have wolves this far south?" Gron asked.

"Not the kind you are thinking of. These wolves are the Rannulfr, a special breed of huntsman that work for Tysta Hund and serve the Council. Although now it's more likely they serve Vangen. We call them the Shield Wolves because of our close ties with the kingdom of Skeldus, the Shield of the Empire. I guess you could say they're like the Night Watch of the Tribe of Docga. Highly skilled hunters, trackers, and woodsmen who are adept at the magic and lore of our kingdom. These leaves will make it harder for them to track you."

"The Rannulfr? I thought Leon disbanded them after the war," Draegan said.

"Men of that caliber don't sit idle for long. I'm sure Tysta put them to work for her as soon as they came home. It's been twenty years but I would hazard a guess their skills are still as sharp as their blades. And who knows what mischief Vangen is up to if he has gotten his hands on them."

Aran squatted down and grabbed a handful of dirt and blew it into the cold morning air. It swirled for a moment and then rose straight up into the forest canopy, turning blood red. "Nothing. They've set traps magic won't detect. We've most likely set a few off just by stepping on the shore. The ointment from the leaves will slow them a bit, but won't prevent them from tracking us altogether."

"Do we stand and fight, or run?" Draegan asked.

"I don't know how many are combing the woods this very moment, but if we've set off any traps, they'll soon come swarming like hounds to a fox," he said, peering into the dense dark forest. "I'm low on arrows. I suggest we move until we can be sure how many pursue us."

The four drove south and west through the thick undergrowth and deeper into the forest, watching the growing light of day fade away. The thick foliage crowded out the sun, leaving dappled patterns of light on the root covered forest floor as the only indication it was day. Several times they tripped and stumbled as they careened at full speed through the twisted oaks and fiery maples of the Vilkas.

They ran all day, stopping only once when Aran thought he heard movement behind them. It proved to be a false alarm, and they pressed on. They continued south and west, crossing streams and doubling back so many times that all but Aran were lost and confused. Ceredyn placed runes on the trees during the few moments Aran stopped to smell the air or study a patch of leaves on the forest floor.

"Nothing so far," Ceredyn whispered to Draegan. "Though if what he says is true I don't know if these seals will pick up the Rannulfr."

"If they catch the reavers, then I'll be satisfied," Draegan said. "Aran's father was a Rannulfr as was his grandfather. If anyone knows their ways, it's Aran," Draegan said.

They continued on, Aran's tread leaving no trace and making no sound as he passed effortlessly through the brambles and twisting branches. Gron and the others crashed blindly through the undergrowth, grunting and stumbling with every step. The dappled sunlight that filtered through the autumn leaves became sparser as they wended their way deeper into the forest. By evening the forest floor was pitch black.

Aran stopped the group near a stream and listened. The insects of the forest slowly came back to life, creating a din that forced the group to raise their voices in order to be heard.

"Stay here and fill your skins. I'll return in an hour. No fire and no movement. Give the Rannulfr nothing to help them find you," Aran said, and melted into the forest.

Gron sat against a tree and began chewing thoughtfully on some jerky. "Not a bad place," he said and began scratching his back against the rough bark. "A little warm for my taste, though." The others headed out and filled their water skins in the stream. When they came back they saw Gron collapsed in the tangle of roots by the tree he was sitting against.

They dropped their skins and rushed to his side. He was unconscious and his breathing was shallow. He was sweating profusely.

"What is it? He's burning up." Draegan asked.

"I don't know," Ceredyn said taking out a small roll of instruments from his pack. Draegan recognized them from the boat, and lifted his hand to his eye. Ceredyn made a small incision on Gron's forearm. "It's not the sealed fire or anything magical. It must be some poison."

"We need to summon Aran," Draegan said. "I would risk it despite Aran's warnings." He placed his hand on the ground and drew a symbol around it in the dirt. "Graywalkers, to me," he shouted into the cacophony of the dark forest. The insects fell silent.

"That isn't good," Ceredyn said, looking around nervously.

A moment later they heard a crashing in the distance. The two dragged Gron's limp body to the edge of the stream and lay against the embankment. The crashing grew louder. Ahead they saw branches begin shake. Draegan drew his sword as Ceredyn wove his hands together in preparation.

Before them a herd of deer burst from the edge of the forest and ran straight at Draegan and Ceredyn. They leaped gracefully over the stream and vanished into the forest behind them. A whistling arrow flew over their heads and hit a lagging doe. The beast hit the opposite embankment with a thud and rolled into the stream, lifeless.

Aran came into the small clearing by the stream and smiled. "Much better than horse," he said. "Or that bitter dragon meat."

"We've got other issues," Draegan said, standing up. "Gron's been poisoned. We found him passed out by that tree," he said pointing.

Aran looked in the direction Draegan indicated and laughed. "Clean the deer; I'll go find some monkshood." He turned to walk back into the forest. "Don't rub exposed skin on anything unless I tell you first," he said and disappeared again.

A few minutes later Aran returned with a tar-like paste that he smeared in Gron's mouth. "Give it a few minutes and he'll be up," he said to the others and sat down to join them. "I saw no signs of the Rannulfr when I was out there," he said indicating to the dense black forest in front of them. "I think we could risk a small fire to cook that deer properly."

"What was that?" Gron asked, wiping the vomit from his mouth. He looked up and saw Draegan and Ceredyn cleaning the deer near a fire. "Meat?" he asked.

"You'll be too sick to eat that for a while. Chew on this," Aran said handing a twisted red root to Gron. He gnawed on it and longingly watched the other three roast great masses of flesh. He let out a plaintive sigh and joined the others by the fire.

"At least I can enjoy the smell," he said, settling in next to Aran.

"No Rannulfr," Aran said between bites of venison. "I wonder if Tysta or Vangen has pulled them out of the Vilkas forest to use them somewhere else in the kingdoms."

"If Vangen is waging a war against the Freehold of Stanrocc and the Clan of the Iron Mountains, perhaps he needed them to bolster the standing army of Fyrian." Draegan shook his head. "Well we've won a reprieve for tonight at least. Rest well. We are likely only a few days ahead of the reavers."

Gron drifted off while the other three made short work of the doe.

***

"Enter." Vangen's voice echoed in the empty council chamber. The great doors swung silently inward, the torchlight of the hall spilling into the darkened room. A lone figure stood framed in the light, casting a dancing shadow over the black table and seal of Skeldus. "What news?" Vangen asked.

Tysta entered the council room, her footsteps barely above a whisper as her light form approached Vangen. She slid a piece of parchment across the table and stood silently. Vangen read it and waved his hand dismissively in the air. "You may leave." Tysta turned and exited quickly, the doors swinging shut behind her.

"So they have outmaneuvered ten of my blood reavers and make their way through the Vilkas," Vangen said, crumpling the paper in his hand. "Perhaps ten times that many of my Night Watch would give them better sport." He squeezed the mass of paper in his gloved hand and it burst into flame.

Chapter 31: The Hunt

Aran awoke before dawn to the chirping of birds. He roused the others and they broke camp, heading southeast, and eating while they walked. The forest changed as they moved further into the interior of the Vilkas. The fiery colors of autumn gave way to more greens and yellows. The air grew warmer as the forest became denser.

By midday they were exhausted. Gron had stripped to his pants and was sweating profusely. He dragged his pack and axe behind him, stumbling as he went.

"Just one drink," he wheezed.

They stopped at one of the countless streams that trickled through the forest, collapsing against a large moss covered boulder as they emptied their water skins.

"This is slower than crossing those swamps in Corvus," Gron said, dousing himself with the last of his water.

"But not as slow as that windblown tundra," Ceredyn replied shivering as he remembered. "Ten miles in one day is a sad feat."

"We've only gone four, and it's now past midday," Aran said. "The way you three lumber through here we may set a new record."

Ceredyn snapped to attention and turned to the others. "They're coming. And quickly," he said in a panicked voice. "I lost count after sixty."

"Well let's see what these Rannulfr are made of," Gron said reaching for his axe.

"Not Rannulfr," Ceredyn said, turning to Draegan. "They're unliving. Reavers. And they're moving fast. I felt them pass just where we entered the forest from the shoreline."

Draegan rose. "We've got a day's lead, unless they're using some sort of *staminis* spell." He turned to the group. "Let's fill our skins and keep going. It's too dense here to take on sixty of anything. We don't have enough arrows anyway." He put on his pack and adjusted the straps. "Ceredyn, set up seals. I want to know exactly how many and where. Place barriers as well. Anything to slow them down or break them into smaller units."

"We should head for high ground and look for a clearing, I don't want them getting in front of us," Aran said. "If I can't find one, you may have to make one," he said looking at Gron. In a flash Aran melted into the forest and moments later the three saw him climbing a gnarled old walnut tree.

"There's a hill a few miles south," Aran shouted from the canopy. "We can make it by nightfall." He slid back down the tree and landed softly. Picking up his pack he said, "There'll be a full moon tonight, which should help us see better," and disappeared into the forest again.

They ran all through the evening, crashing through the undergrowth. Their faces and clothes were torn. Needles and barbs belonging to all manner of strange plants stuck in their flesh and tattered clothing. When they arrived at the clearing in the late evening they collapsed, exhausted.

"Do we have enough time for a nap?" Gron asked hopefully, sweat streaming down his reddened face. "A quick bite?"

"You want to eat with one hundred reavers on our tail?" Ceredyn asked.

"One hundred?" Draegan asked incredulously. He stood up and looked around the clearing. "Ceredyn, we need you to set up seals and barriers. The strongest you can. Aran, if you know of any traps, now is the time to make use of them. I'm going to carve a conflagration rune over this whole area. I've never tried one this large before so it may not be as powerful, but with one hundred reavers we need everything we have." He unsheathed his blade and began walking along the edge of the clearing carving marks every few feet in the ground on tree trunks.

When he had finished crafting his spell he joined the others in the middle of the clearing, listening to the insects and watching the stars. "They're closing the distance," Ceredyn said. "Another hour or so before they're here."

"We need a way out of here in case they prove too much for us," Draegan said, looking over his shoulder. "Gron, would you be so kind," he said nodding his head.

Gron took the World Render and walked to the far end of the clearing. "Such a waste for a good battle axe," he said lofting the great weapon with his right hand and bringing it down on the nearest trunk. With ferocious might he tore into the densely packed trees. Oaks, beeches, maples, and walnuts all fell with surprising ease beneath his blade.

An hour later Gron returned to find the others still waiting in the clearing. "Good. I didn't miss anything." He motioned behind him as he sat down and took a drink from his water skin. "Cleared out a few hundred yards."

"When this is all over, you can sell your services to the gardeners of Dullahan," Ceredyn said. "They always need help with pruning in the summer." Gron laughed and sprawled out on the grass, trying to find stars he knew. Clouds began moving in, dimming what little light they had in the clearing.

"I want them to pour into this clearing and then I'll set off the conflagration spell. If it doesn't work or they push through, we can retreat down the path Gron cleared and hopefully keep them packed tight," Draegan said. "We'll attack, fall back, and repeat."

They waited in silence for a few minutes listening to the night noises of the forest. Ceredyn sat up. "They're near," he said, his eyes focused deep into the forest. "And they're having trouble with the barrier I put up by the creek." He looked at Draegan. "It's the same barrier I've used before. They had no problem finding us in the past, because of your blood. Now they're milling about, almost unsure of where to go."

"What would be different this time?" Draegan wondered.

Gron slapped his thigh. "Well this is going to be a long night," he said, elbowing Draegan in the ribs. "One hundred. Something to tell the grandkids."

Aran held out his hand to silence Gron and craned his neck to listen. "They found our trail. They're following our footsteps, tracking us like animals."

Ceredyn was concentrating on a scroll he had laid out before him. "They're dead, like the reavers we've encountered before, but somehow they feel different when they pass my seals." He turned to his pack and brought out a book flipped it open and laid it on the scroll. He read for a moment, and then looked up. "We know them. They're the Night Watch."

There was a stunned silence. Draegan was the first to recover from his initial disbelief and spat on the ground. He unsheathed his sword and stood up. "How deep does Vangen's madness run? He must have killed them all and used his dark arts to make them into reavers. Now Vangen would have us kill our own comrades-in-arms."

"He always had darkness about him," Aran said, "He shames his father's memory."

"I never liked Vangen, but this, this is beyond reason," Gron said. "He expects us to kill our friends?"

"Well they're already dead," Ceredyn offered. "But they still seem different than the others. They can't find us, or should I say Draegan, as easily."

"He doesn't have any more of my blood," Draegan said. The gathering clouds thickened, obscuring the moon and sending the clearing into darkness. "We'll need a light," he said and began chanting an illumination spell. A ball of bluish white light formed in the air above him, casting unnatural shadows across the small clearing. At the edge of the forest branches began to move.

"The first ones are here," Aran said pointing to the forest.

In front of them shadowy figures began to push through the undergrowth, shambling into the clearing. The four recognized the black and silver garb of the Night Watchmen immediately.

"It's the twins, Dalus and Dalthyd," Gron said pointing at the nearest reavers. "I always knew twins were bad luck. This means the prophecy is true."

Ceredyn shook his head. "Only you would believe the prophecies of a mad man, and get the wording wrong too. Islak said it was 'two children will harbinger the end,' not that they were twins. And he made a thousand other prophecies that contradict that one."

"We have more pressing concerns than the rants of Islak. These Night Watchmen aren't our companions any longer," Draegan said. "They harbor souls that are not their own. We must look past the uniforms and show them no quarter."

Reavers began pouring into the clearing until roughly thirty stood at the forest's edge. "Ready yourselves," Draegan said as he slowly began circling wide from the group. Gron threw his axe over his shoulder and began walking in the opposite direction from Draegan.

The noise of the forest quieted as a soft breeze blew through the trees. Above, the mass of clouds that had concealed the moon parted, letting the white light spill into the glade as Draegan's illumination spell died out. The reavers who had stood in the clearing hissed and howled as they fell to the ground, thrashing and sputtering, and clawing at their bodies. Thick black liquid poured from their twisted mouths. An instant later they burst into flames.

"That was no spell of mine," Ceredyn said. "Could the moonlight be enough to cause that?"

"You tell us," Draegan said. "The others are waiting in the forest. You have some time," he said looking up and seeing the clear night sky.

Ceredyn hunched over his scroll and shut his eyes tightly. He began to rock back and forth with his hands clasped together at his chest. A moment later his eyes opened and he smiled.

"They're weaker. The souls of the first reavers were not perfectly bound to their hosts, but these hundred were even more hurriedly crafted. The bodies are newer and the souls haven't settled in as well, though this group carries weapons and moves faster," Ceredyn said. He paused and thought for a moment. "If the moonlight is enough to stop them, then we shouldn't need blood and bone to kill them."

"Then let's have at them," Gron said, fire building in his eyes.

"They're still undead," Ceredyn said. "We can't pin or bind them, but the *ferian* spell should work with Aran's arrows or simple weapons."

No sooner had Ceredyn spoke then four bolts flew into the forest. Four more followed at such a rapid pace that Ceredyn looked up to make sure they all came from Aran's bow. "Anytime you're ready, Aran said looking down at the stunned mage.

Ceredyn clapped his hands and his eyes turned white as the eight arrows burst into flame, consuming the corpses they were buried in. The flaming bodies of the reavers ran into the glade and collapsed in fiery heaps on the grass.

"The clouds are rolling in and I don't want you empting your quiver," Draegan said. "Sixty Night Watchmen are still far too many for my taste. When they push into the glade, we can fall back down the path Gron cleared and thin them out in a more reasonable fashion."

The four waited and watched the edge of the forest teem with movement. The reavers waited in the shadows, watching the sky and hissing with impatience. Another warm breeze blew through the glade, stirring the leaves and carrying the embers from the nearly forty dying fires into the blue-black sky. The clouds began to overtake the moon, plunging the clearing into darkness once again.

"Now," Draegan shouted as a profusion of reavers burst into the glade at full speed, howling at their quarry. The four companions turned and ran for the path Gron had cleared. Once the other three had passed him, Draegan turned and stopped at the edge of the path weaving his hands together. He shut his eyes and clenched his jaw as he breathed words through his teeth. Most of the reavers had emptied into the clearing when Draegan broke his hands and shouted. His good eye rolled back in his head.

A massive pillar of white fire erupted from the glade, shooting hundreds of feet into the black sky. An instant later it was gone, without a trace of smoke. Draegan turned and plunged down the path to catch up with the others.

"What was that?" Ceredyn asked as Draegan caught up with them.

"Conflagration spell, slightly modified," Draegan said between breaths. "Bigger than I've ever tried before."

"A fire spell, no matter the size, won't hurt them," Ceredyn replied. "Why waste your energy?"

"I wasn't trying to kill them. The heat liquefied the ground. Turned it to tar. Should make crossing difficult for them, if not impossible," Draegan said slowing the group down to take up positions on the sides of the path. "Same thing you did with the ice and the wolves."

Ceredyn stopped next to Aran who was busy hacking branches from a sapling near the edge of Gron's path. He closed his eyes and folded his hands. "There are about twenty stuck in the mire you created," he said. "Looks like they'll be there until daybreak, when the sun should make short work of them. The rest are coming around the edge of the clearing. They'll be here soon."

Aran tossed hastily sharpened stakes across the path to Draegan and Gron. "If Ceredyn can take them out with my arrows, you might try spearing a few with those. I only have eight shots left."

Draegan and Gron looked at each other and began cutting and sharpening more ill-fashioned spears. "Place the *ferian* mark on each one," Draegan said. He turned to Ceredyn who was constructing a barrier. "You'll have to teach me how to remove the soul. If Vangen keeps sending legions of reavers after us it'll be a help to have two doing the work instead of one."

Ceredyn nodded in agreement while he continued to chant. "They're here," he said and took his position behind Aran.

The Night Watchmen came streaming down the path, howling and raking their twisted claw-like hands against anything within reach. Those that still carried swords and daggers dragged them in the dirt as they ran. When they approached the barrier they slowed and began milling about once more.

Draegan and Gron hid in the undergrowth on the side of the path waited for the reavers to bunch together, and then Draegan raised his hand, signaling to Aran. Aran stood and loosed arrow after arrow at blinding speed into the mass of reavers. Each arrow found purchase with a sickening thud. Ceredyn clapped his hands together and shouted as eight former Night Watchmen were swallowed in flames.

The four sprang from the side of the path and continued down it at full speed, deeper into the forest. The remaining reavers regained their senses and pursued, howling and hissing as they ran after their four targets.

"A barrier would help," Draegan shouted.

Ceredyn stopped, wheeled around and planted both his hands on the path. The reavers plunged in a frenzied mass toward him as he chanted, keeping his eyes locked on the ground beneath him. The foremost reavers were clawing at each other, desperately trying to get within reach of Ceredyn. They were inches from his face when Gron charged into the swarm lifting three of the reavers off the ground, impaled on stakes, and tossing them into the oncoming pack. Draegan speared a fourth reaver who had dodged Gron's attack and pinned him to a tree. The creature clawed frantically at the air.

"Now would be a good time," Draegan said. "Before they remove the stakes."

"The barrier is up," Ceredyn said, standing up and looking around, slightly dazed. "Four more? Got it," he said and clapped his hands together and shouted. The four reavers sputtered and hissed as they grasped furiously at the sharpened spikes that ran through their bodies. The other reavers circled the edge of the barrier slowly, testing it every so often and retreating a few steps.

"Why aren't the four speared reavers burning?" Draegan said. He looked at Ceredyn who was trembling on his feet. He rushed to his side to steady him.

"I've got it under control, Draegan," he said and planted his feet, clapped his hands and shouted once more. The reavers crackled in the blazing fire, their arms and legs jerking ineffectually as the flames quickly consumed them. Ceredyn smiled and passed out.

"He's at his limit," Draegan said. "Gron can you take him? Aran, we'll need some of your medicine, but not here. The barrier won't hold for much longer. A *staminis* spell should put enough distance between us and buy the time we need."

The three made the familiar marks on their throats and turned down the path at full speed. They ran through the undergrowth, branches whipping past their faces, brambles tearing at the tattered remains of their clothes. Aran led them continually downhill and southwest. A few hours before dawn he shouted back at them.

"We're at the Sinnas. Won't risk crossing it until dawn," Aran said. The other two came crashing through the forest and spilled out onto the clearing by the bank of the Sinnas River.

Gron placed Ceredyn on the grass and leaned over him, catching his breath. "He's still out," he wheezed.

Aran came over and looked at Ceredyn. "He's in bad shape. I'll need something," he said and disappeared into the forest.

"Gron you watch him, I'll go cut some more spears. Yell if Aran returns," Draegan said and went to the forest's edge and began hacking at saplings. A few minutes later he returned with an armful of serviceable body length saplings and branches.

Aran had returned and was grinding a root into a paste. "This should work if exhaustion is the problem," he said and smeared his fingers inside Ceredyn's mouth. "But it'll take a few hours to be of any use. He needs sleep."

"We need him awake. None of us can kill those things on our own. And his seals are far stronger than mine," Draegan said.

"He'll be out for a while. Waking him now is useless," Aran said.

"Then we'll just have to hold them off until daybreak," Gron said. Draegan shot him a worried look. "I lost count of how many are left. Can't be more than ten, right?"

"Thirty," Draegan and Aran said at the same time.

Gron slumped to the ground in a defeated heap. "I hate these long nights," he said and began ineffectually sharpening a stake with his one good hand while trying to steady it with his feet.

An hour later the three had close to a hundred hastily crafted spears. Aran was hardening their points in the fire with his powder when he heard the night birds stop chirping.

"They're coming," he said and began handing out the stakes to Draegan and Gron. The edge of the forest came alive as the reavers poured out into the glade. They fanned out and watched the three carefully. When they spotted Ceredyn's unconscious form on the ground they began moving forward slowly, black spittle bubbling from their mouths as they gnashed their teeth.

Aran stepped forward and pulled a rope that was hidden in the grass. With a thunderous crack, a massive oak tree splintered, popped, and crashed onto a group of reavers, pinning them to the ground. The creatures dug their fingers into the bark and hacked at their five ton captor with their blades to no avail.

"That's nine less," Aran said. "And they're still in one piece for Ceredyn to work his magic on them."

"That would be useful if Ceredyn were awake," Draegan said.

The remaining reavers paused, then continued pressing toward the three. Gron stepped forward with his giant axe slung over his shoulder. He planted his feet in the loamy earth near the river and sunk the head of his axe into the ground.

"If you want that crow, you'll have to go through me," he said and spat on his hand. Heaving the axe out of the ground with his good arm he took a deep breath and let out a tremendous roar. Thick veins rose in his skin, snaking their way down his corded forearm toward the handle. The carven serpents began to loosen themselves from the axe and coiled around Gron's forearm. The bit of the blades began to glow red. With his weapon high above his head he charged forward, bellowing, and plunged the blade deep into the earth a few feet in front of the group of reavers.

Massive plates of rock and dirt heaved upward from the shockwave. Several reavers stumbled to the ground as jets of flame poured from the axe and spread through the splintered and cracked ground, consuming anything they touched. Draegan and Aran grabbed Ceredyn and dragged him to the edge of the river. They turned and saw Gron standing in the center of a web of fire, surrounded by reavers clawing at the sundered ground, their bodies consumed in blazing fire.

Ceredyn opened his eyes and saw the flames. "What did I miss?"

"Gron split the earth, killed twenty reavers with one blow, and saved our lives," Draegan said. "We did save a few for you to take care of though." Draegan pointed to the fallen oak tree and the trapped bodies of the Night Watchmen.

Ceredyn stood up and stretched. "I still don't feel well. I suppose now is as good a time as any to teach you the *ferian* spell," he said and walked with Draegan over to the oak. He showed Draegan the counter mark and taught him the words and signs as they heard Gron laughing heartily while chastising the burning corpses in the background.

At daybreak the four made camp and slept until noon.

Chapter 32: The Black Forest

The four crossed the River Sinnas and then made their way steadily uphill all afternoon. The humidity increased as the foliage lost any hint of autumn. The ferns and broad leaves of the Vilkas gave way to black earth beneath twisting oaks so tightly knit together the travelers were forced to rely on illumination spells to see.

"It only gets worse," Aran said over his shoulder. "You'll soon see why it's called the Black Forest."

"It's not because it's pitch black?" Gron asked.

Aran smiled and kept wending his way through the low hanging branches. In several places the four had to crawl due to the tangle of trees and roots. As the sun set they broke into a clearing and looked around. Thousands of feet below and behind them they saw the Sinnas River twisting like a shimmering orange-red ribbon through the Vilkas forest, the setting sun glinting off its waters.

"I didn't realize we'd climbed so high," Ceredyn said looking down into the valley. "I can't even see where you felled the trees."

Gron tapped him on the shoulder and gestured farther up the hill. Ceredyn turned his gaze from the valley to what lay ahead.

"I'd say it was going to be a long night, but luckily for you Aran needs to make preparations before we head into that," Draegan said, catching Ceredyn's eye and nodding toward Gron.

Ahead of them the bare rock of the hillside climbed up steeply for a few hundred yards before it ended abruptly in a wall of forest. There, mammoth trunks of ancient trees erupted from the ground and sailed into the darkening sky. The canopy was lost in the haze of reddish purple clouds.

"They're thicker than the pillars in the council chamber," Ceredyn said as he stared straight up at the trunks reaching toward the sky.

"They say Sage Docga the Hunter planted this forest after the War for Athar ended. It was an otherworldly place until the rending of Athar." Aran took his pack and continued up the hillside, climbing over the loose rocks and boulders. "It became poisoned and now it is a cursed place. To enter it unprepared is certain death. Which is why I need you to wait here while I scout ahead."

"We'll make camp here then," Draegan said as Aran climbed the loose rock on the hillside and was swallowed by the Black Forest. "Set up seals and barriers. Aran should return shortly."

Gron made a fire and he, Ceredyn and Draegan sat together and ate while watching the black wall of the tree line for any movement. Behind them they could hear the din of the Vilkas deep in the valley below as the insects, frogs, and other nightlife awakened. Ahead of them not even the slightest breeze disturbed the trees. The Black Forest was utterly silent.

Aran returned a few hours before midnight, carrying a bundle of branches and roots. He threw them on the rocks next to the fire and collapsed next to the others. He was bleeding from cuts on his face and hands.

"It knows we're here," he said and smiled wryly as he searched in his pack for a tin of salve. He applied it liberally to his scrapes and winced as he put his hands in the fire. Gron looked at him questioningly. "Burn out the toxins," he said through clenched teeth. He pulled his hands out and took a breath. "The whole place is poisoned. The trees are black because they contain the venom of Iss."

Aran began grinding the roots into a paste as he placed the branches over the fire. "Don't breathe the smoke," he warned. "After I mix the ashes into this paste we'll apply it before we go in. It won't last more than a day or two so we'll have to move as quickly as possible on our way through to the Wolf's Teeth Mountains."

"What's the paste for?" Gron said sniffing at the smoke from the fire and recoiling.

"They say the forest is alive. It can sense life that isn't its own, and will seek to destroy it. It's an old tale, but one I believe. This paste will help conceal us from the forest and buy us more time to find a way out and over the Wolf's Teeth," Aran said.

Gron laughed. "A living forest? It can't be worse than the pines up north." Aran smiled and pointed with his hunting knife to the dark flittering outline of a bird circling above their fire. Gron looked up and watched the bird as it flew up the hillside and landed on a black branch. It chirruped once, and then was silent.

Gron waited in patiently, straining to listen for more. A moment later the bird dropped from the branch and thudded softly on the forest floor. "Maybe it just lost its balance," he said and searched through his pack for some jerky.

"You can't use magic in there either," Aran said. "We'll need to use the *staminis* spell out here and rush in quickly. No illumination spells either, so I'll have to guide us." Aran sat back and leaned on his pack. "The paste won't be ready until tomorrow morning, so let's rest while we can."

"You've earned your sleep," Draegan said, looking warily at the forest. As the other's drifted off he kept watching the forest, listening to the silence and staring up at the stars. He drifted off an hour before dawn, but his sleep was short lived as the eye shocked him awake with another vision.

"Over the mountains," he said, rubbing his eye. "White heat and a black temple." He rose, said nothing else, and shouldered his pack.

The others got up and made the mark for the *staminis* spell. Aran applied the sooty paste to the three and then to himself. He placed a pinch of powder in each eye and looked up at the sky for a moment while tears rolled down his cheek. He blinked a few times and put powder in one eye of the other three. "Don't have enough to spare," he said. "Follow closely and don't touch anything."

Aran was off, running up the barren hillside while the other three followed close behind. They entered the Black Forest just as dawn broke, the massive pillar-like trees swallowing the misty morning rays. A few feet into the forest the darkness was complete and enveloped them in a shroud of shadows. They ran all day and through the night. Steadily upward they climbed, never pausing, watching the forest speed past them with the grayish black vision of Aran's powder. As they travelled, the colossal trees marking the edge of the forest gave way to tangles of smaller trees with branches so twisted and knit together it was impossible to tell one tree from another. The ground became rockier as roots twisted and rose from the earth making it difficult to run without faltering.

By dawn of the second day the forest had become so dense the four could no longer move fast enough to make the *staminis* spell worthwhile. They broke the incantation and paused for a moment to drink from their water skins in silence. Aran gestured for them to keep from talking. He handed out the last bit of powder for their eyes and motioned for them to follow him.

Aran slid through the branches and over the rocks with considerable ease as the others struggled to keep up. The heat began to build as they changed direction and headed due south. By evening the group was dehydrated and moving sluggishly. The elevation change was so drastic they were reduced to climbing on their hands and knees to keep the tangle of branches and roots from touching their skin.

They continued to push on until a little after midnight when Ceredyn's eyesight began to falter. He had fallen further behind during the evening and realized too late that his powder was wearing off. He squinted and saw the other three clamber over a boulder that was woven in on all sides by tightly knit branches.

He reached into his belt for the vial and fumbling with it as he tried to uncork it, dropped it onto the forest floor. As he reached down to pick it up his bare wrist scraped against a gnarled tree root. The root tore into his flesh as though it was made of rough iron. He instinctively pulled his hand back and forgetting himself cast a small spell to staunch the bleeding. He barely stifled a scream as thorns from the root he was standing on sprang out and pierced his leg above his boot.

Instantly the forest awakened. Barbs and thorns extended as if on springs from every branch and root. The bark of every tree began oozing a foul smelling black tar that reeked of decay and death. The whole forest seemed to close in on itself making what were already tight spaces near impregnable.

Aran wheeled around and saw Draegan and Gron behind him. "Ceredyn," he said and rushed past Gron and Draegan who followed behind.

"I guess we can talk now," Gron said.

"And use magic," Aran shouted over his shoulder.

"Perhaps you'd like to put that axe to work on making this place a little more hospitable," Draegan said.

Gron smiled, unbuckled his axe and began cleaving large swaths of the spiked black branches to the ground with his strong one-armed grip.

The three found Ceredyn collapsed on the ground, roots and vines slowly circling his limbs. Gron hacked them to pieces and Aran pulled Ceredyn to safety on a bare rock.

"Hack us a way out of here," Aran said. "I figured something like this would happen, though I didn't really expect it to be him." Aran reached in a leather pouch on his belt and pulled out a small dried blue flower. He crushed it and shoved the crumpled petals into Ceredyn's mouth. "That buys us a few hours. We need to get him out of here, and back to the Vilkas forest," Aran said.

"Keep pushing to the Wolf's Teeth," Draegan replied. "We're not turning back."

Aran cursed under his breath and threw an ampoule of oil to Draegan. "If you're so adamant above moving forward then this will speed things along."

Draegan smashed the ampoule of oil onto his blade and lit the sword on fire with a quick spell. Gron hacked violently away at the forest with brutal swings of his axe, felling trees with single blows. Draegan put his flaming sword to use keeping smaller branches and roots from tripping Aran who was carrying Ceredyn's unconscious body over his shoulders.

Their progress was slow and the three were consumed with exhaustion by dawn. They stopped for a moment to allow Aran to drink and check on Ceredyn.

"He's still sleeping. The blue nightshade will keep the poison from spreading too quickly. But it also risks killing him too. We need to get out of here so I can do something more than prolong his suffering."

Draegan held his burning blade aloft and looked around. They were completely enveloped in darkness. The Black Forest was bristling with thorns and poison at every turn.

"How far until the edge of the forest?" Draegan asked.

"Another day at this speed," Aran said, wiping the sweat from his brow.

"Do you have enough medicine to cure both Ceredyn and Gron?" Draegan asked. Aran looked at him blankly. "Our berserker friend can get us out of here faster."

"You would put both their lives at risk?" Aran asked.

"And yours. And mine," Draegan shot back. "We have no other options. The faster we can get to out of here and to safety the better our chances. If Gron can use his channeling to push through this forest twice as fast then it's our best chance. Every minute we spend here makes us vulnerable to the bile of the Black Forest. And if you or I get hurt, there will be no one to carry us to safety."

Aran set his jaw and looked at Draegan. "Yes I have medicine enough left for Gron and Ceredyn."

Draegan caught up with Gron and explained his plan. A few minutes later Gron's skin was nearly on fire as his hulking frame tore through the trees as if they were spring grasses. Draegan and Aran followed behind, keeping an eye on the flying shards and splinters of tree trunks and roots that came sailing in their direction.

By nightfall the three collapsed on the bare rocks of the Wolf's Teeth Mountains. Behind them the Black Forest trembled and bristled with hate, its thorns and barbs trying desperately to grasp its escaped quarry.

Aran tended to Gron and Ceredyn while Draegan made a fire. He looked with trepidation at the forest behind him and the mountains that lay ahead.

Aran sat down next to him and stared at the fire. "They'll be better by tomorrow." He paused for a moment and waited in silence before turning to Draegan and continuing. "You could have turned around. We'd be back at the Vilkas now. There would be plants I could have used and water from the Sinnas. Now we're stranded here with this wicked forest blocking our retreat and a wall of mountains ahead of us," Aran said and spread his bedroll.

Draegan sat up and watched the fire die out as the darkness pressed in around him.

"Turning around would have been easier in the short term, but would have ruined any chance of stopping Vangen. Fresh herbs and water will do us little good when the Empire is overrun with reavers. No, this was the right choice. And I am glad to have you still with me."

Aran huffed and lay down while Draegan stared blankly at the glowing coals.

Chapter 33: The Black Temple

Draegan watched the other three stir as the dawn broke, turning the purple black sky a soft rose. The temperature had dropped drastically when they exited the forest and now a biting wind blew through the scree they had camped in, kicking up swirls of dust. He pulled his cloak tighter.

"Morning already?" Gron said as he sat up. His back cracked and he fell flat on his bedroll. "Going to be a long day," he said staring up at the brightening sky. Aran got up, rolled Gron over, and pressed a large blue leaf between his shoulder blades. Taking a stick from the burned out fire he used the ash to draw a mark around the leaf. Gron's skin briefly glowed blue as he inhaled sharply. "That'll wake a person up," he said as he sprang up and prepared his pack.

Ceredyn was not so quick to rise. His eyes had yellowed during the night, and his skin was a sickly white. "Do you have one of those leaves for me," he asked, his voice barely above a whisper.

"You've got enough poison flowing through you right now that if I put a *korda* leaf on you, you'd be dead in a few hours," Aran said as he secured his pack. "They amplify whatever is happening in your body. We'll wait until you're on the mend before I risk it."

The four started up the scree to the base of the mountains. Ceredyn's *topos* spell led them to a slot canyon that brought them to a passable ridge line. They followed it for hours, ever upward, scrambling and climbing as the day progressed until evening. They stopped when they reached the sheer granite walls of the Wolf's Teeth.

Aran found a pool of standing water to refill their skins as the other three made camp. The wind had picked up during the day as thick clouds rolled in from the west, covering the waning moon.

"Have you sensed anything from your seals," Draegan asked Ceredyn who was huddled next to the fire, shaking in the cold night air.

"I don't have the strength to keep all the seals," he said.

"I need you to put one here. Drop the others if you must," Draegan said motioning to the camp. "Tomorrow we have to climb over that into the unknown. I want to know if anything is coming from behind."

"Nothing's going to make it through that forest," Gron said, licking his fingers of the last of the meat. "Those three reavers will be waiting here when we get back."

"I wish I shared in your optimism," Draegan said. He turned and sat down. "Let's get some sleep."

The next day they awoke early and prepared their rope for the climb.

"Wish you would have found another tunnel under these things," Gron said as he fastened a length of cord around his considerable waist. "Going up with one hand is going to be harder than I thought. Can't even tie a proper knot."

For the remainder of the day they scaled the cliff face, battling the biting wind. Gron's size and Ceredyn's continued sickness slowed the pace. It wasn't until late afternoon that they crested the mountain. The sun was setting behind them lighting what lay before them on fire with reds and golds. Below them the Wolf's Teeth cast great shadows over the rocky canyons and arid ground that stretched for miles until it turned to a sea of golden sand near the horizon. In the distance they could make out the shape of something small and dark.

"That must be the temple," Draegan said pointing to the horizon. "It must be immense for us to be able to see it from such a great distance."

"That can't be more than a day's journey," Gron said squinting. "Maybe two."

Aran sighed and looked nearer to the base of the mountains. "It'll be longer than that with all the canyons and gorges we have to cross. I can't imagine any of them have water in them either. The wind is hot and dry."

The four moved off the ridgeline where the warm wind was rising up from the canyons. They made camp behind an outcropping of rock and settled in for the night.

"I'm concerned about the heat," Aran said to Draegan. "We don't have much water, maybe two days if we ration carefully, and I doubt there's much down there." He paused and lowered his voice to a whisper. "Ceredyn is improving but still weak and Gron's wound opens up every time he uses that axe. He can't go on losing blood like that."

Draegan was silent for a moment. He watched the color bleed from the sky as the sun sank below the horizon. He turned to Aran. "I hear your concern. But what would you have us do? Turn back? Give up? If we do this, Vangen wins."

Aran smiled and shook his head. "I understand. But what is our goal? We put ourselves through this crucible to what end? If we collect all these foul Artifacts and dispose of Vangen, what then? We will have succeeded in undoing the work of the priests of Vatn. We'll have brought these hateful objects back into Fyrian. Will you bury them? Sink them into the blue depths? Something else?"

"I will end Vangen. With him gone, the world will return to what it was. The land my fathers, and you, fought for during the War for Unity. An Empire at peace, carved from thousands of years of war. There will be no need for these 'hateful objects' as you say. Let the priests of Vatn have them. Or let the stable boys have them. They will be useless in a world that does not hunger for war."

"A noble thought, but ill conceived," Aran said, turning the shafts of his arrows in the fire. "Men are frail. The temptation for power and greed lurks in every heart. The Sages themselves fell victim to it. Will you prove stronger?"

Draegan looked sharply at Aran. "You sound like Vangen. Your vision of man is base. I hold our kind in higher regard." He watched the Tear of Helian rising in the darkening sky above the mountains in the west. "Perhaps your vision of man is based on what you see in your own heart. Perhaps it is your weakness and frailty you fear. Perhaps you wish me to turn back, to talk me out of my quest so that you may have the Artifacts for yourself." Draegan pulled his cloak around him and stared at the fire.

"Words such as these reflect poorly on both of us. Though we have only three Artifacts already they are molding us to their image. I see it even now. The cloak you wear has a dark air about it, as if it shrouds you from compassion and empathy as readily as it does from the light. You have changed much since you first began wearing it," Aran said and laid his bedroll next to Gron who was already snoring.

"So you would have it from me?" Draegan asked, glaring at Aran.

"I would have the old Draegan return. The Draegan who would have spared the owners of the inn rather than toss them like kindling into the fires of your vengeance." He nodded toward Gron as he spoke. "The others do not use their Artifacts as constantly as you. I fear its foul magic works on you every moment of the day and night." He shook his head. "I would never desire it from you, only that you do as Gron and Ceredyn and carry it in your pack."

Draegan turned away without comment and became lost in the chaos of Islak's visions, grasping the clasp at his neck for comfort as the maddening clouds and apparitions washed through his mind. After Aran had fallen asleep he sighed and removed the cloak, folded it carefully and placed it in his pack after attaching his father's pin to his belt. He watched the stars for some time and fell asleep, undisturbed.

***

The four moved in silence the next day. Aran found a path down the mountains and into the high desert. They moved across the dry canyons as the hot wind sucked the moisture from their skin. By evening they were out of water. They continued through the night and crossed another canyon, hauling Gron, who couldn't scale walls with one hand, and Ceredyn, who was still too weak to climb. By daybreak they had made it to the edge of the high desert where cracked and parched ground gave way to the sand of the dunes.

As the sun rose over the horizon the group made an effort to stay in the soft curving shadows of the tallest dunes and avoid the increasingly punishing heat. The sand turned from a reddish gold to white as the sun ascended into the cloudless sky. By noon the four were baking in their dark clothes, their skin burned and blistering, and their lips dry and broken. The wind assailed them with a constant barrage of sand that worked its way into every piece of clothing and tore at their exposed faces.

By sunset the four were stretched thin, when Ceredyn lost his footing on the ridge of a dune and slid to the bottom.

"We'll make camp there," Draegan said, pointing at Ceredyn, dazed and struggling to climb up the dune. The four set up camp and collapsed with fatigue, speaking little until the sun had sunk below the horizon.

The temperature dropped precipitously at night, sending a chill through the camp. Aran passed around a tin of salve to apply to their burnt skin.

"It's freezing," Gron said, passing the tin to Draegan.

"It'll feel cold, but it speeds the healing," Aran said.

"I'm almost starting to miss those eternally wet and miserable marshes," Gron said, glancing toward Ceredyn.

"Don't speak of water," Ceredyn said and smiled weakly.

Before dawn the four set out in the chill of the morning. Aran had collected a few drops of condensation, but they proved too little to make a difference. The companions' eyes were sunken and they spoke little as they made their way south, crossing the dunes toward the black temple on the horizon.

Shortly after noon in the baking heat of the sun Draegan stopped on the crest of a dune. The others paused and looked up at him. "I see it," he rasped from his parched throat. His lips barely parted, the skin having become glued together in the sun. The others looked at him as he gestured emphatically for them to climb the dune and join him on the crest.

In the distance they saw the Black Temple, looming impossibly large among the dunes. It was surrounded by a patch of green and brown that undulated gracefully in the heat.

"Mirage," Ceredyn said barely above a whisper.

Aran stopped. "I smell water," he said and with new found energy raced across the dunes toward the temple.

The other two sprinted after him, Ceredyn doing his best to hobble after them. After a mile of crossing the dunes they found Aran on his hands in knees in the middle of a sparkling stream flowing in a perfect square around the perimeter of the temple in a man-made channel. He pulled his dripping wet face from the water and stood up as the others approached.

"Stop," he said raising his hand. "Don't drink it."

"Are you mad?" Gron asked and lumbered into the water next to Aran.

"It's poison," Aran said. "I was too impulsive." Gron stared at him in disbelief. "It's poison," Aran said again, whispering to himself.

Ceredyn wove his hands together and looked at Draegan. "He's right. The water is as black as the foul tar dripping from those thorns in the forest. It only looks pure to the eye."

Gron leaped from the shallow channel and stood next to the others, shaking his boots off on the grass and sand. "So all this is an illusion?" he asked.

"No, it's real," Ceredyn said. "And deadly."

Before them the water flowed a few feet deep in a brick-lined channel around the perimeter of the temple. Inside the square described by the channel, palm trees and green grass provided dappled shade from the scorching sun. Beyond these, the obsidian temple stood on a series of steps that poured from all four sides and lifted the structure three stories into the air. At the top of the steps massive fluted columns held aloft a peaked roof with a pediment on the gable. The temple was devoid of any other ornamentation. The black stone seemed to absorb the sunlight, keeping the temple in a state of perpetual shadow.

"What can we do to help?" Draegan asked, offering his hand to Aran.

Aran climbed out of the seemingly clear water and into the gardens where he sat against a palm tree. He took a blue flower from his belt and crushed it in his hand, giving some to Ceredyn and swallowing the rest as he closed his eyes. "I won't be of much use to you in the temple," he said. "It could be days before I'm back to my feet." He nodded at Ceredyn. "I assume it's the same toxin from the forest. Just leave me here."

"Gron, you wait here with Aran, Ceredyn come with me," Draegan said and headed for the temple steps.

A few minutes later the two returned to the garden and found Aran and Gron asleep beneath the same palm tree.

"I'm sorry to disturb you old friend, but we have need of you," Draegan said, shaking him slightly. Aran struggled to shake off his sleep as the group ascended the stairs to the temple entrance with Gron carrying Aran's slack frame on his back.

The columns of the temple were as large as the massive trees that guarded the entrance to the Black Forest. The interior of the temple was dark, yet open on every side. Viewed from the inside, it was nothing more than a series of columns supporting a roof, with no walls or inner rooms, yet the setting sunlight didn't penetrate more than a few feet past the outer ring of columns.

"I don't know what's waiting for us in there, but this might hold a clue," Draegan said pointing to a white stone carved with symbols. "Ceredyn says it's in a language he's never seen."

Aran hunched over and caught his breath, looking at the stone with heavy lidded eyes. He said, "It's the ancient tongue of my tribe, of which I have scant knowledge." He blinked slowly and with obvious effort stood straight. "I will do what I can to translate the little I know," he said, staring at the stone tablet.

An hour later Aran motioned for them to join him. He was sitting on the ground leaning against one of the mammoth columns.

"It's a warning from Manath the Hunter," Aran said in a hoarse whisper. "He claims to have failed. The evil that lies in there," Aran said, pointing to the bowels of the temple, "has corrupted all his work. He proved too weak."

"Not very helpful," Gron said peering into the shadowy innards of the temple. "We might as well take a look in there and see what he was talking about."

Draegan nodded. "Vangen has the sword Carnis Fornax. We have in our possession the axe known as the World Render, the Shadow Walker, and the Black Horn. Either the bow know as the Dark Ichor resides in there or it's the whip called the Burning Chains. And whichever it may be, we must claim it." He turned to Aran. "We'll come back for you. Rest for now."

The group took several strides towards the temple. "It's empty as far as I can tell," Ceredyn said.

The three stepped beyond the inner ring of pillars into the darkness. They moved cautiously, ready at any moment for an unknown horror to pounce from the shadows. Instead, a ring of braziers in the middle of the temple suddenly came to life with blood red flames. They cast just enough light to see a raised platform inscribed with a seal in the center of the temple and a small flight of stairs leading up to a landing. There among the dancing shadows sat a great black hunter's bow.

"The Dark Ichor," Draegan said. "Of course. This place and the Black Forest make more sense now."

"Enlighten us," Ceredyn said.

"When the Elder Gods of Darkness chose their six blades to lead their armies in the War for Athar, it was Syn Thain, the Hand of Plague, who gifted this bow to his champion Talus Sen, the Spreading Darkness," Draegan said eyeing the weapon with wonder. "The Chronicle of Fire suggests that this bow contains the venomous blood of Syn Thain and feeds its dark sickness to each arrow it shoots. Whoever is pierced by one of its arrows becomes infected with plague, spreading disease as well as death. Some say this weapon alone felled more of the forces of Light than the other Artifacts combined."

Ceredyn looked at the bow and then back at Draegan. "I've seen what happens when you grab one of these things," he said nodding toward Gron, "and I value both my hands. But I don't sense any traps or seals placed on it."

Draegan furrowed his brow and stepped through the ring of braziers. He headed for the stairs, when he turned suddenly to face a scraping noise coming from behind the group. The other two turned as well, drawing their weapons. Together they looked into the darkness as the noise became louder.

"I didn't realize I was so intimidating," Aran said as he limped into the light. He placed a hand on Gron's shoulder and caught his breath. He looked up at Draegan. "I'll take the bow if you don't mind," he said and smiled as he hobbled uneasily past the braziers and toward the stairs.

Draegan bowed and stepped aside as Aran half crawled and walked up the stairs to the landing. At the top he took a deep breath and straightened himself, smiling down at the group. Reaching out, he wrapped his hand around the grip and collapsed in a screaming heap on the landing.

The bow had sprung to life as he touched it, releasing hidden spikes that pierced his hand. The three started to rush up the staircase when the entire temple began to quake.

"You two get out of here," Draegan shouted and flew up the stairs to the landing. He grabbed Aran and turned to carry him down, when Aran grabbed his shoulder.

"It's too late for me," Aran said. "There was more on the stone I didn't tell you. Manath failed because he wouldn't give his life. I did, and gladly." He smiled weakly as the great columns began to crumble, sending clouds of black dust into the air.

"Save your breath and let's get out of here," Draegan said.

Aran was looking beyond Draegan, staring at something in the distance. "The curse is lifted," he said as the bow clattered to the ground. Its foul spikes had retracted, taking the hard edge away from the gracefully curving weapon.

"He walked the Western Path, as will I," Aran said, barely audible above the rumbling of the temple. "Stop Vangen, but I beg you not to use these accursed weapons. You cannot wield them for good. Evil cannot be righted with more evil."

A massive slab of the ceiling separated and fell behind the stairs. "Hold on to me," Draegan said and reached for Aran.

"Leave me," Aran shouted and pushed Draegan aside so that he tumbled down the stairs. Draegan stood and made to go back for Aran. "No Draegan, I am lost," Aran said. "I took too much of the water in my haste and foolishness. The poison courses through me and is beyond the reach of any medicine or magic we have. Now I give my life so that you can live to defeat Vangen. Do not make my sacrifice hollow by foolish bravery that can change nothing."

Draegan took one last look, then grabbed the bow and rushed out of the temple as it collapsed in on itself, sending clouds of black dust high into the evening sky.

Gron and Ceredyn were in the garden by Aran's pack, under the palm tree.

"Where is he?" Gron asked.

"He wished us well," Draegan said and turned to look at the pile of black rubble behind him. "That tomb does him no justice. He fought with my father and now has died an unsung hero of the Empire." He clenched his fist tighter around the grip of the bow. "Vangen will pay dearly."

The three stood in silence watching the black dust rise into the reddening sky and feeling the temperature drop as the stars began to flicker in the eastern sky.

"We'll camp here tonight," Draegan said breaking the quiet. "I have no plan for tomorrow."

An hour after they had made camp Ceredyn was looking through Aran's pack. "I don't know what half of this stuff is, and the other half I don't know how to use properly." He turned to face the others. "I really should have listened more carefully when he told us his tales in the barracks. This man was a treasure trove."

Gron walked off to the edge of the garden where the channel marked the beginning of the desert. "The water smells different," he yelled. "Less sweet."

Ceredyn wove his hands together and paused for a moment. "It's clean. I don't know if this is a trick or illusion, but it's clean," he said excitedly.

Draegan pushed his way past Gron and scooped a handful to his mouth. He laughed. "If it's an illusion, it's a good one. This water tastes better than any wine," he said and buried his burnt face into the stream. The others followed him into the water and they drank until they were sick.

At nightfall the three made a fire under the palm and talked about Aran until well past midnight before falling asleep.

Chapter 34: The Failed Council

"As you can well understand the House of Corvus works tirelessly to aid your efforts," Arius said from his seat opposite Vangen in the Council Chamber. "Though our network of Ravens is stretched thin keeping the five kingdoms in check with their misinformation. Should they falter in their task of keeping your subjects under the impression that you…"

"You need more gold?" Vangen said, cutting him off. "You of all the council members understand your place best, Arius. Do not test the limits of my patience with your thinly veiled attempts at blackmail. You are in a precarious spot, old man."

"We have proven loyal and patient Vangen," Tysta said, "but you push us beyond our limits. We cannot keep the truth from the people much longer." Tysta brushed a lock of hair behind her ear. "The Tribe of Docga has for thousands of years been on good terms with the Kingdom of Skeldus, but you test my equanimity."

Vangen leaned back in his chair and sighed. "You are, of course, right. You two have proven wiser than the traitor Baledin and of greater vision than Maluk of Stanrocc. Time grows short and patience grows thin."

Vangen rose and headed for the great doors. "Now I must leave you two as I play host to a most anxiously awaited guest." Vangen slowed his stride as the doors swung inward. He turned to face the two at the table. "You will have your reward."

Vangen exited and waited until the great doors of the council chamber had sealed. Weaving his hands in an archaic symbol and speaking a single word he heard the muffled screams of the two in the sealed chamber as he headed to his study.

Chapter 35: The Western Path

After sunrise the three filled their water skins and carved Aran's name and clan sigil into the trunk of the palm they had slept under.

"Where are we going next?" Gron asked. "To be honest, I'm not looking forward to going back through that forest."

"The eye has been silent. I have no idea where the last Artifact hides, but it certainly isn't in this desolate place," Draegan said. "Before he died, Aran said he would walk the Western Path, as Manath before him." He looked at Ceredyn. "It may be too literal, but what do you see west of here?"

Ceredyn sat and cast a *topos* spell. "Sand and heat in all directions, though west has more salt."

"The sea?" Draegan guessed.

"Perhaps," Ceredyn said. "It's not much to go on, but I agree with Gron. The Black Forest was an ordeal we were lucky to pass through once. Without Aran and his wood lore it's a sure death to try again."

"So is staying here," Draegan said. "We head west then, to find the sea."

For three days they crossed the dunes. The days burned and baked them, the wind tore at their faces with sand, and the nights froze them. They were out of water by the second night. The three spoke little. They made the most progress in the mornings and evenings, but with no cover to protect them during the intense heat of midday they still kept moving.

By dawn of the fourth day all three were exhausted from the demanding pace set by Draegan.

"If this heat doesn't kill us, he will," Ceredyn said to Gron.

"Save your spit for something useful," Draegan snapped. "A *topos* spell would be nice."

Ceredyn grumbled under his breath and sat in the shadow of a dune, out of the wind. He folded his hands and concentrated for a moment.

"Water," he shouted and pointed excitedly due west. "The sea," he said and ran by Gron and Draegan over the dune and out of sight.

The other two chased after him and after cresting a dune saw the sun glinting off a vast expanse of water in the near distance. The three ran the last few miles across the dunes and onto the shore. Small grasses grew near the edge of the dunes, and further north along the coast they could make out palm trees.

"You can turn this into drinkable water I assume," Draegan said between breaths.

"Of course, it's a simple. Just a matter of…" Ceredyn stood stock still and stared up the shoreline.

"What is it," Gron asked and squinted in the direction Ceredyn was looking.

Draegan threw his pack on the wet sand and cracked his back. "Persistent, for sure. But it ends today." He drew his sword and motioned to Gron.

"The reavers?" Gron asked. "I still can't see them. Didn't Aran have the bones?"

"I have them," Ceredyn said and tossed a few of the bones to each of them. "Draegan, you know the spell, but without Aran here I'll need you two to keep them off me." He sat and drew several marks in the wet sand. Taking out a scroll he unrolled it and began chanting.

The reavers continued down the shoreline toward them. Draegan and Gron moved up toward the dunes forcing the reavers to group together near the water. When they were within a hundred yards of each other, Gron and Draegan stormed forward, herding the three reavers into a tight group. The corpses hissed and clawed at their attackers, spraying black bile from their contorted mouths.

"We need to mark these ones first," Draegan shouted to Gron. "I'll pull one out and you occupy the other two."

Gron charged at the mass of arms and teeth and sent two reeling back while Draegan deftly marked the other with his hunting knife. They continued in this manner until all three were marked.

"I wish Aran was here to put these bones in them," Gron said, pulling a shard from his belt and circling a reaver uneasily. Gron and Draegan found their marks and plunged the bones into the lifeless flesh three times without incident.

"Ceredyn," Draegan shouted as the two ran back to where he still sat in the sand. With a clap and a shout from Ceredyn the reavers burst into flames and fell to the sand. The waves swallowed them, though they continued to burn, turning the blue water orange and red as they glowed beneath the foaming surface.

"That puts an end to that," Gron said, puffing. "So now what?"

"I hope you're right," Draegan said. "Though I'd be surprised if Vangen stops after this." He watched the flickering orange and red lights beneath the blue green water fade as the undertow pulled the corpses out to sea. "Let's head up to that grove of palms."

The three settled in the shade of a palm that hung low over the beach. Here the sand of the dunes gave way to grasses and rocks. The beach was littered with broken pieces of coral and shells. Ceredyn began the process of purifying the sea water. He looked up from the fire at Draegan.

"You never answered Gron," Ceredyn said. "Now what? Only the Burning Chains remain, but where?"

"This thing is usually quite adept at keeping me from sleep," Draegan said, tapping his left temple, "but lately it's been nothing but black haze and red flames," "We can't afford to wait for inspiration. Vangen pillages the Empire and kills at will while we meander about the whole of Athar. I think it's time we head back to Dullahan and put an end to his madness."

"We have four of the six Artifacts. Vangen has at least one, if not both," Ceredyn protested. "How exactly do you propose to stop him?"

"Even if I had them all it would prove difficult," Draegan said. "I met with only a fraction of his power in his study when I faced him, and we've encountered hundreds of his hideous offspring since then. If he can give life to the dead then I wonder if he has also become deathless himself."

"Only one way to find out," Gron said as he rummaged through Aran's pack. "Looking for some fishing line and maybe a hook. Ah, there it is. Good man, that Aran. I miss him already." Gron stood and fumbled with the delicate operation of trying to tie a hook on a line with one hand. He gave up and handed the mess to Draegan.

"As I was saying, there's only one way to find out if he's immortal," Gron said, hiking up his belt as he stood. "We'll have to kill him and see if he stays dead."

Ceredyn smiled. "He has a point," he said as he tasted the water in his skin. "These should be good. Drink."

The three emptied their skins and Ceredyn began the spell all over again as Gron cast the line futilely into the waves. The sun was setting, turning the foamy whitecaps orange. Draegan sat on the trunk of the palm and watched the droplets of water shimmer in the air as the waves crashed and broke over the boulder at the edge of the shore.

"We're going home tomorrow," Draegan said. "We have to face him sometime. The longer we wait for Islak's eye to talk to me, the more people he murders, the more villages he burns, and the more terror he spreads through our kingdoms." He slid off the tree and looked at the grove of palms from the waterline. "This time we'll make a proper raft."

The three began work before dawn. Gron felled the trees and Draegan shaped them into planks while Ceredyn made rope and cordage from grasses and bark fibers.

"I think I've killed more plants than people with this axe," Gron said. "I hope this blade gets a bite of Vangen before it's all over."

By the evening tide they had pushed off and begun their journey home. For nine days the current carried them north and west. There were no storms, only clear skies and a burning sun. The three had built a small shelter in the middle of the raft from the canvas of Aran's pack. It fit only one person, so they took turns getting burned in the noon sun. They fished for food and Ceredyn purified the sea water. Ceredyn commandeered the contents of Aran's pack and conducted arcane experiments on them to discern what the various pastes and poultices were. He set Gron's beard on fire twice and had to dive into the ocean on more than one occasion to stop a fire from spreading up his cloak.

"I still know about as much as when I started," Ceredyn said. "I wish those hounds of Docga wrote books like proper mages. Oral tradition leaves so much room for error." He threw up his hands and let the wind take the ashes of his latest inquiry.

"They seem to get it right," Draegan said from inside the tent. A mass of clouds shrouded the sun and Draegan joined the others on the deck.

"What is your plan when we land in Skeldus," Ceredyn asked. "Are we to storm Dullahan and call out the king to present himself to our tender mercies?"

Draegan sat next to Ceredyn and sighed. "We may very well have to. I can enter and leave the castle at will thanks to my cloak. If the priests of Vatn couldn't keep me out, I doubt Vangen can either. But I can't take you with me." He began idly picking at the cords that bound the rough-hewn logs.

"I wouldn't dare use this," Draegan said lifting the bow from his back. "Aran was right. The Dark Ichor is useless in our quest. I can't risk poisoning our people and unleashing a plague upon the five kingdoms even to kill Vangen." He watched the horizon pitch up and down. "I should sink it to the bottom of the sea," he said absentmindedly.

He turned and looked at Ceredyn and Gron. "Your Artifacts, however, will prove most useful. We've seen what Gron's axe can do to tower walls and cursed forests. I doubt the enchanted walls of Dullahan or any of the four gates can withstand the might of the World Render."

"But what of Vangen's army?" Ceredyn asked. "Knocking down walls is a much simpler task than fighting off tens of thousands of soldiers and who knows how many reavers."

"My hope is that the reavers are occupied in the north and east of the Empire, picking up where we Graywalkers left off," Draegan said. "If Vangen would use the standing army of Fyrian against us then I would not risk so many casualties. Those men are innocent." He pointed at Ceredyn's pack. "Your horn will prove invaluable if he chooses that path. Sound it and freeze them with fear as we make our way inside the gates."

Ceredyn nodded thoughtfully. "Even if we make it into the castle and confront Vangen," he said. "What is the plan for dispatching the most powerful mage you've ever encountered?"

"Chop his head off," Gron said, his toothy smile shining white through his red beard. "Wizards don't do well without them." Draegan looked at him thoughtfully for a moment, smiled, then nodded in agreement.

For two more days they drifted in peace, Draegan's eye revealed no visions, allowing him to sleep for the first time in many weeks. He dreamed of Issa, his father Havek, and Leon.

By dawn of their eleventh day at sea the current shifted and brought them in sight of land.

"We're near the harbor of Skeldus," Ceredyn said. "Do we continue up to the mouth of the Orichal?

"No. We take the overland route. We'll keep close to the river and cross on the south side of Lake Sias," Draegan answered.

The three drifted near the rocky coast as it turned north east. Under an overhanging group of oaks they found a small inlet and put ashore.

"Sink the raft after we get our supplies off," Draegan said, stepping onto the shore. No sooner had his foot touched the ground then he fell and curled into a ball, clutching his head and swallowing his screams. Ceredyn and Gron watched from the raft.

"Heaven's Mirror," Draegan coughed out as he tried to find his feet. "Lake Sias holds the last Artifact."

"I guess Vangen will have to wait," Gron said as he tossed his pack onto the shore.

"We were going that way regardless," Ceredyn said, grabbing his pack and hopping to dry land.

The three settled down in a thick grove of pines a few hundred yards from shore. They made camp and slept until nightfall, when they followed the harbor northeast to the mouth of the Orichal River. By midnight of the next day they had made their way to Lake Sias, passing undetected though bands of soldiers patrolled the King's Road and were posted in every village along the way.

"Heaven's Mirror," Draegan said as he watched the moon and stars undulate briefly in Lake Sias's inky black water and then settle back into a perfect reflection of the night sky. "Hard to believe that something so evil lies beneath its surface."

Lake Sias stretched out before them, smooth and black in the faint moonlight, its water lapping softly at the shore. On the far eastern edge a ring of small hills rose up into the night sky, framing the lake.

"So where is it," Gron asked trying to peer beyond the polished surface of the lake. "Is there another one of those black temples down there?"

"I don't know," Draegan answered. "I saw a hollow cavern, and this lake immediately after. I have the impression the Artifact lies at the bottom."

"There is a spell to breathe water, but I don't know it," Ceredyn said. "I do know a spell that can buy us time to dive down and explore, but it won't last more than a few minutes."

The moon was setting when the three slipped into the icy waters. Ceredyn illuminated his knife blade and guided them downward. From the surface the small bluish white light resembled a gently falling star as the other two followed Ceredyn down to the lake bed.

Among the rocks the three looked around for any signs of an Artifact. Their air supply was running out as they felt their lungs burning. Draegan fought the urge to gulp lungfuls of the cold clear water.

A few feet away Gron began flailing his arms frantically. The two swam over to find him pointing wildly at the base of a boulder. There in the lake bed and partially obscured by a boulder, a rusty grate let out a small stream of bubbles.

The three looked at each other and immediately began pushing the boulder. Gron dug his feet into the loose dirt and set his shoulder on the rock, heaving with all his strength. The boulder rolled enough to clear the grate. In an instant the metal of the bars crumbled and sank as Gron's axe smashed them to pieces.

Diving down and grasping at his throat, Draegan followed the others into the darkness, watching the rock sides of the tunnel slowly turn into rough hewn blocks and finally mortared stones in the light of Ceredyn's glowing knife. The tunnel curved sharply upward and the three burst to the surface swallowing air and water as they struggled out of the underwater tunnel and into an arched chamber.

"I'm never going to eat a fish again," Gron wheezed, coughing up water as he dragged himself from the pool onto the large flagstone floor of the chamber.

"Fish can breathe underwater," Ceredyn said between breaths. "I doubt they have the same experience as you."

"Quiet," Draegan whispered. He pointed ahead and Ceredyn lifted his blade. In the faint light they could make out a vast chamber with rows upon rows of carved pillars supporting a vaulted ceiling that soared in the darkness. The sound of their breathing and water dripping from their clothes echoed in the dank space.

"Is this another temple?" Gron whispered.

"No," Draegan said. "I think this may be the cistern of Dullahan. Thousands of years ago the city of Dullahan was besieged by a briefly united army of the four kingdoms. The story is told how the castle withstood the siege for over a year. When the siege broke no one could understand how the people of Dullahan got their water." He turned to the other two. "This must be it. The engineers and mages created this space to pull the water from the lake and siphon it back to the castle."

"Ingenious," Ceredyn said. "But where is the Artifact? I sense nothing."

"Can you find the center of this place?" Draegan asked.

Ceredyn nodded, and in a moment they were off, walking toward the center of the vast chamber and trying desperately to see beyond the edge of the illumination spell.

"All this work for a water tank," Gron said, examining the stonework. The columns were carved with figures and scenes from famous battles, spiraling ever upward and vanishing in the darkness of the chamber. Several of the columns were themselves depictions of famous generals, warriors and mages.

"Truly remarkable," Draegan said.

After an hour of walking Ceredyn stopped. "This is it," he said pointing straight ahead. Before them a round of marble rose a few feet from the flagstone floor. A faint shaft of light illuminated the white stone from above.

"Nothing," Draegan said. "It's gone." He turned to Ceredyn. "Is it an illusion? A trap?"

Ceredyn pulled out a scroll and wrapped it around a column. After a few minutes he said, "It's not here. There's still a residue, so it was moved recently."

"Vangen," Gron said. "He must have beaten us to it."

"Then he has two of the six Artifacts to our four. Carnis Fornax and now the Burning Chains of Pyr the Red Scourge." Draegan looked into the darkness and cast another illumination spell. "There has to be another way out of here." He lifted the orb of light high above his head and craned his neck to see. "The conduit tunnels. Over there," he said pointing.

Gron and Ceredyn raced after him as he sprinted across the chamber. "If this was used to store water for Dullahan they had to have a way to transport it. I only hope the pipes are big enough for us to fit."

He slowed as he saw the far wall of the cistern chamber begin to rise up before him. In front of him eight massive tunnels bored into the bedrock of the lake. Each shaft was large enough to comfortably allow a battalion of soldiers to march through.

Ceredyn and Gron caught up with Draegan and stared in awe at the size of the tunnels.

"A *topos* spell would be appreciated, Ceredyn," Draegan said as he tried to peer down the gaping tunnel entrances.

"It's about three miles to Dullahan, from here, if these things go straight," Ceredyn said gesturing at the tunnels. "Though I have no idea where they lead or why they would allow such an easy egress into the castle."

"We'll just have to find out," Gron said.

They headed down one of the central tunnels. The flagstones were worn smooth, making their footing precarious. They moved slowly up a slight incline the entire time, with Ceredyn checking every hundred feet for seals or barriers.

"If Vangen knows this is here, he's sealed it," Draegan said. "I don't want to alert him of our presence until it's absolutely necessary."

After an hour of slow progress the tunnels began to narrow. After another hour the tunnels had become so constricted the three were hunched over, Gron on his hand and knees.

"Just like the tunnel under the Frozen Maw," Gron said, grunting as his wounded hand struck the stone floor.

Ceredyn stopped. "It just gets smaller and smaller," he said, pointing ahead. "I haven't found any seal yet, but I wonder if he needs one in here. Not even a child could pass through what lies ahead."

Draegan sat on the cold, damp floor. "Is there another way out? I'd rather not try the lake again," he said looking back down the tunnel toward the chamber. In the steady light of his spell he saw an odd shadow on the roof of the tunnel a few feet behind Gron. "There," he said pointing, "What's that?"

Once Gron had managed to turn around the three retraced their steps and saw what was causing the break in the uniformity of the tunnel.

"An access hatch," Draegan said, peering into a vertical shaft that led up from the tunnel. "The air smells dead up there."

"It's either this or we go out through the Sias and risk being seen," Ceredyn said. "Although we'd also have the gates of Dullahan to contend with." He paused for a moment. "Let's try this first."

Rusty iron bars were driven into the stone of the shaft creating a ladder, allowing them to climb easily to a grate that barred their exit. After Gron had tried shouldering it open to no avail they regrouped at the base of the access shaft.

"It's too narrow up there for me to swing my axe," Gron said. "Plus I can't hold on and swing at the same time with only one good hand."

"No need," Draegan said. He took a slip of paper from his belt and unfolded it. Taking out his knife he drew blood and made the shadow walking symbol on the paper. Climbing up the bars he slid the paper through the grate and came back down.

"I'll pry it open when I'm on the other side," he said and slapped his palm on the dank flagstone. A cloud of roiling black smoke enveloped him as the world distorted and he was gone.

When he felt solid ground beneath his feet he opened his eyes and pushed through the haze for the grate. Finding it he unsheathed his sword and began to lift the plate ring. There was a snap, followed by a loud click and the grate swung open with a rusty groan.

Ceredyn and Gron came up through the shaft and stood next to Draegan while taking in their surroundings. They were in a dimly lit, barrel vaulted chamber a few stories high. The chamber disappeared into the darkness in front of and behind them, and was intersected at ninety degree angles by hundreds of smaller vaulted chambers.

"What place is this?" Ceredyn asked.

Draegan looked around in the faint light. Small alcoves were carved in the walls, running the length of the chamber. The air was damp and fetid and he felt a chill run through him. "These must be the catacombs of Dullahan," he said.

There was a faint sound of footfalls at the far end of the chamber as a figure slowly emerged from the shadows. "Indeed they are, brother. And if I had known to expect visitors, I would have cleaned the place up a bit," Vangen said, snapping his fingers to illuminate the entire chamber.

Chapter 36: The Beast of the Blade

"Vangen!" Draegan shouted. He gripped his sword in both hands and stepped in front of Gron and Ceredyn. His blade shone a dull green, reflecting the sinister light that seemed to emanate from the damp walls.

"Hello dear brother," Vangen sneered from the far end of the main hall. "I see your journey has come full circle and yet it has not relieved you of your penchant for entering through the sewers. Your odd habits aside, I believe you left as four, yet I count only three. Tell me what happened to your faithful hound, Aran?"

Draegan took another step forward and pointed his sword at Vangen from across the vault. "Don't feign interest in the life of one man while you send your profane servants to kill your fellow countrymen," Draegan yelled.

"My fellow countrymen?" Vangen said in mock surprise. "You give me cause to smile, which I need so dearly in these sour times. I thank you Draegan. Your presence here has been missed," Vangen said and bowed slightly. "My countrymen, as you so cleverly put it, are in fact my subjects. Need I remind you yet again that I am the Emperor of Fyrian? As such I have need of my subject's services. My reavers collect them and bring them here," he said gesturing to the alcoves in the walls, "where I am able to put them to better use than farming or boot mending, or whatever meager existence it was that they scraped from my land."

Draegan looked into the shadows of the alcoves and saw the pale skin of thousands of corpses stacked on top of each other. He recoiled in horror. "I give you one opportunity to turn yourself over to the mercy of the people," he said thrusting his sword in Vangen's direction. "Turn yourself over to me and stand for your crimes before the Council. I promise you safekeeping until you are sentenced."

Vangen laughed derisively. "You are more fun than Baledin. I had no idea how your sense of humor had grown during your meanderings across Athar." Vangen looked up thoughtfully. "Though I do miss that oaf more than I care to admit. A shame I had to kill him. Insubordination, you know," Vangen said absentmindedly. "I will have to do the same to you." He paused. "Oh but not yet. This is too fun. You promise me safekeeping, as if anyone can do me harm. Quaint."

Vangen took a step forward toward the three and looked around the chamber. "Though your mention of my crimes wounds me. When did preserving peace become a crime? I was unaware that building a better Empire was also a crime. It was my ignorance I suppose that led me to improve on our father's work." He continued walking forward slowly, as he considered Draegan's words. "Yet you would have me stand before my subjects and let them judge me for the actions I took to secure the greater good. You think them capable of understanding the measures I took for their betterment? That would never do. Would you have a child judge his father?" Vangen put his hands on his hips. "As usual your plan is ill-conceived."

Ceredyn wove his hands together and began chanting. Vangen raised his black gloved hand and brought it down sharply to his side. "Silence," he snapped. "I will not stand your feeble attempts at spell-weaving in my workshop. The thought of you profaning the birthplace of my new Empire with the cursed tongue of your people sickens me." Ceredyn's hands fell to his side and his eyes clouded.

Gron had unbuckled his axe and stepped in front of Ceredyn. "I'll crush your soft skull with one hand if you don't release him," Gron said, bristling with rage.

"The bear cub speaks," Vangen said. "Though I would council not using your remaining hand. Your uncle tried with both of his hands and I proved the stronger man. Better to put that magnificent axe to use. Let me see it wielded with all the rancor you can summon, barbarian," Vangen hissed. "I should dearly love to test it against my blade."

Draegan held out his hand to stop Gron. "You would do well to listen to him, Vangen. Or heed your own words and keep silent. We have seen the atrocities you have committed. I gave you a chance to face your malfeasance. Which path will you walk?"

"An ultimatum?" Vangen laughed. "You are hardly in a position to insist. Will you swing your sword while quoting from the priests of Vatn? Will you attack me with your frustrated and impotent rage? Or will you run into the shadows once again? I proved the superior warrior in our last encounter and while you have exhausted your strength in your travels, mine has only grown. Your time as the best swordsman in Fyrian has ended."

Draegan began walking forward, his sword at the ready. He moved slightly to his left and followed the wall. Gron picked up Draegan's unspoken cue and began pressing forward along the opposite wall.

"As much as I would like to continue this conversation, I have an Empire to run," Vangen said, snapping his fingers and plunging the corridor into darkness. "You see I have my own problems," he said removing the hilt of his sword from his cloak. He ran his hand down the length of the invisible blade and the black fire poured from the open mouth in the guard. The dancing flame cast an unearthly light in the chamber.

"Carnis Fornax hungers. Fet Reth used this blade to great acclaim in the War for Athar, felling tens of thousands. Each soul it fed upon was joined with the blade, making it and the wielder stronger. But I have done something no Sage could ever do. I command the magic that gives the blade life. I have discovered how to pull out the souls that dwell within it and use them to build an army of unliving soldiers." Vangen stared at the dancing flame. "My reavers of Iss. But now it hungers again and I must feed it." Vangen looked up to see Gron and Draegan within a few hundred feet of him. "Alas, you three would do little to assuage its craving, so I must leave you and join the war at the front, like my father before me. Carnis Fornax will slake its thirst in battle once again."

Vangen turned and walked toward the back of the chamber. "I won't leave you alone though," he said over his shoulder as he headed for the spiral staircase leading up to his study. "I put you in the company of my first experiment. It is a little crude, but it should prove effective in battle. Once it is done with you, I will bring it to the front with me." He began climbing the staircase. "I will return before I leave for the Iron Mountains to collect your Artifacts. I'm truly thankful for the work you've done and the thoughtfulness you showed by bringing them to me, albeit one short. But I have taken the liberty of acquiring that one myself."

Draegan cast an illumination spell high in the air, bathing the cold, wet stones in a bluish white light. Behind him he saw Ceredyn frozen in place, his body motionless and his eyes blank. Ahead he saw the Vangen's cloak whipping behind him as he ran up the staircase.

"I'll go after him," Draegan shouted. "You stay with Ceredyn."

Draegan took one step and felt the entire chamber shake. He stopped and listened as pebbles and dust settled onto the flagstone floor. He paused and took another step. Again the entire structure trembled.

"Over there," Gron said, pointing down one of the numerous side tunnels that led off the main corridor.

The rumbling grew into a rhythmic thumping, crescendoing to a roar as they stared in disbelief. A huge white mass came crashing into the main hall from the side corridor.

Draegan and Gron ran back to Ceredyn and saw the horror that stood before them. In the faint blue-white light a towering, shapeless mass of arms and eyes, legs and mouths protruded at unnatural angles from a roiling accretion of putrid flesh, tendons, and bones fused into a hideous abomination. The creature stood still in the center of the hall, its multitude of arms and legs flailing as its hundreds of eyes rolled and wandered in all directions. Its howling mouths leaked black bile that burned its rotten white skin. Boils and scars covered the beast, and red streaks showed where it had begun tearing into itself in desperation.

"It's as big as a house," Gron said. "I don't know where its head is or I'd decapitate the hideous thing and put it out of its misery."

The beast turned slowly toward Gron's voice as he spoke. Its legion of mouths let out a wailing scream and the creature began to heave all its arms and legs in Gron's direction.

"It heard you," Draegan said. "It's too big to get around. Back down the access shaft."

The lumbering creature charged down the hall as Draegan struggled with the grate. "It was just open," he said pulling vainly at the iron bars. With a thunderous crash the mass of white flesh slammed into a support column and shattered the stone, halting its progress momentarily as it shook off the rubble.

"The floor was wet, so I turned it to ice," Ceredyn said, released from his stupor. "I don't know what Vangen did to me, but once he left I came back into myself."

"Glad to have you back. Can you bind or pin it?" Draegan said watching the arms and legs of the creature begin to move in unison to try and right itself. He reached into his pack and dug frantically for his cloak. He rose and threw the garment over his shoulders in one motion, fastening it with the pin he took from his belt. He shuddered slightly, feeling the chill of the catacombs mix with the cooler air created by Ceredyn's ice spell.

"Not without one of Aran's arrows or the bone stakes stuck in it," Ceredyn said.

Draegan pulled one of the remaining bones from his belt and nodded to Gron. They charged at the writhing mass that was still trying to gain purchase on the frozen flagstones. Draegan carved multiple *ferian* symbols in its rancid skin while Gron followed behind, dodging arms and snapping teeth as he plunged the handful of bones into the beast.

The two ran back to Ceredyn who sat by the grate, concentrating on a rune-filled scroll. Draegan shouted at him and he rose, clapping his hands and yelling the words of the spell.

Ceredyn suddenly screamed in horror and fell back on his hands, crawling away from the creature as it finally picked itself out of the rubble and found its three assailants.

"Hundreds," he gasped as Draegan lifted him to his feet. "Hundreds of souls are trapped in that thing. I could only get a few. They all came rushing at me, trying to get out. It's an amalgam of corpses and souls."

"I can give them release," Gron said as he lifted his great axe and ran at the beast.

The creature was once again propelling its hideous bulk down the corridor as Gron raced toward it, yelling and brandishing the World Render in his good hand. When he was within a few feet of the beast he leapt into the air and brought the hulking axe down with savage ferocity into the center of its mass. The blow stopped the beast's forward momentum, but its abundance of limbs grabbed at Gron, lifting him effortlessly from the ground and hurling him back toward the grate where the others stood watching.

"It's strong," Gron said, picking himself off the flagstone floor. He raised his hand and caught the axe the creature had removed from itself and hurled at the group of companions. "Got a good arm too. Too many good ones, I guess. Puts me at a severe disadvantage," he said, raising his stump in the air.

"Let's start with those, then," Draegan said. "Shave its limbs off one by one and it won't be able to back us into the tunnel." Draegan and Gron moved to the sides of the vault. "More light," Draegan shouted to Ceredyn.

Ceredyn cast another illumination spell. The creature squirmed in the light and clawed at its lidless eyes. Gron and Draegan ran at it and began hacking at its limbs. With the beast distracted by attacks from different directions, Gron easily lopped off arm after leg, stepping out of the way as they fell to the floor, as they still vainly tried to grasp at him. Draegan had a harder time of it. He had managed to remove an arm and was working on another when the black, oozing stump of the first arm began to sprout anew.

"It's growing back its arms as quickly as we sever them," Draegan shouted across the creature to Gron. "Fall back."

The two ran back to Ceredyn who had retreated further into the tunnel as the monstrosity lumbered forward. "It can grow them as quickly as we can cut them."

"I have an idea," Gron said. The others looked at him. "I'll bury it." He took off his shirt and removed his necklace, tying it to his belt. He removed a claw from the chain and said, "Run past it. Turn it around and I'll come at it from behind, and drop the ceiling on it." He chewed the claw and clenched his fists as his skin began to give off tremendous heat and a slight red glow.

Draegan sprinted toward the beast and turned at the last moment, diving for the side of the vault as he dodged the creature's thrashing arms and legs. He dove through a tangle of limbs and sprang up behind the beast. The monstrosity howled and began turning itself around to face Draegan.

Gron's skin was steaming in the dank catacomb, his veins pulsing along his rippling muscles. He bellowed and stormed at the creature, his axe held high. He brought the black blade down on a support column with a deafening roar. The chamber trembled as a mass of rocks fell from the ceiling onto the beast. A cloud of black dust rose from the rubble, obscuring Gron's view. He could hear the creature hissing and howling as the dust settled. He looked up at the ceiling, and stomped his foot on the flagstones. A massive keystone the size of a wagon loosed itself and plummeted into the back of the creature, pinning it to the floor.

"Well done," Draegan yelled form the other side of the beast.

Gron picked up a massive boulder and approached the creature, intending to bludgeon it to death when a series of arms snaked themselves out of the rubble and grabbed him by the ankle. Gron fell to the floor as the beast dragged him closer to one of its slavering mouths.

Draegan shouted and started climbing over the pile of rubble when a crack in the ceiling caused him to look up. Another arch collapsed as Draegan jumped back, barely avoiding being crushed. The massive stones of the arch fell and sealed off the tunnel, cutting Draegan off from the others. He clawed frantically at the debris, clearing only enough space to poke his head through.

He saw Gron being dragged toward the beast as Ceredyn ran to help.

"Axe," Gron bellowed, clawing frantically at the flagstone with his one good hand. Ceredyn rushed to the axe, struggled to lift it and staggered under its weight toward the half-buried beast. He let the heft of the Artifact carry the blade downward, neatly severing the arms that bound Gron.

Gron stood and pried the grasping hands from his leg, tossing them into the heap of debris and flesh. His eyes began to return to their normal icy blue as he held out his hand for the axe.

"How can you touch it without being consumed by the fire?" Gron asked.

"You and I share the same flesh and blood," Ceredyn said, pointing at the scar on his arm. "When you took the axe, I stopped the pyrrhic fire by binding you with my tattoo covered skin. The ink in my tattoos are my blood, which now serves as a barrier, keeping the fire from consuming you, but affording me the ability to touch the World Render without having to pay the price you did."

"Clever crow," Gron said, taking a step toward him. "Now hand me my axe."

"It's all yours," Ceredyn said, letting the weapon drop to the ground and stepping back. Gron started forward, curiously eyeing

Ceredyn who quickly wove his fingers into an ancient symbol and smiled.

Gron screamed and fell to the ground. He gnashed his teeth and gripped his forearm as the bandages that bound his wound burst into flame.

"On second thought, I'll keep the axe. Along with the horn. The bow too," Ceredyn said, bending over to pick up the weapon. The serpents carved on the grip coiled, then relaxed as Ceredyn lifted the weapon to his shoulder.

"You can't mean it Ceredyn," Draegan shouted from behind the pile of rocks. "The evil of the Artifacts is clouding your better judgment."

Ceredyn smiled. "Oh but I do mean it. As I've done so much for you three, it's only fair that the spoils go to the one who put in the most work."

"Traitor," Draegan yelled. He began clawing furiously at the debris that stood between him and Ceredyn. "You coward."

Ceredyn turned and began to walk back to the access grate where the companions had dropped their packs.

"You deceitful crow. Who paid you to betray us?"

"It's painfully obvious, Draegan," Ceredyn said turning and facing Draegan as Gron frantically smashed his bloody stump into the flagstones, trying to stop the fire from spreading up his arm. "Vangen."

Ceredyn looked down at Gron and scowled. "Spend your last few moments of life with some amount of dignity, savage," Ceredyn said as he kicked Gron in the ribs. Gron howled in pain and curled into a ball as the fire kept burning its way up his arm. Ceredyn turned to Draegan. "Tell Vangen I apologize for the inconvenience, but I've decided to take the Artifacts back to Corvus, to the Council of Rune. He is welcome to seek them there."

"I would expect a crow like you to have no honor," Draegan yelled. "You turn on everyone, like a rabid dog."

"Honor? No. Power? Yes," Ceredyn said. "You were raised in the most powerful of the five kingdoms, and by the hand of the king no less. What you failed to see with your privileged upbringing was that the suffering of the rest of the kingdoms made your life of luxury possible. For thousands of years, since the Council of Dullahan and the Rending of Athar, the wretched House of Corvus has been marginalized. Our land is an unusable waste, our kingdom small and worthless, and yet we are pillaged by these heathens from the north," Ceredyn said, kicking Gron once again. "And you men of Skeldus, with all your wealth sat in your plush palaces and did nothing to aid us. Over the years we have had no choice other than to survive by wit and sorcery, selling our services to the highest bidder in the never ending wars. Now there are no wars. Now we have nothing. But we have become the greatest mages in Fyrian. Now we seek the power that we have never had. We deserve what Skeldus kept from us. We deserve Fyrian."

"You are as mad as Vangen," Draegan shouted, still clawing at the rubble. He pulled so furiously at the heap that in his rage he loosened a large stone that tumbled down, closing himself off completely from Gron and Ceredyn.

"Your effort in helping the House of Corvus spread its wings and achieve its birthright, just as Sage Corvus the All-Seeing prophesied, will be noted in the history books," Ceredyn shouted to Draegan, but his voice was lost in the collapse of the rubble. Ceredyn turned to walk back to the grate when Gron's hand shot out and grabbed his ankle. With a twist he sent Ceredyn sprawling to the ground as he pulled his way toward him, his bloody stump bubbling and hissing in the black fire that crawled slowly up his arm toward his heart.

Ceredyn turned and drew the curved knife he wore at his belt. He kicked and slashed at Gron, taking off two fingers from his remaining hand. Gron continued to crawl toward him, scraping his body along the floor, the fire spreading as his flesh sizzled in the flames and his joints cracked in the aftermath of the berserker spell.

"You don't have much time left," Ceredyn said as he kicked Gron off him and scrambled toward the axe. Grabbing it he rose and brought the mighty blade down on Gron's flaming shoulder, severing his injured arm completely. Gron screamed in agony as he watched his severed arm be consumed in the Pyrrhic fire.

"Despite what Draegan says, I have some little honor in me," Ceredyn said. He stood over Gron who clasped his bloodied hand over his shoulder trying desperately to stop the blood from spilling from his body.

"You saved my life, though I'm not saving yours. You'll die down here from that wound, but not from the fire. A more dignified death is your repayment for my life." Ceredyn turned and fled down the tunnel for the grate.

Gron watched him grab the bow from Draegan's pack and with the axe and horn, Ceredyn disappeared down the hatch and into the darkness beyond.

Chapter 37: The Dark Artifacts

With no way to get to Gron, Draegan screamed in frustrated rage as he scrambled off the opposite side of the rubble pile and down onto the flagstone floor of the catacombs. Half-buried arms of the beast clawed at him from the rubble as he sped past, the creature's limbs still flailing ineffectually under the mass of rocks and debris.

He made it to the stairs and ascended them at full speed. They spiraled upward carrying him into the darkness of the massive vault. The stairs wound into a claustrophobic opening in the bedrock beneath the castle. He cast an illumination spell and saw the steps terminate on a small landing beneath a hatch a few stories above him.

"Another access hatch," Draegan said. "How far beneath Dullahan am I?" He took a piece of paper and hastily scrawling the shadow walking rune, he folded it and placed it up his sleeve before testing the door above his head.

It swung up easily, the iron hinges making only a slight creak. Peering through the opening he saw darkness. A moldy smell mixed with the dampness from the tunnel behind him. He stepped cautiously from the hatch and felt the ground beneath his feet. The stones had changed from rough hewn to smooth.

"You may enter," a voice said from the darkness. Amber light began to emanate from a small candle, giving a faint glow to Draegan's surroundings. As his eyes adjusted he saw piles of books stacked haphazardly around a circular room. A single window, blackened by soot, was the only break in the myriad maps and charts that hung on the wall. Behind a heavy oaken desk saddled with countless tomes and scrolls sat Vangen, hunched over a book and busily writing in the dim light.

Draegan planted his feet and swiftly reached for his sword. "Give me a moment to finish," Vangen said, keeping his face buried in the pages of the book as his pen hastily scratched its way across the surface. As Vangen uttered the words, Draegan's sword became unfathomably heavy, dropping him to one knee. His hand was fused to the grip as he struggled vainly to both stand under the weight of his blade and release the weapon.

"What sorcery is this?" Draegan stammered as he strained against the invisible chains that seemed to be binding him to the floor.

Vangen put his pen down and snapped the book shut. "You are standing on a binding seal, albeit a modified one. Something similar to this would have worked on my first set of reavers but you and the crow lacked the vision to experiment," Vangen said, looking over at Draegan through the pile of books that surrounded him. "Well, enough with the pleasantries. Where is the rest of your merry band?" Vangen looked around the room. "First you lose your hound and now your bear and your crow."

Draegan coughed as the spell tightened around his chest, squeezing his ribs with every breath he drew. "I have lost Aran and Gron, but it's you who have lost Ceredyn." Draegan struggled to raise his head so he could look Vangen in the eye as he spoke. "Your crow flies home to his roost with the Artifacts. The Council of Rune and the House of Corvus has betrayed you. Once I'm done with you, I will hunt him down for Gron and for the Empire."

"I have always enjoyed your adherence to the arcane notion of duty." Vangen smiled. "An almost filial piety, first for our father and now with his untimely passing it has shifted to the Empire.

Draegan tried again to stand, but felt the invisible bonds constrict with every movement he made. He glowered at Vangen with a wicked fire in his eyes.

"I see your anger, brother. It does not become you." Vangen stood behind his desk and gazed around his study, as if seeing it for the first time in the flickering light of the candle. "It reminds me of father when he looked at me." He looked back at Draegan, still laboring under the crushing weight of his sword. "Enough of your obsequious genuflections. Your mock fealty softens even my heart. Perhaps it is time I show you mercy and enlighten you to the truth."

Vangen lifted his hand slightly as he circled his desk, inspecting the maps and charts that covered the study wall. Draegan rose to his feet, though he was still held by the chains of Vangen's spell. His hands were bound to his side as if in irons and his legs were pressed together, holding his body stiffly upright with a balance that was not under his control.

"I have always hated you," Vangen said. "But killing you outright was never the answer. I learned at a very tender age that base murder alone was not satisfying. It lacks a greater purpose and makes one a slave to impulse." Vangen stopped walking and looked at Draegan. "I was ten when I killed my mother. She had made the foolish decision to tell my father about the books I had been reading and the forbidden skills I had been acquiring."

Draegan looked at him in horror. "You killed your own mother? She loved you more than anything, and for that you murdered her?"

"It was she who brought me those books," Vangen said, stabbing his finger at the air. "If anyone was guilty it was her." He lowered his hand and took a calming breath. "And so she was duly punished."

Vangen began slowly circling the room once again. "Seeing how the great lion of Athar was made low, dragging himself around the castle after her untimely passing brightened my spirits. But then you came to her funeral with your father. I don't know how much mead they drank that night or whose idea it was to pawn you off on father, but you proved a most joyous gift for him. An unexpected offering. You brought him the happiness that I never did." Vangen stopped and wheeled to face Draegan. "It cheered him to no end to see you excel where I fell short in our studies," Vangen said, his eyes narrowing as he sneered at Draegan. "And so I decided to kill you."

"But I had learned that without a thorough plan, actions can have unintended consequences, your recent adoption being my chief example. So I resolved to devote the next ten years to architecting your fall."

Draegan wriggled in his invisible bonds. He craned his neck upward, raising his chin as if keeping his head above water. "You're an abomination Vangen. Even as a child your heart was black. Release me and I will end your suffering."

"In due time, dear brother," Vangen said. "Though it pains me to think you aren't the least bit curious as to how I composed my grand design. Would it shock you to know that I sent you after the Artifacts on my behalf? Would you begin to grasp the extent of my foresight if I told you I plotted your every step since you fled Dullahan so many weeks ago with your friends? Would you descend into madness to know that nothing you have done has been without my consent, and that your very presence here at this moment was exactly as I had crafted it?"

"You're mad. Delusional. You've been consumed by your own ego and lust for power," Draegan said. "My will is mine alone, and I will prove it by cutting your heart from your body."

"To control you as a puppet, as I am now, would lack the elegance I desire. No, I merely guided you, prodded you when you needed motivation, and kept you on course when you began to drift." Vangen circled back to his desk and ran his hand over the leather cover of the book he had been writing in when Draegan appeared. "It's all in here, everything I've learned and all my deeds to this point," Vangen said. "This will surpass the Chronicle of Fire as the new and complete history of Athar."

Vangen dragged his fingers slowly across the heavy cover and looked up at Draegan struggling under his incantation. "Long before you left for Draken's Hold last year to visit your true father and share with him the glorious news of your rapid ascension to Captain of the Night Watch, I was sowing the seeds of your demise. I had been to the Isle of Vatn many times, pouring through the archives when I encountered the very vault where you found Islak sleeping. I left the eye for you, but only after I learned how to implant visions, my visions, into it. The Black Tower and Temple, the Island of Fire and even the old cistern beneath the lake where all of my doing. I had discovered Islak's book long ago and knew the locations of the Artifacts."

"Then why not hunt them yourself," Draegan hissed between clenched teeth.

"I was needed here," Vangen said raising his arms and gesturing toward the castle. "I can't run an Empire and disappear for weeks at a time. Nor would I be foolish enough to risk my own life. I knew where they were but not how to get them. You were always the pragmatic one, so I left that task to you and your companions." Vangen smiled as he watched Draegan ball his hands into fists and strain against the unseen fetters. "You proved quite capable in gathering my Artifacts, for which I have already thanked you."

Draegan laughed bitterly. "For all your talk of control and power, you overlook the fact that your Artifacts are gone. Ceredyn has taken them."

"I have already accounted for his treachery." Vangen planted his hands on his desk and leaned across it toward Draegan. "After all

I have told you, you still do not grasp that all this," Vangen said, his eyes narrowing as he waved his hand above his head, "was my intent?" He stood again and straightened his cloak. "I want the Artifacts to be disseminated throughout the kingdoms."

Vangen laughed as Draegan stared at him, dumbfounded. "Here, let me show you. Perhaps this will speak more eloquently of my plan," Vangen said as he walked to the soot covered window and waved his hand over the glass. In the wavering light of the single candle Draegan saw images appear in each pane of dark glass. Vague shapes took from, humanlike and moving rapidly.

"There," Vangen said pointing at the window, "our hated crow is being set upon from all sides by my few loyal Rannulfr. Once they tear him limb from limb they will carry the World Render to the Clan of the Iron Mountains, and take the Dark Ichor to The Tribe of Docga in the south. I feel the Black Horn would best be used by Arius and I do owe him something for the use of your friend Ceredyn, the Rookery's greatest prodigy." Vangen pointed to another pane of glass. "And here you see that even as we speak the Burning Chains, which I recently acquired in the cistern beneath Lake Sias, are arriving in the Granite Hall, from a rogue group of Rannulfr that believe they have stolen the Artifact from me and are defecting to the Freehold of Stanrocc."

He turned to Draegan and the window again turned a dull black. Draegan continued to stare at the soot covered glass, while the candle guttered.

"That leaves my blade, Carnis Fornax, and the Shadow Walker, your cloak that I so generously gifted to you, to the kingdom of Skeldus," Vangen said returning to his desk. "And you will need to master them both in the coming war."

"You've undone all the work our fathers shed blood for," Draegan shouted, clenching his fists so tight his nails began to dig into his palm. "You would plunge the whole of Fyrian into bloodshed just to spite your father."

"And you," Vangen replied. He looked up from the desk at Draegan and watched him struggle against his bonds before taking a flask of dark liquid and spilling it on the desk. He ran his hand through it, making various runes and sigils before clapping his hands together and uttering words that sounded of death.

"You speak the dark tongue of Iss?" Draegan whispered.

The whites of Vangen's eyes turned black. "I can, although it takes practice and a sharp knife," he said, sticking out his tongue which Draegan noticed was split in two as it rolled over his cracked lips. He pulled it back and grinned at the disgust on Draegan's face.

Draegan felt the warm blood begin to pool in his clenched fist. He strained against the binding spell, working his arm in tiny movements until the paper in his sleeve slid into his hand. With a flick of his fingers he cast the scrap outside the edge of the binding seal and pressed his bloody palm against the fabric of his thigh. He felt the floor pitch upward as the light of the candle was swallowed in the spiraling darkness.

An instant later Draegan was on the floor, covered in a black mist and a thousand cuts all over his body. He curled into a ball and tried to control his breathing as his body was racked with spasms.

"That was a warning, though I hate to punish you for your creativity," Vangen said as he pushed a lectern toward the wall, upsetting a stack of books in the process. "You cannot shadow walk out of this room. If you do, you will surely die. And as you are now learning, shadow walking inside my study will prove quite painful." Vangen turned to face Draegan who was beginning to raise himself from the floor. "It took me a considerable amount of effort to figure out how to prevent your cloak from functioning properly in this space. You really should be more impressed Draegan. I have discerned a method for stopping one of the most powerful magical Artifacts in the history of Athar. Will you not admit that I am greater than the Sages?"

Draegan rose and drew his sword, his head still reeling from the pain of the cuts. He took a moment to focus his eyes and let the room steady itself. He saw Vangen near the door, pushing aside a mountain of books, half of which tumbled to the floor as he shoved the remainder in front of the door's locking mechanism.

"I'll walk through that door with your head in my hands," Draegan said, leaping over a pile of scrolls. He brought his blade down with merciless brutality in a flashing crescent of white light. Vangen wheeled and stumbled back against the door. A black flame erupted from his hand catching Draegan's sword and stopping it inches from his neck. The air around them chilled as Draegan felt the black fire of Carnis Fornax pulling at his body. Vangen set his jaw and flung Draegan back with a single swipe from his arm.

"You're quicker than I recall," Vangen said circling away from the door and stretching out his left hand to feel the stone wall of his study behind him. "I shall pay you more heed." Vangen backed away as Draegan pressed forward through the books, Vangen continuing to knock them over as he stepped cautiously backward. "I keep forgetting you had your sword blessed by your wife. If only Issa could see you now. Though of course it is quite difficult to do that when one is dead."

Draegan let out a bloodcurdling scream and launched himself at Vangen. He bellowed as he hacked wildly at Vangen with unbridled rage. Vangen deftly blocked each blow, continuing to circle against the wall, pushing aside heaps of books as he made his way back to his desk.

"Spare me your righteous indignation. You should thank me I didn't take her life with this blade and make her into a reaver. I could have easily sent her after you, forcing you to kill her for a second time," Vangen said. "I took the higher ground and ended her life swiftly, though she did manage to first give me a message I have since forgotten to relay to you." Vangen watched Draegan's eyes fill with hate as he spoke. "Did I not mention she came here seeking you while you were out hunting the Artifacts?"

Draegan stopped his violent onslaught and stood frozen amidst the piles of books. "Tell me what she said, then I will end you swiftly," Draegan hissed.

"You couldn't kill me even if I let you. I am beyond you in ways that would take a lifetime to explain." Vangen moved to his desk and set his flaming blade down. He held both his arms wide and smiled at Draegan. "Come here and I'll tell you her secret," Vangen said.

In a surge of darkness, his cloak flying about him Draegan rushed at Vangen, his silver white blade flaring briefly in the dim light before plunging it into Vangen's chest, burying it up to the hilt. Vangen took a breath and closed his arms around Draegan, gripping him like iron to his chest. Draegan went limp as he felt he felt the invisible chains of Vangen's binding spell weave their way through his body once again.

"That blade cannot kill me dear brother," Vangen whispered to Draegan as he stepped backward, the sword sliding out from the wound. "You see," Vangen said pointing to his heart, "you have pierced me through, yet I live."

"Tell me what she said," Draegan said as he stood frozen behind the desk.

Vangen looked up from his desk. "To be honest I have no recollection of what she said. I only remember the surprise and pain on her face as she fell to the ground, dead."

Draegan screamed in rage. "I'll find a way to end you."

"No need to worry yourself, Draegan, I have already devised a way," Vangen said rifling through a mass of scrolls on the ground behind the desk. "I asked you once before to kill a member of the Council. You failed in your attempt on my life, as was my plan. This time, howver, you will succeed." Vangen found a tattered piece of parchment and spread it on the desk. "You need only act the part I have written out for you, and act it well."

"You're a greater fool than I thought if you think I'll play any part in your wicked schemes. My whole purpose since I've left has been to end your reign. When I saw you kill Issa through the eye of Islak, I resolved that the end to your reign would be as violent and painful as my powers of imagination would allow. You will not be brought before the council, and you will not be judged by the people. I will end you here and now. Only then, when your sickness has been cut from the Empire will we have peace in Fyrian."

Vangen smashed his fist into the desk. "Have you heard nothing? Can you see nothing?" Vangen took a breath and calmed himself. "There will be no peace in Athar, dear brother. Every step I have taken, everything I have done has ensured that Fyrian is plunged into a state of war."

"And let me guess. You will sit on the throne, bringing the kingdoms to their knees as they consume each other," Vangen said.

"Wrong again. You will, Draegan."

Draegan stopped struggling against his bonds for a stunned moment. Vangen continued. "You will kill me and ascend to my throne in this time of war as a usurper. The four kingdoms each now wield a Dark Artifact and Skeldus commands two. Even now, the malevolence of these grand weapons poisons their wielder's minds. By sunrise every nation will be at war, seeking above all else, to claim the two which you possess. I am afraid, brother, that your options are limited. Each of the kingdoms knows the power of what you possess, and hungers to seize the Artifacts for themselves. You will be hunted for your cloak and my sword. If you run, they will find you. If you stay, you can lead Skeldus to battle as the king, and watch as thousands of your subjects march to certain death on the battlefield. This is what I have left you with. Run and be hunted or stay and rule an Empire torn to pieces by a war that will surpass that of the Sages."

"Why throw away your life so recklessly?" Draegan asked. "If you hate me so much, why let me kill you? Would you rather not stay and watch me suffer?"

"I have said before that I am beyond you in many ways. Your myopic vision cannot see beyond this world. You view death as an end, rather than a beginning." Vangen looked down at the desk and smiled to himself. "I have designs that encompass more than Athar. In time, if you play the part I have written for you successfully, and read what I've written in these tomes you will begin to grasp the extent of the plans I've laid."

Vangen drew his fingers across the scroll and watched it absorb the liquid from the desk's surface. He placed the burning blade on the parchment, its black tongues of flame licking at the paper which began to glow a bilious green. The paper ignited and the green fire spread from the desk to the floor, coruscating around the room, dancing between piles of books and over heaps of scrolls until it circled the study and came back to the desk. The room smoldered with a pallid green light as the cold fire carved an ancient glyph throughout the room.

Draegan tried to make sense of what he saw. "A *ferian* spell?"

"Modified. Heavily," Vangen said turning his gaze from the flames back to Draegan. "At last I see the hint of understanding growing in your face. You finally realize that you never had a choice. I have spent these past ten years not only raising you up to great heights, but crafting a scenario in which you have no escape. You must fall." Vangen took a step back from the desk and into the perimeter of the green fire.

"The council will know of your treachery."

"The council is dead, dear brother, and by your hand no less. At least that is the rumor. News of their untimely passing along with mine is spreading through the kingdoms as I speak. By dawn every villager will whisper of your heinous crimes in the Council Chamber. They will tell of how you took the Dark Artifacts into that sacred space and profaned it with the innocent blood of four nobles and your own kin in order to assume my throne. You will be hated, hunted and reviled. The four kingdoms will once again find a common enemy in you. You will rule a besieged land as you are attacked on all fronts."

Draegan strained against his invisible shackles.

"Or you can run. Hide. Shun what I have given you and live your precious few remaining days as a famed coward while the four kingdoms rush into this hollow country and brutally conquer the people you claim to love so dearly."

Draegan ground his teeth. "There is always hope. I won't believe your lies."

"Yes, hope. Always hope. It will make your suffering so much sweeter," Vangen said with a mawkish smile. "The peace of my father died with him. So too did your hope. All that is required of you now is to focus your frustrated hate, take my blade and end my life," Vangen said as he raised his hand.

The invisible chains that bound Draegan slackened and he caught himself as his weight returned to his legs. In an instant he grabbed the hilt of Carnis Fornax and pulled it back as he lunged at Vangen who stood motionless, arms outstretched and head tilted back, watching him with black eyes and a cruel smile. Draegan charged at him but at the last moment, wheeled around behind Vangen and bent him back toward him with his own forearm and drove the flaming blade through Vangen's chest and into his own.

"You are wrong. I choose to play neither king nor coward," Draegan hissed in Vangen's ear. He felt the frigid flames of the sword hit his chest and spread around his torso, vanishing into his cloak. His blood went cold as he felt the sword pulling at him, trying to draw him into itself. "I choose to die with you."

"You never had that choice," Vangen whispered as his lips parted in a thin smile. "Father was far too generous with his gifts. That pin should have been mine, not yours."

Draegan let go of the hilt, stepped back and watched Vangen collapse to the floor, the green flames of the *ferian* spell gently lapping at his body as he lay in a crumpled heap. The black flame pierced his corpse completely. Draegan looked down at his own chest, dumbfounded, and felt his clothing for any signs of damage.

"How is this possible?" Draegan yelled as he watched Vangen's black eyes drain and turn a milky white.

Vangen's mouth twisted into a cruel smile. "Far too generous. It should have been mine, now I curse you with it," Vangen said as his mouth bubbled and frothed with bile and blood. A rattle of air escaped through the liquid and Vangen went limp as the green fire consumed his body. In a few short minutes the fire died and little remained of Vangen's body.

Draegan stood motionless in the study for hours, staring at the ashes of his brother, until the rays of the sun pierced the layers of soot on the study window, bathing the room in a muted glow. He slowly reached for Carnis Fornax and gathered the cold cloak around his shoulders feeling a chill creep through his bones as he walked past the smoldering embers of Vangen. Taking a seat behind the heavy oak desk, he folded his arms and watched the sunlight filter through the window.

Chapter 38: Vatn Awakes

Ieros finished his ablutions and donned his white robe as the sun rose through the small window in his monastic cell. Being the head librarian of Vatn for the last sixty years afforded him the luxury of not having to sleep in the dormitories with the other priests and acolytes. He used his precious privacy to rise and greet each day in his own way, out of the sight of his brothers and sisters.

But today he would not be walking the gardens in silent meditation before breakfast, for he had an urgent matter to attend to. He hastily scrawled a note on the simple desk that was one of the few items in his stark room. He tucked the parchment in his belt and headed directly for the common hall where he posted it for all who entered for breakfast to see.

"The library will not open today. I apologize for the inconvenience, Ieros."

He turned, left the hall and headed down the marble stairs that spilled into the meticulously maintained gardens at the foot of the White Temple. He circled the base of the mountain the Temple was built upon and took a seldom used dirt footpath toward the shore where he turned south and slipped into a thicket of undergrowth. Ieros pushed his way through the dense vegetation for a few minutes until he came to a small inlet where a weatherworn boat bumped gently against the shore.

"I haven't made this journey in quite some time," he muttered under his breath as he stepped into the boat with surprising ease, considering he was nearly a century old. Untying the boat he pushed off and began paddling across the open sea to one of the many tiny uninhabited islands that dotted the southern coast of Vatn.

The sun was high in the sky when Ieros stepped out of the boat and dragged it to the white sand shore. He secured it to a tree and headed directly into the close-packed vegetation beyond the thin strip of shore on the tiny island. After a few minutes of walking he came to a small clearing and leaned against a tree to catch his breath. He mumbled a few words under his breath and the brush in the clearing began to wither. Beneath the decaying thicket Ieros saw the familiar worn flagstones inscribed with a sigil he'd not seen in many years.

He smiled softly, the lines in his face showing his age as he placed his hand in the center of the stones. They glowed briefly and began to groan in protest as they slid apart to reveal a staircase that spiraled downward into darkness. "Why do I never remember to bring a torch," he said and began his descent.

Ieros reached the bottom of the stairs and pushed through a set of solid iron doors that yielded to his touch. The doors swung silently inward to reveal a cavernous stone hall chiseled from the bedrock of the island. The vaulted ceiling swept up for a hundred feet where great chandeliers of black iron held thousands of candles that gave the massive chamber a warm glow. At the far end of the hall a fireplace large enough to swallow a herd of cattle held a fire that seemed piteously small in the grandeur of the space. In front of the fireplace a lone figure sat in an unadorned wooden chair behind a small bench and eating from a bowl. He looked up from his simple meal at his visitor.

"Enter Ieros, and eat with me. It's been many years since we broke bread together," came the gruff voice as it echoed through the hall.

Ieros began crossing the length of the hall. "Vangen has fallen and Draegan has risen in his place. The Dark Artifacts are lose in Fyrian once again, Isirah."

"I know."

"Then you know why I have come," Ieros replied as he approach the fireplace.

"What can be done at this late hour, old man? Fyrian has fallen. Athar is lost. All will return to shadow and dust," Isirah grumbled and picked idly at his bread as he looked at Ieros standing by the fire. Both listened to the fire sputter in the silence before Isirah spoke again. "You've grow old in the past thirty years."

"And you've grow hopeless," Ieros snapped. "To think I trained such a cynic."

"Then what would you do, Ieros? War will consume Fyrian soon, then Vatn. What hope have we?"

"We have Issa's son."

What happens next? If you'd like to be the first to know when more stories from the Dark Artifacts are published, please sign up for our mailing list here: http://eepurl.com/JRSZL

I thank you for reading this book. If you enjoyed it, please take a moment to tell others by leaving a review.

If you're interested in reading more about the world of Athar and the characters in it, please take a look at these other books:

The Rise of Isarn (Book 2 of The Dark Artifacts) – release date Dec 2015

About the Author

T. R. Edwards is a life-long fantasy fanatic. He is a web-designer with a degree in the visual arts. Mr. Edwards currently lives outside Philadelphia with his wife and two kids, scanning the horizon for dragons.